I Called Him Dancer

A Novel

By G. Edward Snipes

GES Book Publishing
Carrollton, GA

Published by GES Book Publishing
Copyright © 2011 by G. Edward Snipes
and
GES Book Publishing http://www.gespublishing.com

Cover Design by Eddie Snipes

ISBN 978-0-9832247-0-9

Contact the author by visiting http://www.eddiesnipes.com

Picture Credits
Front cover photo by Yuri Arcurs via
http://www.dreamstime.com

Table of Contents

Preface

When people see a breathtaking performance, it looks like natural, raw talent. The truth is, behind the performer is a long road filled with struggle, pain, and hardship. In front of every winner is a mountain of failure they must first climb and conquer. The greater the mountain, the sweeter the taste of success. Michael Camp is an award winning dancer. Beyond his short-lived success, stands a valley of despair with terrain so rugged, his very life will hang in the balance. If he survives, the mountain awaits. It has been said, unless a seed falls into the ground and dies, it cannot blossom into life. Can Michael Camp trust enough to die, when life seems out of reach?

Tralena Walker and Tom Webster first noticed the man called Dancer, and wrote about his challenges in their music. Read the song of the man we know as Dancer, and then follow his story as we finish the song.

"DANCER"

I always call him Dancer
'Cause he had all the moves
But he kept on changing partners
Each time his steps improved
We'd all sit there and wonder
Which one of us he'd choose
We all thought he was a winner
'Cause we'd never seen him lose
To the young girls down in Bristol
He was all that we dreamed of
But he was always careful
Not to fall in love

He'd say, Love ain't made for dancers,
That's the pity of it all.
You might see me stumble,
But you'll never see me fall.

(CHORUS)
'Cause dancers ain't real people
And we don't have real hearts.
I know that I should love you,
I just don't know where to start.

The last time I saw Dancer,
Was on the evening news.
He was wearing some old trench coat,

And someone else's shoes.
He'd gone about as far,
As his dreams would let him go.
He was out there washing windshields,
Up in the New York snow.
Now when people ask about him,
I always smile and say,
The last time I ever saw him,
He was working off Broadway.

(CHORUS)
'Cause dancers ain't real people
And we don't have real hearts.
I know that I should love you,
I just don't know where to start.

COUPLET
They call him a homeless person,
But there's so much they don't know.
He's a disenchanted dancer,
And the music's way too slow.
Written by Tom Webster and Tralena Walker

Chapter One

A homeless man pulled his tattered coat closer to his neck, trying to block out the early morning chill while walking toward Central Park. A woman stood before him, looking at a display outside the Majestic Theater. His eyes were drawn to the display and saw an actress in the picture wearing a fancy ballroom dress. A chilling cold ached through his body, and his legs froze in place, but forgotten memories warmed away the chill as he admired the posters outside the Broadway theater.

"It's a good play, isn't it?" The man in rags turned to face the woman. By her stylish long gray coat, he could tell she was accustomed to the finer things of New York.

The woman gave an uncomfortable smile and walked away.

With trembling hands, the man ran his fingers across the theater display. Grime smudged onto the clear sheet of acrylic guarding the words, *Return of the Phantom. A High-energy sequel to Broadway's longest running play.* He started to leave, but stopped again at the next poster. A gold frame held the lovely picture. With the tip of his finger, he outlined the face of Christine Daaé.

"Alina hasn't changed." He tapped his finger on the man wearing the phantom's mask. "Looks like there's a new Erik." Leaning close, he examined the picture. "Yep. That definitely isn't Antonio."

A deep sigh escaped from the pit of his stomach. "Things should have been different." He tried to imagine his face in the picture, half hidden behind the mask. Patting the display like the shoulder of an old friend, he turned and lumbered down the street toward his favorite tipping spot just off Broadway.

The vagrant stood at the corner of 54th Street, looking at a marquis with a longing stare. The picture of the Return of the Phantom still lingered in his mind. The glamour of the Big Apple and the names in lights proclaim the success of those who have reached stardom. In this place, dreams still come true. The entertainment industry may have changed, but here, the golden age of theater spills into the modern day.

Pedestrians covered the sidewalks, peeking into windows and hoping to glimpse one of the celebrities that bring the theater district to life. The vagrant stood on the corner of 54th and Broadway, watching as people hurried past, and hoped someone would show a little charity. Each person hurried their pace when they neared the bearded man in rank clothing.

The homeless man shrugged off their indifference. He would earn his keep without them. Hunger pangs stabbed at his stomach, but the agonizing craving in his body always took priority over meals. His body screamed for relief and he felt as though his chest would implode from the weight pressing on him. Trembling fingers ran through his matted brown hair, and the man shifted from one foot to the other while watching cars creep by. He leaned against the building and again ran both hands through his hair. He rolled the snags through his fingertips. Jumpy legs wouldn't give him a moment of rest, so he walked a few paces and waited for the light to turn red.

When the light changed, he walked to the first car and raised his spray bottle. He ignored the woman shaking her head and dodged her angry stare. He sprayed the window, cleaned it with a squeegee, and repeated the process on the other side of the windshield before walking up to the driver. The woman refused to roll down her window.

Heartless wench.

He reached across the windshield and pretended to flick off a piece of dirt, dragging his muddy sleeve through the driver's line of vision. Looking at the smudge, he said, "Oops." He smiled and raised his hands in an innocent gesture. "Maybe you'll be homeless one day and see how it feels," he grumbled under his breath, and walked toward the next car.

Raquel neared the end of her drive from Tennessee to New York. Traffic stopped, and she took the opportunity to review her directions. *The next turn is the Lincoln Tunnel.* Her heart beat faster, and she wondered if it was excitement over her new opportunity, or the hope of finding Michael, who had been missing for more than two years. He'd been the inspiration behind Raquel's dream to perform on Broadway.

I actually made it! The thought of being on stage in New York caused a bright smile to sweep across her face, but the cheer receded into heartache. She needed to find Michael. Only then could she fill the hole in her lonely heart.

After exiting the Jersey turnpike, Raquel followed the signs toward the Lincoln Tunnel. Traffic slowed as a flood of cars trickled through the tollbooths blocking the entrance to the tunnel. While she inched along, her thoughts raced back to her hometown of Bristol. Her stomach knotted at the thought of Robert. A shiver crawled down her spine and she had the urge to glance over her shoulder. He couldn't be following her, but she still couldn't resist the urge to check.

What's the stalker doing now?

She could envision him dialing her old cell phone number, and shrieking in rage when he found it disconnected. She had played Robert's game, letting him believe he controlled her while she planned her escape. How long did he sit at the cafe before realizing she'd given him the slip?

Is Robert calling her parents, demanding to know where she had gone? Hopefully, her mom wouldn't slip up and tell him she'd moved to New York.

"Man! Traffic is rushing like molasses on a cold morning," she complained as she thumped the steering wheel.

Raquel pulled into the tollbooth, paid, and sped into the tunnel. Another clog of taillights and exhaust stopped her. She glanced at her watch.

Good thing I gave myself an extra hour. Can't take a chance on being late for my first meeting with my new producer.

Her attention returned to Tennessee, but she forced Robert out of her thoughts. It would do no good to escape his iron grip if she left her mind in his grasp. She pushed her long brown hair behind her ear and thought about Michael. How her heart skipped the first time they danced together. When the quiet and shy boy took the stage, an awe-struck class watched him become a different person. A horn honked from behind, startling Raquel out of her musings. She pulled ahead.

I need to keep my focus on the road.

"I always knew he would make it big." Raquel's own voice almost surprised her. Her heart lifted at the idea of finding him in one of the Broadway theaters. *Does he still love me? Did he ever truly love me?* She couldn't keep the doubts from digging at her heart.

Accustomed to the fresh air of rural Tennessee, Raquel almost gagged at the smell of exhaust in the tunnel. She tried to focus on something positive, hoping to distract herself from the suffocating smell.

Michael's talent had placed him on the fast track to stardom, and Raquel had spent four years trying to catch up. Their goal was to dance together again. Excitement had filled his voice when he called to announce his new leading role in the Return of the Phantom, but soon after his calls quit coming.

Why? Did he have a new life and love? Her heart ached at the thought, so she pushed it away. *There must be another explanation.*

The scruffy man approached another car waiting at the red light, cleaned the windshield, and garnered a tip. He gave a dissatisfied stare at the money. *A dollar? The guy is wearing a suit. I know he can afford more than a buck.*

At this rate, the day would end before he could make enough money to survive. He felt his rage growing, fueled by his desperate cravings. An almost overwhelming urge to smash through the window and strip drivers of their valuables came over him, but he wrestled down the feeling. When would he get a break? There were few friendly faces to greet a man down on his luck on Broadway.

Traffic continued at its agonizing pace, but Broadway crawled into view. Raquel's shoulders grew tense at the passing of each minute. With her extra hour gone, she now feared being late for her meeting.

A man near the intersection ahead distracted Raquel from her frustrations. She watched the vagrant in rags as he bounced from car to car with a squeegee and a spray bottle, cleaning windshields, and gathering tips.

A friend had warned her to always tip street washers. Though cleaning wasn't invited, they expected payment. Raquel grabbed her purse and fished for cash. She pulled out a bill.

I doubt he has change for a twenty.

Other than the money she needed for parking, Raquel could only produce a dollar and some change. She poured the change into her palm and wrapped it in the dollar as the vagrant drew near. With the precision of an experienced windshield technician, the man rushed to the passenger side, sprayed the window, and drew the squeegee across it.

When the man reached for the center of the windshield, Raquel's heart stopped, frozen in a moment of shock. The window washer's crystal blue eyes looked familiar. Excitement and confusion gripped her heart, causing her pulse to quicken. Filth and a burst of whiskers obscured his face, but did she know him? Her mind rebelled at the thought, but her heart trumpeted with recognition. She tried to get a good look as the vagrant hurried to the driver's side to finish the job. In a moment, he stood at the car window with an extended palm.

Raquel brushed her hair aside and looked up, examining the man's face, searching for Michael's features behind the grime. The man refused to look at her, but glanced back and forth as though scanning for unknown threats. She started to hand him the money, but held it for a moment and tried to get another look at his eyes.

"Dancer?"

The man's eyes widened for an instant, then narrowed. The whiskers around the corners of his mouth raised slightly. "There ain't no dancers here, lady."

Raquel stared for a moment. "You just look like someone I know as Dancer. Aren't you Michael? Michael Camp?" Suddenly, she felt embarrassed by her question. How could Dancer be a vagrant? He is certainly a Broadway star by now.

"I'd do the Tennessee two-step, but it will cost you extra."

The voice and the eyes seem like Michael's, but that's impossible. Raquel refused to accept the thought and began to deny her heart's realization. Her thoughts warred against reason, trying to decide whether to accept the reality standing before her, or the image of Michael she'd expected to find in New York. She opened her mouth to speak again, but a blowing horn interrupted her. The car ahead had moved thirty feet.

The driver behind her rolled down his window to voice his complaint, but the sounds of car horns obscured his words as more drivers joined the protest. Words fled. Raquel handed over the money and pulled forward, followed by the line of impatient drivers. The man walked toward the traffic light, preparing for a new line of cars and reluctant tippers. When Raquel turned the corner, she adjusted her mirror to keep the man in sight until a building obscured her view.

Raquel parked her car and took a final glance at her watch. "Ten minutes late," she moaned, then slammed the car door. Racing to the production office, she fought to push down her emotions, but she couldn't get her mind off the windshield washer. Raquel wanted to reject the idea that he could be the man she loved, but couldn't mistake those blue eyes. Could this be why she lost contact with him two years ago?

Her mind raced through the possibilities—and the impossibilities. *Is it possible that one of the nation's top dancers is now homeless? If it is Michael, how could he have ended up cleaning windshields off Broadway?*

Chapter Two

The biting New York wind stung Raquel's face, sending chills through her body. People strolling down the sidewalk didn't act cold, but to her the temperature felt ten or fifteen degrees colder than Tennessee. She pushed through the office doors, and a young lady directed her to her meeting room.

Raquel regained her composure. She understood the need to have stage presence, even in a meeting. Willing the homeless man and the stress of being late out of her thoughts, she focused on showing herself to be a professional caliber dancer. A deep breath helped her conjure up a face of confidence, and she headed down the hall to meet her agent and producer.

Clacking heels announced her approach to everyone within earshot. *As if being late weren't enough, now I sound like a wounded horse.* The office door stood half opened, and she peeked into the room. "I'm looking for Joseph Rodney."

"Come in," Joseph said as he rose to meet her. The talent agent had first introduced himself after her performance at the Knoxville Theater. He wore a blue long sleeve shirt and black slacks. With his sleeves rolled halfway up his forearm, he had a rugged look. To her, his look seemed out of place in New York. But she liked it. If he'd been wearing jeans, Joseph would have looked like someone from her hometown of Bristol.

"I'm sorry I'm late. This is my first time driving in New York and finding parking was harder than expected."

Joseph gave a warm smile. "So what do you think about New York traffic?" Raquel gave a wry look and shrugged. "The first taste of traffic is a big culture shock for most people," Joseph said. He ushered her toward the table. "Raquel, you remember Marcus Davenport? He was on the panel when you flew in for your audition. He's the producer you will be working for."

Marcus had a wiry frame, a thick black mustache, and curly black hair. His light brown eyes were focused with intensity, but when he smiled, it gave Raquel a sense of reassurance. Before speaking a word, the producer's kind eyes and intense expression communicated assurance, confidence, and control.

The producer stood and offered Raquel his hand, "Good to have you on board with us, Raquel. I don't like a lot of social distractions when I am evaluating new dancers, so I don't say much during auditions. Some call it a quirk." He motioned for her to have a seat before sitting back down. "Let me start by making it clear that in this business, promptness cannot be over stated. I know this is your first day in New York, so I will give you a bye, but from this point on, if you are scheduled for a meeting at four, be prepared at four," he looked at his watch and said, "not fifteen after four—not even two after four. Be early and you'll be safe. If I can't trust performers to be on time, I can't rely on them in the production."

Raquel opened her mouth to speak. She wanted to explain how she planned to give herself more than an hour to spare, and could not have known it would take so long to get from the Lincoln Tunnel to Broadway, but the man's intense gaze disarmed her. Words fled, so she just gave a quick nod.

She listened as he reviewed her portfolio, and explained her starting role as a secondary dancer. He explained his fair approach, and that many opportunities existed to move up for those who worked hard and performed well. She had thought a single theater made up Broadway, but Marcus surprised her by explaining it consisted of about forty theaters, each producing their own musical at any given time.

Marcus wasted no words. The producer gave Raquel a

quick information dump, said for her to be at the Belasco Theater at seven in the morning, then excused her from the office. A sense of awkwardness filled the air, and she looked at Joseph. The shrug of his shoulders said what she needed to know. It had only been five minutes, but the meeting had concluded.

Mixed emotions flooded her mind. The feeling of letting Marcus down needled at her after she arrived late for the meeting. Sorrow shoved her earlier excitement aside. She would have to make up for her disappointing first impression. The earlier encounter with the street washer also came to mind. Leaving home, horrible traffic, the street washer—she'd had enough for one day. And she still had to find her apartment in this confusing city. A sudden longing for home came over her, and Raquel felt her lip begin to quiver.

Was this a big mistake?

Raquel blinked back a tear trying to escape, and allowed herself to be distracted by the photographs adorning the hallway walls. A faint odor indicated the place had recently been painted. She touched one of the gold trimmed pictures, then worked down the hall, looking at the plaques, awards, and history decorating these walls. For a moment, she stood there, soaking it all in. Raquel wondered if she was standing where many great stars once walked, and where many dreamers desired to stand.

How did a girl from Bristol end up in the theaters of Broadway? She wondered if Michael had stood in this hallway. What would she give to stand here with him? She let the thought soak in. Her heart felt weighed down by the thought of the window washer being Michael. *Maybe it wasn't him, but just someone who looked like him.*

"It's a special place, isn't it?" Raquel jumped and turned to see her agent, Joseph, standing nearby, and studying the displays. She hadn't seen him come out of the office. "Sorry. Didn't mean to startle you."

"It's okay. I was just lost in thought."

Joseph gave a pleasant smile and turned to the wall again. He ran his hand along the edge of a plaque. "I remember the first time I walked down these halls. It is inspiring, isn't it?"

Raquel looked at a picture of a beautiful woman she didn't recognize. In the photo, a line of dancers adorned the stage behind the woman. They were out of focus, but she could tell they were soldiers from The Nutcracker. "Yes, it's magical." She pointed to the photo and said, "I'll be dancing The Nutcracker. It must be special to be on center stage like that." She ran her fingertips along the carved gilded picture frame.

Joseph nodded while he moved to examine the photo with her. "It's still a work in progress, but Marcus is turning this new office into quite a museum."

"Oh? This is new? I thought I was walking the hall where these dancers once walked."

"You'll do that when you step into the Belasco. But then again, I don't know what this space was used for in the past. It might have been a star studded walkway years ago."

Raquel stepped down to the next picture and her eyes returned to the wall. "It still feels magical. Seeing the stars framed in gold. I can almost see them dancing."

Joseph stepped forward to join her. "Every performer wants to see their legacy displayed on these walls." He looked at her and asked, "How do you feel about your new opportunity?"

"Excited. Maybe a little scared." She shifted her eyes from the wall to Joseph. "Can I ask you a question?"

"Sure."

"Have you ever heard of a dancer named Michael Camp?"

Joseph's eyes looked upward as he searched for any memory of the name. "It doesn't ring a bell. Has he been on Broadway?"

"Yes. He came here a couple of years ago. He was once a Grand Prix winner and was recruited out of Pahl School of Dance. He's from my hometown in Tennessee."

Joseph stroked his chin and said, "The name doesn't ring a bell. But then Broadway is a big place." He turned to face Raquel. "Is he a friend of yours?"

Raquel nodded. "Yes, and I thought I saw him." She looked down at the polished floor. It was like glass. Hardly a scuff in sight. "He was washing windows. I lost contact with him about two years ago and thought the man cleaning my windshield looked like him." She lifted her eyes from the floor and looked at Joseph. "It doesn't seem possible, so it's probably someone who looks like him. Is there a way to find out if he's performing in any of the theaters?"

"It is. I know some people in the other theaters. I can ask around."

"Could you do that? I really would like to find him."

"When I get a chance, I'll ask if anyone knows him. Michael Camp, right?" Raquel nodded. "I've got a dinner engagement. Would you like to join me?"

Raquel gave a kind smile, but shook her head. "I truly appreciate the offer, but no, thanks. I've got to get moved in to my apartment."

Joseph flashed another smile and touched her shoulder. "No problem. I'd better run, then. Maybe I could show you around New York some time. It can be a bit overwhelming when you're new."

"I might take you up on that." Joseph's eyes sparkled above his smile. She could tell he wanted to be helpful.

"Great! I'll get with you sometime next week. Good luck on your new opportunity, and call me if you have a need." Joseph gave a final wave and disappeared down the hall.

"I think he likes you."

Raquel's eyes darted to a man wearing a full-length black leather coat, also touring the hall of memories. When Joseph left, he stepped toward Raquel. "What?" she asked.

"I'm a pretty good observer and I think he likes you," the man said.

Raquel felt herself blush. "No, he's my agent. He's just being helpful."

"I see," he said. His knowing smile said he didn't see things the same way as Raquel. The man stepped closer and extended his hand. "Hi, my name is Richard Barnhouse." She instinctively reached out and he gave a firm handshake. "I'm a reporter doing a behind the scenes story on Broadway and have a few minutes before a meeting. Do you mind if I ask you a couple of questions?"

The man's face had chiseled features, and his shining smile made her feel more at ease. A warming fragrance caught her attention. *I've got to give him credit. He has good taste in cologne.* She inhaled deeply. "Okay, I guess. But I'm about to leave, and need to take care of some things."

"Great! I won't take up much of your time," he said while pulling a voice recorder out of his pocket. "You don't mind if I take voice notes do you?" When she hesitated, he followed her eyes to his recorder. "I can write things the old fashioned way if you wish."

After looking back up, she shook her head. "No. That's okay."

"Great! I couldn't help overhearing you talking about a former Broadway dancer who's homeless. Can you tell me a little about him?"

Something tightened in the pit of her stomach. The idea of humiliating Michael caused bile to rise in the back of her throat, and her thoughts rose onto her tongue like a bad taste. Bitter words spit from her mouth. "No. I don't want to talk about it. Sorry."

Unfazed, he continued probing. "Did I hear you say he was a former Grand Prix winner? What type of competition is that?"

The decision to speak with this man had been a mistake. Time to make a polite exit. "I'm sorry. I have to go take care of some things." Noise from her heels clacked as she hurried down the hallway.

"His name was Michael Camp, right?"

Regret pounded her while hurrying away. Caught up in her own world, Raquel hadn't thought to look for anyone else when talking to Joseph. Now she had to get as far from the reporter as possible—and hope the damage hadn't already been done.

If I had only known he was nearby. In this city, I need to learn to keep my mouth shut.

Outside the office, traffic packed the streets. The thought of weaving through the tangle of cars unnerved her, but the new apartment awaited. This was turning out to be a long day.

After a good rest, I'll be able to think clearer. Maybe I'll run across Michael again.

In vain, she tried to put herself at ease, but in her heart she knew rest wouldn't come until she found the truth, and discovered what happened to send the dancer's life into disarray.

Chapter Three

It had been a long day. Michael couldn't get the encounter with Raquel out of his mind. All evening his thoughts raced through his life. He'd left the past behind, but now it had followed him to New York. Shame filled him at the thought of Raquel. How did she recognize him behind the mask of facial hair? The thought of her seeing him in this condition disgusted him. In the future, he would be careful to avoid her.

The sun crept out of sight just before he arrived at his hideaway under the bridge. Several months ago he'd found this crevasse and taken up shelter here. No one ever came around this area at night. The perfect spot to escape from the world. Some of the other homeless guys lived in shelters, but Michael preferred to be alone. None of these guys were friends. He had acquaintances, not friends. One thing he'd learned early in life is people can't be trusted. Relationships cause pain, and anyone trying to get closer than arm's length is trouble.

After pulling a rank blanket over himself, Michael stared into the darkness. Time rolled by, but his thoughts chased sleep away. First, the poster this morning had haunted his memories, then Raquel this afternoon. The past had returned in full force today. His life should have been different.

"Why is life cruel and hard to some, but generous and kind to others?" he complained to the bridge above his head.

Most of the time he pushed the past from his thoughts. Pain remained his enemy—and his companion. It had been with him since birth, and walked with him ever since. He hadn't allowed the memories to haunt him for a long time, but now his heart longed for the days on stage.

Cold stung his hands when he placed them on the concrete to raise himself up. The bottom of the bridge banged into his skull. Michael massaged his head. He cursed the bridge. And the pain. And the numbness of his soul.

Broadway once appeared to have been his destiny, but life blind-sided him on that one. Life teased him with talent, dreams, and the pretense of opportunity. Almost as soon as he stepped onto the Broadway stage, fate snatched it all away. Fate took away his mother, his friend, and his life of dancing.

Anger surged in him as he ran his hands through his hair, then pulled cold fingers over his face. "Why is life so unfair?" he shouted into his palms.

With a long sigh, the disenfranchised dancer leaned over his knees, while his mind forced his thoughts into the past.

The dream had begun when Michael was six years old. He lived in a cheap, one bedroom apartment. He remembered watching through his childhood eyes as his mother, Loreen, rushed about while getting dressed. She snatched up things she needed for her evening out. In his mind, Michael could hear the stove timer buzzing, and saw his mother hurrying to the kitchen to pull a TV dinner from the oven. He smelled the aroma of the Salisbury steak dinner as his mother entered the room and placed it on the old coffee table.

The sour memory of his mother's boyfriend, Derk, still left a bad taste in the back of his throat. He remembered the man glaring at him with annoyance as his mom arranged the table. Michael watched him fidgeting at the door, and feared Derk would lose his temper again. Derk made him feel unwanted and always seemed annoyed at his presence.

"Honey, your supper is ready, but you need to let it cool off." Michael's mother took him by the hand and hurried him to the sofa. "You have three videos to watch." She turned him to face her, and held up a finger. "Don't go outside."

"Loreen. We need to get going." Derk sighed impatiently and shifted from one foot to the other.

Loreen leaned down to kiss Michael good-bye. The smell of her perfume and makeup lingered for a moment. He liked her perfume, but didn't like the makeup smell. His mom looked pretty until she caked the makeup on her face. He also didn't like the blue stuff that gave her clown eyes.

"I've got to go," his mother said as she pushed a video into the VCR. "We'll be at a party, so it might be late." She grabbed the keys and disappeared behind the apartment door with Derk.

Michael poked at his peas and carrots. He hated both. At least he could eat the dessert first since his mom wasn't here to correct him. He gave a blank stare toward the TV. Now that he was six, the three preschool videos in his collection seemed boring. Besides, at his age, he didn't need to watch shows about learning to count, and he'd watched these shows so many times he could recite them from memory.

The window caught his attention, and he looked outside to see if there were any other kids his age in sight. Just a handful of men milling around.

Do other kids sit alone on Saturday nights watching dumb old baby shows?

He pulled a board game from under the sofa, and played with the pieces while songs about numbers echoed in the background. His old toys had been left behind when he and his mom left their old apartment. When going home, his mom spotted police and she drove away. They never went back to get his toys. Michael didn't know why they ran, but his mom promised she would get new toys. Two apartments later, this game remained the only thing he had.

The shows were too boring, so he poked the eject button

and flipped through the stations. News, two grownup-looking movies, and dancers with music. Too bad they didn't have cable TV. Music and dancing looked like the best option, so he left it on the public broadcasting station. Every half hour, the performance paused for a call of viewer support, whatever that meant. Michael went back to his game where colored pieces began their quest to make it around the board, trying to avoid an attack from hordes of peas and carrots.

The music stopped and a man with a microphone began his call for pledges. His words sounded proper, and Michael thought he had a strange way of talking. The man kept waving papers at the camera and talking about people who had already given money for shows like this. He announced that someone named John waited with the lead dancer, and the camera switched to a table where two men sat. John wore a yellow suit. He leaned back and raised his eyebrows when he talked. The man Michael had seen dancing now sported a black shirt and sat beside John. The questions were boring, so Michael returned to the battle on carrot hill, only looking at the TV when something grabbed his attention.

"What made you want to become a performer?" Michael heard the boring man ask, and he glanced to the TV.

The dancer's eyes brightened, and a big smile flashed across his face, "When I dance, I feel like I come alive. Even when the lights are off and the audience is gone, I dance. I would dance even if it was only for me."

Michael's ears perked up at the dancer's words. He wished he could feel that way. Other kids played baseball, soccer, and football, but his mother never took him anywhere. Rarely did he even make it beyond the field behind his apartment. The more the dancer talked, the more excited the man became.

John continued. "What do you like most about dancing?"

"What do I not like about it?" His eyes sparkled as the smile returned to his face, "I suppose, the thing I like most about dancing is, it allows me to close out the world around me. It's like I'm entering another world. The pains of life cannot enter there, and I am free to live. When I dance, it is just the music and me. It's an escape from the sorrows of life."

Suddenly, the dancer's words seemed to speak directly to Michael.

Michael blinked as he stared at the TV, listening to the discussion between the announcer and the dancer. Michael wondered if he could make the world go away like the man on the stage had said? He scrambled through the stack of VHS tapes, looking for a blank tape. Derk had a pack of blanks used to record football. Michael pulled out the kiddy show and shoved a blank cassette into its place. He fumbled for the remote and pressed record.

Just before the broadcast switched back to the performance, the dancer said again, "When I dance, I come alive!"

The words reached into the room and gripped Michael's heart. He watched the man dancing to Celtic music, amazed at how the dancer leaped and seemed free from the world.

Michael pushed the game under the couch and laid on the stale cushions, watching the performer in this amazing new world. *I want to find another world. I want to be like him!*

The sound of Derk's voice stirred Michael out of sleep, but he began to drift away again. A rough shove forced him back into consciousness.

"Get up! We need to sit there," Derk growled. Michael rubbed sleep from his eyes. Pain jolted him when the tips of Derk's fingers thumped the top of his head. "I said, get up!"

Michael scrambled up, and almost gagged at the smell of alcohol saturating Derk's breath.

Derk acted nice to his friends, and except when drunk, he seemed kind to Michael's mom. But Derk hated kids, and he took every opportunity to remind Loreen of this. His favorite words were, "Go away." The small apartment didn't give Michael many places to go, but he did his best to stay away from Derk.

"Get off the couch and let your mother sit there," Derk barked.

Michael obeyed as the drunk motioned for his mother to sit on the sofa. Michael stood on wobbly legs as his eyes demanded to return to his dreams. "Can I go to your bed?" Michael asked his mother with a sleepy voice.

"No!" Derk snapped. The couch was Michael's bed, but Derk often woke him up when wanting to sit there. He turned to Loreen, "Can't you send the brat away? He's getting on my nerves, just standing there. Staring like some kind of a fool."

Loreen looked at Derk for a moment, then turned to Michael and said, "Go sit at the table. We'll be going to bed soon." Her words were slurred and she smelled like alcohol, too. Michael noticed how tired she looked. He stared for a moment before she softened her voice and said, "Go on now. Sit at the table. You can have the sofa in a few minutes."

Michael crawled into the chair, drew up his knees, and leaned over them. He drifted in and out of sleep while listening to Derk and his mother talk about this evening's party. Eventually, sleep overtook him.

His arm slipped off his knees and Michael had a sensation of falling. He jerked awake and looked around, trying to orient himself. Darkness surrounded him in the silent room. He slipped off the chair and took his place on the couch. Pulling a sheet from the back of the sofa, he thought again about the man on TV. As sleep returned, he wondered if he, too, could escape his world through dancing.

Michael opened his eyes to see sunshine streaming through the window. He heard voices and leaned on the windowsill to peek outside. A small crowd of kids played tackle football in the grass between his apartment and the one across from him. Most of the kids looked older, but one boy looked to be Michael's age. He ran, waving his arms screaming, "I'm open," but the older kids never threw the ball to him. The boy looked up and their eyes met. The kid waved and Michael waved back.

The apartment was quiet, so Michael turned on the television to see if he had recorded the show from last night. The final half-hour of the performance was on the tape. Celtic music played while the man jumped and spun in front of a line of girls in black skirts. The man had the fastest feet Michael had ever seen, and when he jumped, he seemed to hang in the air. Michael studied the feet of the man leading the performance and modeled his steps after him. He rewound the tape, watched, and imitated the dance again. A sound of someone stirring in the bedroom caught his attention. Michael ejected the tape and hid it under the sofa. He didn't want his tape to be overwritten by Derk's football games.

Each morning, Michael pulled out the tape while Derk slept, and mimicked the steps of the dancer. Once he'd memorized the steps, he began imitating the man's arm motions and spins. After learning the moves and no longer having to remind himself of each step, he felt something growing inside. The man was right! He did seem to leave the world behind when he closed his eyes and danced in the rhythm of the Celtic music playing on the television.

"Well look at that!"

Derk's voice jolted his mind back into the real world. Michael looked at the TV and back to Derk.

"What are you? Some kind of a queer?" Derk sneered as he turned back to the bedroom. "Loreen, are you raising a boy or a girl?" He walked toward the TV and Michael thought he looked like a giant towering over him. "Don't you know dancing is for girls? Girls, and girlie men. Is this what you want to be? A sissy? A girlie man?"

Was that the type of man he saw on the TV? A girlie man or a sissy? Real men don't dance? Derk ejected the tape and walked to the trash. "No!" Michael cried. His attachment to the tape confused him, since it contained something he could never become. He wasn't a girl or a sissy, so this meant he couldn't be a dancer, but he still felt connected to the performance on the tape.

The cassette made a soft thump as Derk tossed it into the three-day-old leftovers growing rank in the trash. Derk turned as he shot a threatening look at Michael. "Don't you even think about getting that tape out of the garbage. You need to be a man. I ain't living with no sissies."

Michael fought back the tears, but he could not stop his face from melting in the heat of Derk's searing words.

"See? You're gonna cry. You're not a man. I think I'll give you something to cry about. I'll make a man out of you yet." Derk stomped toward the bedroom, his frightening voice echoing in Michael's ears.

Michael decided not to be there when Derk returned. He unlocked the door and ran down the steps of the apartment. Sharp pebbles burrowed into his bare feet, but he continued running until out of sight, hoping Derk didn't follow. After rounding the corner, he sat on the cold curb, buried his head, and let his bottled up feelings flow out with the tears.

"What's a matter?" A voice called out. He looked up and saw the boy who had waved at him a few days ago.

"Nothin'."

"My name is Tommy."

Michael wiped his eyes on the back of his hands, trying

to regain composure. "My name's Michael."

"Why are you crying?"

"My mom's boyfriend got mad at me," Michael said.

"For what?"

After dropping his head again, he said, "You wouldn't understand. He just thinks I'm a sissy."

Tommy sat next to him, "Yeah. I hate it when people call me that."

Michael looked up, surprised at the admission. "Why do people call you sissy?"

"I like to sing. My gramma used to sing opera. She taught me how to sing since I was four. I like it, but people bully me and call me sissy because I sing opera - like my gramma."

"What do you do when they pick on you?"

"I keep on singing." Tommy smiled. "I used to tell my gramma I didn't want to sing anymore because I'm getting bullied. She told me to keep on singing. Gramma says bullies can't sing and they are just jealous. People who can't sing want to keep us from singing. Don't let them drag you down, just keep singing. She must have told me that a thousand times."

"My mom's boyfriend saw me dancing. I saw a guy on the TV who says dancing makes him feel alive. He said it is like being in another world." Michael scraped the remaining moisture off his cheeks, then wiped his fingers on his pants. "So I started dancing. I watched him and started doing what he does." He dropped his head and said, "Then Derk came out and said I was a sissy. He threw away the video and was going to get his belt. His belt hurts a lot, so I ran. He says boys don't dance, only girls and sissies."

Tommy nodded as he looked at Michael. "My gramma would tell you, just keep dancing. I wish I could dance."

"Hey! If you teach me how to sing, I'll teach you how to dance."

"Okay," Tommy said with excitement in his voice.

"Want to come to my apartment?"

Tommy had records that taught how to hit notes with his voice. Michael enjoyed trying to sing 'ah' to the various pitches the instructor gave on the CD. The two boys laughed and giggled when one of them would screech a note beyond their range. When he began learning, Michael screeched most of the notes, but Tommy seemed to hit all but the highest notes easily.

Over time, Michael began to hit more of the notes as he improved with practice. Sometimes he thought he hit the notes, but Tommy scrunched up his face. Tommy's mom also helped when they disagreed about Michael's performance. She was a good singer too, and helped the boys with their singing.

One day, Michael sat at the dinner table with Tommy and his family, and wished he could have a life like this. Michael had never seen a family that got along together. Tommy's mother and father seemed to care about him, but Michael had never experienced what a family felt like. Tommy liked going home and he didn't get threatened for no reason at all. His little sister was a pest, but even her pestering was nothing compared to living with Derk.

The boys finished eating and Tommy's mom took the dishes from the table and said, "It is time to start getting ready for bed. Michael will need to go home."

Tommy looked at Michael and smirked as he announced, "Me and Michael have something we want to show you first. We want to do a show."

"Okay, but it will have to be a quick one," his mother said.

The family moved to the den. All eyes were on the two boys as they stood before the semicircle of chairs and a couch. Tommy looked at Michael and a giggle slipped out, causing Michael to giggle with him. He put his hand over his mouth until the snicker went away. Tommy opened his mouth and sang, "What's playing at the Roxy?"

Michael spread his arms and returned in harmony, "I'll tell you what's playing at the Roxy."

The two young men sang and danced their way through 'Guys and Dolls' with a make-shift dance routine. Tommy's father and mother gave a standing ovation, and his little sister followed their lead.

"That was very good!" his mother said. The sincere pride he saw in her eyes struck Michael. "Thanks for the show, but it is time for Michael to go home now."

While walking toward the door of Tommy's apartment, Michael felt a hand on his shoulder. Tommy's dad said, "You and Tommy gave a fine performance. I think you two make a great team. I was really impressed."

Never had Michael heard anyone praise him. It felt good, and something about performing made him feel alive. He rushed up the stairs to his apartment, excited to tell his mother about the show.

"Mom! Mom!" Michael called with excitement as he burst through the door. His heart dropped when he saw the stack of boxes. He looked around the empty room, then to his mother. "We're not moving are we?"

"Get in the car, we are leaving now," she said. Desperation etched in her voice.

"Why? I don't want to go."

"Just get in the car, I can't explain right now," she said as she led him back to the door.

Derk finished carrying boxes down to a truck he'd borrowed. Michael climbed in the car beside his mother. His heart ached as he thought about Tommy, and he wished he could have said good-bye. His friend would never even know what happened.

"Meet me after you drop him off," Derk said as he climbed in the truck and pulled away.

"Drop me off where?" When his mom didn't answer, he asked, "Where are we going?" His mother just stared ahead as if drawn by something Michael couldn't see. "Mom?"

Her only words were, "I'm sorry, Michael." No explanation. No emotion. He looked out the window, wondering what lay ahead. Something in his stomach told him this wouldn't be a happy night.

Chapter Four

Michael watched the dusk turn to darkness during a drive that seemed like hours. The car turned into a neighborhood and he saw a decorative red brick wall. A light lit up a sign that said, *Wind Song Community*. The car made a second turn and hurried down a winding road for a few minutes, and then his mother turned the car onto a driveway.

His mom reached into the back seat, retrieved a small suitcase, and handed it to Michael. "Come on. You are going to stay with Uncle James for a while."

Loreen had three brothers, Joe, James, and John. James lived the closest to their location. She rang the doorbell, waited a few seconds, and rang again. The porch light came on and James opened the door.

Uncle James was a round man with a square goatee. His fuzzy navel flowed out from underneath his stretched-out T-shirt. Michael watched as his uncle looked at his mother, down to him, and back to his mom. Michael felt small and out of place holding his suitcase like an orphan.

"What is this?" James said as he looked down at him again.

"I'm leaving Michael with you," his mom said as though this was something James should have expected.

"What do you mean, you're leaving him?"

"Derk doesn't—" she stopped her words and looked down at Michael. "I can't take care of him, so I'm depending on you."

A long scowl spread across the face of James as he folded his arms in defiance. "Loreen, I can't take him in. This place is barely big enough for the two of us. We don't have kids. I don't know how to raise kids. Besides, he's your son and your responsibility."

Loreen turned and retreated from the porch, while Uncle James called her name and rushed after her. Michael fidgeted on the porch as he watched his mother get into her car. "You can't leave him here!" Uncle James shouted as the door slammed and the car backed out of the driveway. He followed the car out to the road, yelling at the vehicle. Michael's mom didn't wave or look back. Michael looked down to his feet as he toed the painted concrete while waiting for Uncle James.

His uncle walked up the driveway, grumbling to himself. He ascended the steps and pushed open the door. "Come on," he said in an annoyed tone, and walked into the house. Michael held the handle of his suitcase with both hands and walked in, avoiding eye contact with Uncle James. Aunt Sue waddled into the room.

Aunt Sue perfectly matched James in height, weight, and appetite. She had a surprised look when she saw Michael. Her eyes darted up to James, "What's going on?"

"It's Loreen," Uncle James said as he tossed his arm in the air. "She dumped him off at our doorstep. She wants us to take care of him."

"What?" She rushed over and looked out the door before turning back to Michael. She bent over and hugged his head, "You poor thing. It will be okay. Everything is going to be alright."

Aunt Sue's tender reassurance gave Michael a wave of comfort. He had held his emotions up to this point, but something about her words broke through his emotional wall, and tears began to perk up to his eyes. He tried to hold back his tears, but couldn't. He fought to stop them, but waves of his pent up emotions began cascading up and out, for all to see.

Aunt Sue took him to the couch and held him as she tried to be reassuring. Her arms could not erase the pain, or keep Michael's shattered world from crumbling around him. He had been ripped away from his only friend, and his mother had cast him off as a hindrance to her and Derk's lifestyle. Uncle James didn't want him, and he made this clear as he ranted around the house.

"James, please be quiet." Sue stroked the hair of her crying nephew and said, "Can't you see he's been shattered? Don't make it harder on him. It's not his fault."

When the well of tears dried up, Aunt Sue gave him ice cream, and turned the TV to a station with cartoons. Aunt Sue and Uncle James had cable TV, and Michael found it amazing to have so many things to watch. She turned the TV up loud and disappeared into the kitchen. Michael could hear them talking, but the noise from the cartoons obscured their words. He felt certain they were discussing something about him.

Michael finished his dessert and crawled onto the couch. He laid down and watched television until his eyes grew heavy. The show with Tommy was only a few hours ago, but already it seemed like a distant memory. He wondered if he would ever see Tommy again. Or when his mother would return.

"Michael, time to wake up." The soft voice of Aunt Sue reached into his lethargic head and pulled his thoughts into the bright morning. The smell of cooking bacon tickled his nose, causing his stomach to growl. He sat up and bullied the sleep out of his eyes with his balled up hands. He blinked and rubbed his eyes again. Trying to regain his bearings, he looked around and saw Uncle James sitting at the table in the kitchen, drinking coffee.

"Eat some breakfast, and then we are taking you to see Uncle Joe," Aunt Sue said, trying to sound enthusiastic.

Michael tottered to the kitchen to join his uncle while Aunt Sue poured a glass of orange juice. She left and returned with a plate of eggs, bacon, and cream of wheat.

Michael wolfed down the bacon and eggs, but only used the yucky white wheat for making swirls with his fork.

Uncle James eyed his artwork with a critical stare. "Aren't you going to eat your cream of wheat?"

"I don't like it," Michael said, then curled his lip and glared at the offending substance.

"How do you know? Do you have taste buds in your eyes? You didn't even try it," Uncle James said as he gave another scowl. Uncle James was good at scowling.

Aunt Sue scurried over and swooped up the plate. "It's time to get your stuff together so we can get on the road," she said over her shoulder as she scraped the plate and placed it into the sink. Uncle James gulped down his remaining coffee and disappeared into a bedroom. He emerged with a buttoned shirt; its tails dangled just beyond his protruding girth. He grabbed the suitcase and disappeared out the front door. He returned and impatiently waved Michael toward the car. The feelings of dread returned as Michael began the trail of silent tears to what seemed like a faraway land, and a house which would never feel like his home.

The three drove in silence until Aunt Sue leaned over the seat and spoke in her usual cheerful voice. "Do you remember Uncle Joe?" Michael shrugged. He had a vague memory of his uncle. He had seen him when the family gathered at Christmas two years ago. "Uncle Joe lives on a farm in Wedowee, Alabama. He has animals and you will have cousins your age. It will be a lot of fun for you."

Uncle James waved a hand in the air. "What kind of name is Wedowee, anyway? Who would name a town Wedowee?"

"I'm sure it's a nice place to live," Aunt Sue said to James. She turned back to Michael and gave a cheerful smile.

Michael wondered how long it would take to drive from Macon, Georgia to Alabama? Never had he been outside of Georgia. Instead of asking, he decided to look out the window. He nodded when Aunt Sue tried to make conversation, but didn't speak. A smile spread across his face when he thought about the show he'd put on with Tommy, but sadness returned when he remembered he would not see his friend again. Why couldn't he live with Tommy? It would be better than going from house to house where no one wanted him. Maybe Tommy's parents wouldn't want him either.

After a long drive, Uncle James turned off the highway and drove along winding roads. After some time, the car turned onto a long, bumpy driveway. The car's clock showed 3:15. They passed a barbed wire fence where cows grazed on the hillside. Michael could smell an odor he had never detected in Macon. He thought it smelled like someone who had not bathed in a whole month. Soon a white farmhouse came into view. It had windows coming out of the roof and a green painted porch stretched across the front and around the sides of the house.

"What kind of a bird is that?" Michael blurted out before his mind could stop his mouth.

"Those are chickens," Aunt Sue said as Uncle James gave a loud laugh. Michael had seen pictures of chickens, but he thought they were supposed to be white. These were orange birds with thick bodies. They strutted around the yard and pecked at everything that crossed their paths. When the door opened, Michael thought he heard one singing.

Three of Michael's cousins stood on the porch with his Uncle Joe and Aunt Beth. They all waved as Uncle James and Aunt Sue squeezed from the car. Michael felt a twinge of disappointment when he climbed out. Aunt Sue had said that some of his cousins were his age, but they were all teenagers.

Aunt Beth came down and gave Michael a warm hug and Uncle Joe took the suitcase. His cousins greeted him while Aunt Beth spoke to her visitors.

"Will you be staying the night?" Aunt Beth asked Uncle James and Aunt Sue.

Uncle James stretched his arms and legs back to life. "Naw. Me and the little woman are going to head over to Talladega for a few days. It's not often we get out to Alabama. Gonna see the motorsports hall of fame and maybe catch a race."

"Won't you stay for the meal?" Aunt Beth asked. "It will be a late lunch, but I had planned for you to eat when you got here."

Uncle James patted his large stomach, determined there was room, and gave a jolly answer. "It is a long ride. I could use a little honey for the journey. I might be able to muscle down a bite or two."

Muscle down a bite he did. Based on the amount he muscled down, Uncle James was quite an athlete. After the meal, Aunt Sue gave Michael a long hug, and soon the car carried the two down the dusty driveway, and out of Michael's life.

Though he hardly knew his Aunt Sue, he already missed her. The emptiness inside echoed with loneliness, and the tenderness of his heart began hardening. Feelings of rejection forced love into the past. He loved his mother, and she had rejected him. He'd found a close friendship with Tommy, but life ripped it away. Love wasn't worth the pain. Though he didn't understand it at the time, he had determined never to allow himself to be vulnerable again. If he didn't love, he couldn't get hurt. Michael would find refuge in the only thing no one could take away - his growing passion for dance.

Chapter Five

Michael stared into the darkness. Through his bedroom window, he could hear the sounds of cicadas and frogs echoing in the night air. The first few nights he had trouble sleeping with all the noise, but he learned to tune out their songs. Life was different on the farm. Non-stop work weaved itself into everything about farm life. Work before school, and work after school. Even a six year old found no escape from the labors waiting for attention.

Uncle Joe put him in charge of caring for the chickens. Each day he got up before the sun to feed and water the chickens, and when he returned from school, he dropped his books on the counter, grabbed a wire basket and began an egg hunt.

Even after Michael had combed through the yard and gathered the eggs in sight, Uncle Joe always found five or six he'd missed. Before supper, his uncle would hand him a basket and send him out to check again. After three attempts, Uncle Joe would walk around with Michael and hint at the location of the hiding brown eggs.

This night, the sounds were almost deafening. Warm air filled the room, but Michael closed the window to muffle the noise.

How did Uncle Joe find the eggs so easily? After rotating the pillow, his head felt cool for a moment. His thoughts began to fog, and his eyes grew heavy. Michael took comfort when he remembered this was Friday night. There would be work tomorrow, but no school.

Michael tried to hold on to sleep, but something shook

him out of the comfort of rest.

"Wake up." Uncle Joe shook him and spoke again. "Michael, it's time to wake up." He opened his eyes, but his mind tried to fade from the conscious world. The youngster rolled over in an attempt to evade his uncle's beckoning call. "Oh, no you don't." After several failed attempts to rouse Michael, Uncle Joe said, "You aren't getting out of work that easy. If you don't get up, a little cold water on your head will stir you into action."

The thought of cold water was almost as effective as the real thing. He rolled over and forced his eyes open. It looked darker than normal. Michael rubbed his eyes. "What time is it?"

"It's 4:30, and we need to get started."

"I thought I could sleep until five. Besides, it's Saturday," he said to his uncle's shadow.

"The farm doesn't take weekends off. Today you are going to learn how to milk a cow." Uncle Joe's cheerful voice made it sound exciting, but Michael wasn't so sure. "We need to get finished before breakfast."

Michael dragged his mind from sleep and his body from the comfortable bed. After pulling on his jeans, he tugged on his work boots and descended down the stairs with his uncle. A glass of water waited for him on the counter. He gulped a few swallows and headed toward the barn. Uncle Joe grabbed two pails, gave one to Michael, and led him to a stall with a large cow.

Uncle Joe pulled up a stool next to the cow, washed the teat, and said, "This is how you do it." He slid the pail under the udder before turning at an angle to give Michael a good view. "Okay, now watch what I am doing. Pinch the teat with your finger and thumb close to the top. Then grip with each finger as you work toward the tip." A stream of milk shot into the stainless steel pail, echoing a sound into the quiet morning. "Now release, and grip it again. What you are doing is letting the milk fill up the teat, and then forcing it out with your fingers. Now you try it."

His uncle stood and motioned to the stool. Michael looked at the massive cow, and then stared blankly at the udder. "Go on," Uncle Joe encouraged. "Sit on the stool and get a grip." Michael sat on the stool and reached toward the udder. The beast shifted, causing him to jump back. "Don't be afraid of her. She wants that milk out of her just as bad as we want to get it."

Michael sat down again. He looked back at Uncle Joe, who motioned toward the udder. The smell of the barn and the ugliness of the udder made his lip curl. Something in his stomach lurched. The hunger he'd felt moments ago fled. Slowly he turned to face the nasty cow. *What is in there wants to come out?*

After getting another gross whiff, he leaned back from the cow and turned to Uncle Joe. "Do I have to?"

"Come on, Michael. You're a big boy. Just reach in and take one of the teats." Uncle Joe put his hands on his hips. "Your cousins didn't have any problem with this. And Rebecca's a girl." He pointed back to the cow's udder.

The four teats hanging from the udder looked like giant earthworm heads rather than a source of milk. He certainly didn't want to touch one. A glance to his uncles confirmed his dread. No getting out of this one. He reached down. The surface of the skin felt rough and rubbery when he pinched it between his fingers and thumb. His uncle continued to prod him and he grabbed one and pulled. Nothing happened.

"Don't yank on them. Pinch it at the top and work down with your fingers."

Michael scrunched his face and reached back in to lay hold of it again. *Why can't we just get milk from the store?* He pinched and pulled. A single drop of milk dripped out. His uncle appeared delighted at the progress and coached him until he finally got a weak, but steady stream of milk into the bucket.

Uncle Joe looked down and smiled. "See? You *are* getting the hang of it. You will be a farmer before you know it." His uncle took the other bucket, and it clanked while he walked to another stall. His voice called over the wall, "You keep milking her until you can't get milk, and I'll work on the others. I'll check on you in a minute."

The happy sound of Uncle Joe's whistling matched the tempo of the streams hitting the bottom of his pail. Michael tugged away, but his cow never made a stream like he heard from his uncle's bucket.

Michael let out a long sigh. Jumpy legs didn't want to rest on the hard stool. Why did he have to do this? *I'll never complain about eggs again.* He slouched forward, and let his tired arms droop down.

A crackle of hay announced his approaching uncle. Michael reached under the cow and returned to milking. Uncle Joe walked to a large steel vat, poured out his full bucket, and then peeked in to see Michael's progress. Milk barely covered the bottom of the bucket.

Uncle Joe gave another encouraging smile. "Keep going. It takes a little time to learn, but you will get the hang of it." He whistled as he disappeared. Soon, the sound of streams of milk hitting the pail joined his tune. After visiting the other cows, he returned to Michael and finished milking his cow.

"You'll catch on before you know it. When you take over this job, always remember the cows can't wait. They have to be milked first thing in the morning, no matter what." Uncle Joe said it with enough conviction that Michael figured there must be a reason, but he didn't ask why.

His uncle poured the remaining buckets into the vat, where they were cooled, and then bottled through a spigot near the bottom. "I will come with you every morning until you get the hang of it. Then I'll let you take charge." He gave Michael's head a brisk rub. "Let's go get some breakfast before feeding the chickens."

When Michael walked in the door, the smells of breakfast danced around his head and his hunger returned. He hurried to the table and watched his cousin pouring milk into each glass. He took a sip and thought it somehow tasted sweeter after his labors. Family members began appearing around the table like flies drawn to the aroma. Aunt Beth placed bowls of food on the table, and then took her seat. All activity paused while Uncle Joe gave a prayer of thanks, then resumed with a renewed vigor as spoons and forks clanked against the plates.

"How do you like life here on the farm?" Aunt Beth asked. She scooped a pile of eggs and shot it onto his plate. Michael shrugged while examining the food and poking yesterday's egg hunt with his fork. He liked the family, but he didn't feel connected. He was an outsider. At least Derk wasn't here. But he would endure Derk if he could be with his mother. Heartache returned at the thought of his mom.

For a moment, he felt like crying, but Uncle Joe reached toward Michael with a plate of biscuits. A welcomed distraction.

The plate hovered for a long moment before his uncle asked, "Do you want one?" Michael took a biscuit and eased it onto his plate. "You've hardly said a word since you got here. We need to get you to open up a little," Uncle Joe said.

The plate of steaming biscuits made its way to the next hungry hand, and then continued to the other side of the table. His aunt made the best biscuits. The fresh butter tasted sweeter than what came from the store. He took a warm bite and looked up, made eye contact with his cousin Rebecca, and darted his gaze back to the food on his plate.

Encouraged by the glance, Rebecca decided to engage him in conversation. "How do you like school?" Michael answered with another shrug as he poked at the scrambled eggs with his fork. "Come on now, we know you can talk. What do you like best about school?"

"I dunno," Michael said as he stared at a slice of bacon. He poked at it, but felt the gaze of his cousin boring into him. He heard his cousin let out a frustrated sigh.

Aunt Beth corrected Rebecca with a sympathetic answer. "Give him time. He's been through a lot. He'll open up as he gets used to living with us."

Her comment carried optimism, but this would not come to be. Michael closed out the world and withdrew into his shell each time anyone attempted to connect with him. Only dance made him feel alive, but he hid this passion from his new family.

Longing to again return to his new found passion and to get lost in its realm of enchantment, Michael looked for an opportunity to get alone and dance, certain it had a role to play in his life.

Chapter Six

Lonely songs from the Rhode Island Reds serenaded Michael while he refilled the chickens' feeders. Worn sneakers dragged through the dust, and curious birds followed him through his morning duties. A cricket leaped from behind the trough, and a school of beaks raced for the fleeing insect. A bird emerged from the throng, holding the trophy high in the air, only to have it snatched from its beak. The violated chicken chased the robber, who swallowed the cricket with a quick shake of her head. In an instant, the birds forgot the insect, and returned their interest to Michael.

The chickens tried to comfort Michael with their songs, but his heart focused elsewhere. *When will mom come back for me? She said it would only be for a while. Maybe she had to find a new apartment again, and she'll come when she's done moving.*

He finished his poultry feeding and reached for the wire baskets to begin the daily egg hunt. The chickens laid eggs in strange places. Most of the eggs were deposited where they roosted, but he wondered why some of the birds made his job harder by hiding their brown-shelled eggs in unusual places.

How long is a while? It already seems like a long time.

He trudged to the sink to wash the eggs, and then set them out to dry. Michael took another trip around the yard, but found no hidden eggs. *How does Uncle Joe always find more?*

With his chores complete, Michael slipped away to the barn on the backside of the property. The simple farm had been in the family for several generations. A two-story house sat in the midst of six large oak trees which provided shade and shelter. A chicken coop stood on the right side of the house with a broken down fence around it. The chickens had pecked every living plant out of the dark soil near the coop, but they found plenty of vegetation around the house.

A grazing pasture rolled up a hill to the left of the house. A large barn housed the cows and provided a place for milking. An open building had two dozen wire stalls where baby calves were sheltered and cared for. Toward the back of the property stood an old horse barn with a tractor shed poking out from the side. The horses had been sold long ago, so the barn now stored feed and tools. Behind the barn were the cornfields and vegetable gardens.

Near the house, Aunt Beth's manicured flower gardens were ablaze with bright colors. Two giant pecan trees marked the corners of the yard. Michael inhaled the sweet fragrance of roses as he walked through the yard toward the barn. Even his mother's perfume couldn't compare to this flowering aroma.

The family dog followed him as it bounded up and down. He picked up a stick and hurled it across the yard, giving the dog the joy of a new mission.

Michael reached the barn, lifted the latch, and gave the barn door a tug. It let out a long, slow groan. He enjoyed exploring the farm and had already found that the old barn held many hiding places. It was crowded on the lower floor, but the loft was open except for a few bales of hay.

Wooden rungs creaked when he climbed up. At the end of the loft, sunlight filtered around the edges of a door. It took some effort to free the hooked latch on the door, but he managed to force it loose and pushed it open. A breeze of fresh air swept away the stale odor of hay, and sunlight chased away the darkness. Michael stepped to the center of the floor, and began reliving the memory of his performance with Tommy. He hummed a tune and closed his eyes, imagining he and Tommy were dancing on a stage.

Uncle Joe strolled through the yard, counting the eggs his nephew had missed. Nearby, Aunt Beth worked with cousin Rebecca, evicting weeds from her flower beds. "Where is Michael? He needs to finish picking up the eggs from the yard." Rebecca pointed toward the barn. "Go get him for me," Joe said and headed into the house to get a wire egg basket.

The barn door stood open, but she didn't see any sign of Michael. Rebecca started to leave, but then heard a commotion above her. It sounded like a wrestling match. She crept up the wooden ladder and peered into the old hayloft. Her mouth gaped. She climbed back down and ran to her mother.

"Mom, you've got to see this," Rebecca said in a pant.

"What's wrong?"

"You'll never believe what shy little Michael is doing in the hayloft. He is dancing up a storm." Rebecca grabbed Aunt Beth by the hand and rushed back toward the barn. "Hurry, before he stops."

Beth eased up the ladder as she scanned the loft to locate the sound of Michael's shuffling. Michael hummed as he danced, eyes closed, lost in a world of his own. "I don't believe it," she whispered down to Rebecca.

"What did I tell you? And he is actually dancing pretty good," Rebecca said with a knowing smile.

Beth shifted to get a better look and a creak echoed from the rung she stood on. Michael stopped and turned. His face flushed when their eyes met, and he looked down. Aunt Beth waited for an awkward moment before speaking. "Uncle Joe wants you. He has found some more eggs."

Beth climbed down and Michael followed. They walked in silence for a while before she said, "You were very good up there. Where'd you learn to dance?" Michael just shrugged and studied the ground.

Joe held out a basket when they arrived at the house. Aunt Beth said, "Rebecca, why don't you help Michael find the eggs today." She took the basket from Uncle Joe and handed it to her daughter. Joe gave a quizzical look, and she gave a glance which told him not to say anything. Rebecca took the basket and walked across the yard with Michael. Joe followed her into the house.

"What's going on?" Joe asked.

Beth reassured him with a smile. "Did you know your nephew is a dancer?" Joe raised a suspicious eyebrow. "You should have seen him in the hayloft."

"Shy little Michael? I don't believe that."

"It's true. He was dancing like a real performer. You would never know the boy in the loft was the same boy who never talks. He looked like someone with no inhibitions. The little boy with the drooping shoulders, who never takes his eyes off the ground, looked like a young man—his head held high. He was actually good." Beth laughed and shook her head. "I wouldn't believe it myself, if I hadn't seen it."

Joe stroked his chin and tried to absorb her words. After a long moment he said, "Do you think we should—"

"Find a place he can dance?"

Joe nodded. "To be honest, I've been very concerned. He seems to be closing himself to the world and everyone around him. I thought farm life would help, but he seems to become more isolated with each day. But if this is something that interests him, maybe there is hope for the boy."

Beth placed her hand on his arm. "Joe, his self-esteem has been shattered and he needs something to draw him out of his shell. Let's see if we can get Michael involved in a program."

"I agree, but this isn't exactly a town with a lot to offer. Do they have programs like this in Wedowee?"

Beth's face lit up. "Actually, there is a studio in town. It will be a challenge to get him there, but we have to do something. If we don't re-engage him, I'm afraid of what he'll become. I can't bear to watch him dry up, and dancing just might be the outlet he needs for his emotions."

Michael's heart leapt when he entered the Wedowee Dance Studio with his Aunt Beth. He was actually going to learn to dance! The two were greeted by a smiling lady in tights.

"Hi! I'm Ms. Thomas. Are you Beth?" the woman asked and reached out for Beth's hand. They shook and then she kneeled before Michael. "You must be our new student." Michael stared at his shoes and didn't look up. Unfazed, the teacher continued, "We are so excited to have you." She reached for a clipboard and handed it to Aunt Beth. "Fill out the new student form at the reception desk and I'll introduce him to his teacher."

The woman put her hand on the small of Michael's back and ushered him into a large room where many eyes turned to greet him. There were two boys and about a dozen girls. The teacher stopped her lesson when Michael walked before the class. "Michael, this is your teacher, Ms. Johnson. This is Michael. Michael Camp."

Michael looked around the room, but avoided the eyes of the students staring at him. Mirrors surrounded the room and wooden bars extended from the walls. A trophy case stood at the front of the room. A broken trophy in the center of the case captured his attention. The otherwise beautiful trophy displayed a victorious dancer, missing its leg.

Ms. Johnson greeted Michael and turned to the class, "Students, be sure and welcome Michael Camp to our studio." She instructed the class to pair up and continue practicing while she worked with Michael. "Do you think you would like modern dance?" Michael shrugged. "Have you ever danced before?" She placed her hand under his chin to lift his eyes off the ground and looked into his crystal blue eyes. "You are going to have to look at me. Have you danced before?"

"A little."

"Do you like it?"

"Yeah."

Ms. Johnson smiled. "You aren't a talker are you? That's okay. If you work hard, your dancing will do your talking." She led Michael to a mat. "Okay, Michael. I want you to show me something you've learned." Michael mumbled his words at the floor, and the teacher raised his chin again. "You need to look at me when you talk, and talk clearly."

"I just know a dance I saw on TV. Me and Tommy danced for a Guys and Dolls song..." His voice trailed off while he returned his gaze to the floor.

Ms. Johnson gently raised his chin. "There is nothing on the floor. You need to look at me." She brushed strands of light blond hair behind her ear and said, "Show me your dance."

Michael felt sick at his stomach. This wasn't like performing with Tommy. It seemed different standing alone. Derk's words rang in his mind, "Dancing is for girls and girlie men."

The dance teacher gave an encouraging smile. "Don't be afraid. We are here to teach you. But to teach you, I need to see what you can do."

After closing his eyes to hide the world, Michael concentrated on the song in his head. He pictured the dancer he saw on the television and stepped forward. In a moment, the world around him faded, and music filled his mind while the dance charged his heart. He danced and turned. The boy's graceful arm motions and polished footwork surprised his teacher. He stumbled for a moment when his sneakers gripped the mat, but quickly regained his composure.

When he opened his eyes, his teacher stared, one brow cocked into a graceful arch. His aunt had walked up, and stood behind her. Her beaming smile made him both embarrassed and excited. Aunt Beth looked down at his teacher. "Not bad for a boy who's never had a lesson, huh?"

"Not bad at all," Ms. Johnson said while rising from her kneeling position. "He's such a shy boy, but when he starts his dance, he loses inhibitions." She turned to Michael and said, "Your movements have a lot of natural grace in them. That is hard for most boys to learn. If you apply yourself, you will be a good dancer." She turned and called a student from across the room, "Marty, take Michael and teach him how to do warm ups."

Beth watched Michael shuffle across the room with the other student. Ms. Johnson said, "I have to say it isn't often I'm surprised. When students come in, I usually see a clumsy child which needs a lot of work just to get to ground zero, but I am amazed at his natural grace. And he has never taken dance before?"

Aunt Beth shook her head. "No. He has been very neglected since he was born, and his mother recently abandoned him. He has a lot of emotional problems and when I saw him dance, I thought this might be a good outlet for him."

"I'm sorry to hear that." Ms Johnson looked across the room and said, "But I do have to say, I'm pretty excited. We might actually have a real dancer in our class." She looked back to Beth. "If he can overcome his insecurities, this young man has real potential."

Chapter Seven

For the next ten years, Michael learned to perform in the Wedowee studio. Soon after turning sixteen, Ms. Johnson approached him during practice. She held up a brochure. "Michael, I need to talk to you about something." Michael climbed to his feet and followed his teacher away from the rest of the class. "Michael, I think you are ready for the next step." He looked at her with curiosity, not knowing what to expect. "I think you should enter the *World Youth Grand Prix.*"

"What's that?"

The teacher placed the brochure in Michael's hand. "It's an international competition where youth from all over the world compete in a Grand Prix - a dance championship. You have talent. Real talent. I think you need to apply yourself one hundred percent and prepare for this competition. Winning prestigious competitions is what gets you noticed, and can launch you into a career of dance. Does this sound like something you would like to do?"

Michael nodded and his teacher gave a tender smile. "Good. I'll talk to your aunt and enter you into the competition. They have ballet and contemporary dance. You're good at both, but I think you are stronger on contemporary dance."

"It's what I want to do," Michael said.

"That's what I thought you would say." Michael turned to leave, but Ms. Johnson remembered another detail, "The only problem is we need to get you to New York." She said it as if it was a minor detail, but Michael thought about how far away New York was from Wedowee, Alabama. How would his aunt and uncle afford to send him to New York?

Excitement over the thought of competing pulsed through Michael. He wolfed down his supper, and rushed to the barn. Climbing up the wooden ladder leading to the hayloft, Michael prepared to commit himself to practicing the routines Ms. Johnson had given him. She worked with him each afternoon, and he spent the last few hours of daylight after supper repeating the routines until he ran out of daylight. All the major dance schools recruited their top prospects from this competition.

At every opportunity, his teacher warned him about how hard the competition would be. The best youth dancers in the world would be competing, and many great dancers failed to make it into the final rounds. She explained being good wasn't good enough. Even being great is often not good enough. He would have to put in the performance of his life, and it would require working harder, and being more dedicated than the competition.

Despite the competitive level he would be up against, she believed he had the ability to overcome the odds facing him. Ms. Johnson had competed as a youth and though she did not make it past the semifinals, she seemed confident Michael could. She believed he had the intangibles that set great dancers above those with mere talent.

He reflected on Ms. Johnson's pep talk. She explained, those who achieved greatness had something within them which illuminated a performance beyond technique, and into the unknown element that strikes at the heart of the audience and judges. He could not reach this level without perfect technique, but technique alone would not lift a dancer to the top. Rarely does a dancer arrive on the scene with the stage presence she believed Michael had.

The teacher had a way of presenting the reality of challenges with enough discouragement to create a fear of complacency, while using her ability to encourage others as a source of inspiration, calling students to reach for lofty goals. Her students were anchored in confidence but fearful of arrogance. Daily she built students up, while teaching that overconfidence was a guarantee of failure.

She pushed Michael to dig deep down for the determination to rise above his limitations. Each day seemed like the process of tearing down what was flawed, and building up his technique, skill, and hope. When Michael became frustrated and felt like giving up, Ms. Johnson would begin building up her pupil. Somehow, she always knew when to take him down a notch or two, and when to stop breaking down and start encouraging.

Dreams are free, but money was tight. Dreams alone would not pay for travel, so Uncle Joe took Michael to the Wedowee Farm and Feed Supply store. Long time family friend, Johnson Parker, agreed to hire Michael part-time so he could raise the money for the dance competition in New York. Since Michael was sixteen and had a license, Mr. Parker hired him to load up feed orders and drop them off at nearby farms. He would get five dollars an hour plus any tips the locals would pay him.

The bags of feed weighed twenty-five to fifty pounds each. Michael had to load them on the truck, deliver them, and then unload them for customers. Backbreaking work wasn't the most exciting activity for Saturdays, but held the only hope he had for getting to New York. After a few weeks, Mr. Parker gave him a fifty-cent raise and two more days to work after school. He now worked fifteen hours a week and had earned nearly one hundred dollars including tips.

With the Grand Prix only eight weeks away, at the most, Michael would earn eight hundred dollars. Less than half of what he needed to compete in New York. Ms. Johnson encouraged Michael to continue working toward his goal even though it didn't seem possible. She kept telling him something would come through.

"Always be prepared," Ms. Johnson would say, "Luck is when preparation meets opportunity." This was her way of saying, if Michael worked hard, it would pay off, even if the odds were small.

The morning of the first day of the competition arrived, but Michael remained in Alabama. He walked down the halls of high school, trying to push New York out of his mind. Michael had known the chances of him making it to New York were small. Though he'd tried not to get excited, he could not help but feel disappointed as he watched his opportunity passing by with each tick of the clock. He'd worked hard every day preparing for this event, and trying to earn enough money to go. Though he had known from the beginning it was a long shot, the thought of his wasted efforts were weighing down on him.

Plopping behind his desk with a sigh, the teacher's voice seemed like a faint echo, blurred from his conscious mind by his heavy heart. He doodled on his assignment paper as his mind squiggled around in random thoughts. He kept pushing the Grand Prix from his mind, but the thoughts about New York climbed over his guarded emotions. All his dreams were now out of reach.

At this moment, hundreds of dancers were gathering as each envisioned themselves holding the Grand Prix in their hands. Michael wondered what it would feel like to win a major competition.

The bell rang.

"Class, place your completed assignments on the stack on my desk," the teacher instructed.

He looked at the meaningless drawings on the paper, and decided to sneak out of the room by placing himself behind the students hurrying into the hall. Outside the class, he dragged along as he headed to math class. The bell soon rang, warning students to find their seats. Another couple of minutes and the late bell would ring. The hallway before him emptied. A boy raced toward his classroom, trying to beat the late bell.

The bell rang. He stood outside the door, wondering how he would be able to concentrate on numbers and equations. He felt dread at the thought. Michael turned and walked away, heading toward the library. In the quietness of the library, he could get lost in thought and withdraw from his academic demands for an hour.

Taking a book off the shelf, he flipped through the pages, examining the dancers of the past. It would be nice to have his life depicted in a book one day, but who cared about wannabe dancers from small town Alabama?

It seemed like only moments passed before the bell rang again. Students began filing out of their rooms, some rushing into the library as they sought books for assignments. He continued flipping the pages and looking at the bios of those who had achieved greatness. Most of these were ballet dancers. He had studied ballet, but his ambitions were for modern dance and theater.

"Michael!" His thoughts were shattered by the sharp voice of his math teacher. "Why weren't you in class?"

"Crap," he said to himself, wondering why he hadn't taken a seat in one of the study carrels where he could be hidden from view. Now he would get detention for skipping class.

"Michael, your aunt has been looking all over for you. You need to report to the office now. You should have left an hour ago."

"What's wrong?" Michael said as his heart raced.

"You have a ticket to New York," his teacher said as she shooed him out of the library. He raced down the hall to the principal's office where his aunt had a panicked look as she paced, but relief washed over her face when Michael approached.

Mrs. Parker had heard Michael was going to miss the competition and persuaded his boss, Mr. Parker, to sponsor the trip. The flight would take off from Birmingham in two hours. It would be a stretch just to make it in time.

His aunt rushed him to the car where his bags were already packed. The car sped up highway 431 toward the interstate leading to Birmingham. The trip would take nearly two hours, so they had to make up time and hope to not pass a speed trap. The car raced onto the interstate, as Michael fidgeted in the passenger seat. Today was the first day of the Grand Prix. The registration and auditions would end at six o'clock this evening, so not only did they have to make it to the airport in time for the flight, but they also needed to land, and make it to the registration in time to enter the competition. It was a small window of opportunity, bordering on the impossible.

The car pulled into the long-term parking at ten minutes until two. Michael and Aunt Beth raced toward the terminal, bags in hand. The lines at the airport were light, but the clock showed 3 minutes until two o'clock when they passed through security. Michael had never seen his aunt run so fast and her endurance surprised him. They approached the counter with boarding passes in hand.

"I'm sorry, the captain has already closed the door to the plane. You will have to take an alternate flight," the woman at the counter said without looking up from her work.

"Can you please double check, my nephew has an international dance competition in New York, and he will not be able to compete unless we get on this flight," Aunt Beth pleaded.

"I'm sorry. You will need to rebook the flight." The woman turned away.

"Please, can you check? This is his only opportunity."

"We cannot board you after the door closes," she snapped with a tone bordering on annoyance. Aunt Beth buried her head in her hands as she plopped her elbows on the counter.

A man approaching from behind overheard the exchange. "Let me check something for you, ma'am." He walked over and picked up a phone. He chatted for a moment and hung up, "The captain hasn't pulled away and has agreed to get you on board."

Aunt Beth gripped the man's hand with both of hers as she exclaimed, "Oh, thank you. Thank you. Thank you."

"Good luck on your competition." He smiled as he let them through the door leading to the plane. Michael couldn't believe it. Opportunity had met preparation, and they were heading to New York. Now he wondered if they could make it to the auditions in time?

Chapter Eight

Michael and Aunt Beth stepped off the subway and looked for the R. Bolger Performing Arts Center. They found it on a map, and hurried up 55th Street. It now pushed five-thirty, and they had just located the center. The workers at the booth where participants registered were beginning to gather their papers together as they prepared to close for the day. Aunt Beth began a discussion with the attendant who informed her that the registration was now closed. The conversation turned heated when she demanded to speak with someone in charge. A worker led her into a room where the discussion continued while Michael waited in the foyer.

Aunt Beth remained persistent, and refused to be denied. After what seemed like twenty agonizing minutes, Aunt Beth emerged with a number, which Michael affixed to his belt before a worker escorted him to the auditorium. The awkwardness of being late seemed worsened by Michael's lack of proper dress. The baggage did not make it onto the plane and would not get to them until the next flight, arriving several hours from now.

Michael stood before a panel of judges wearing a T-shirt and blue jeans. He looked around to see the professional looking dancers gracefully bounding around with tights, tutus, and theatrical outfits. He alone stood in the audition room in street clothes. The graceful movements of the girl next to him sent a wave of doubt through his mind.

I look like a hick from Alabama. Why am I here in New York standing in tattered jeans in front of snooty judges?

A judge motioned for him to come forward. A woman looked down to a piece of paper, then looked up, peering over the rims of her reading glasses. "You are Michael Camp?" He nodded, feeling even more unsure as he stood before three scowling faces behind the judge's table. "Why are you not appropriately dressed?" Three frozen faces stared, awaiting his response.

"I-I didn't know I was coming until the last minute. Then the plane lost our luggage," Michael said, wondering if his voice sounded as shaky to the judges as it did to him.

The woman in the middle pulled off her glasses as she stared into his soul. She finally spoke, "You don't carry a spare outfit when you travel to compete?" She gnawed on the earpiece of her glasses as she waited for a response.

Michael shrugged, then spoke the only words that came to mind. "I'm sorry. This is my first national competition, and I've never flown before."

"I would suggest, in the future, you be prepared. You need to expect the unexpected." She continued to stare. Michael shifted from one foot to the other. The woman raised her eyebrows and sighed, looked down at the paper before her as she made a scribble. "Very well," she conceded. "What are you going to perform?"

"Don Quixote," he squeaked nervously. Ms. Johnson had him prepare for the competition by learning Don Quixote since it's a favorite of the ballet community. When he passed the auditions, he would perform the contemporary dance.

The woman's eyebrows arched again as if announcing her skepticism that such a dance could find its way into small town Alabama. The two other judges turned to the woman as if seeking reassurance such a performance was acceptable from a southern redneck. She gave a weak nod. The stone faces returned their gaze to Michael as the judge allowed his absurd request. "Very well then. You may proceed."

The dancer closed his eyes for a moment, blocking out everything but the music in his mind and the world of dance. Michael stepped into his routine and launched into the air with a leap that felt like it defied gravity. He stepped through the dance he'd practiced so many times it now seemed to be a part of him.

For the moment, Michael seemed to be in a world beyond the judge's station in New York. The dance made him feel alive as he tuned out the scenery around him, only reminded of his location by the ungraceful flapping of the legs of the blue jeans. For a moment, he wondered if his performance would be overthrown by his worn jeans, but forced himself to push all thought from his mind but the dance.

Michael launched into the highest leap he could muster. He landed, completing his routine with a pirouette, then stopping before the judges on one knee with his arms raised high. He opened his eyes, expecting the judges to be impressed with his unexpected performance. Three faces without expression looked down at him. Nothing but a blank stare. Had he impressed them? Did they hate his performance?

Each of the three judges looked down to their clipboards and jotted mechanically. Without emotion, the woman in the middle of the table looked up from her writing and said, "That will be all, thank you."

His mind raced to find something to interpret, but the faces and voices before him were like blank pieces of paper. Perhaps his hick town performance didn't compare to the refined dancers these judges saw everyday.

"You may wait in the auditorium. Those who advance will be announced at eight," the woman said, then returned her attention to the papers before her.

Walking away from the judge's table, Michael had a foreboding feeling. Instead of walking out like a victor, the head judge made him feel small and his performance seemed unimpressive. As he exited the auditorium, Aunt Beth clasped her hands together and rushed to meet him.

"How did you do?"

Shrugging his shoulders, Michael said, "I dunno."

"Well, how do you think you did?"

"I felt good when I danced, but the judges didn't seem impressed. I don't think they liked it," he said as he tried to distance himself from the cold auditorium. "They didn't like my clothes."

"Did you tell them our luggage didn't arrive yet?"

"Yes, Aunt Beth," Michael said with an annoyed sigh. He really didn't feel like rehashing the exchange. "I told them but they said I should have been more prepared. I really don't want to talk about it. I don't think the judges liked me very much."

His aunt tried to comfort him with the usual reassuring words people say when someone falls flat on their face. Everyone always claims trying your best is good enough, but it never makes losing feel better. It really boils down to succeeding or failing. Working long hours for months always seems like a waste of time when you fall short of a goal. Words can't change this fact.

He didn't feel like eating with his stomach in knots, so he waited in the auditorium while his aunt went for a snack. The odd looks of several dancers reminded Michael that his clothes were not appropriate for the competition. For a moment, he entertained the idea of getting away from this building and away from the people with scornful looks.

Now, time for the agonizing wait. Michael had the urge to pace around, but with his clothes, he decided to remain seated where fewer people would cast their glances his way.

Just after eight o'clock, the judges filed in as a spokesman called the meeting to order. There were several pre-trial events around the US and the world, and today's auditions would only advance fifty dancers to the stage performance competition. Before moving on to read the names of those advancing, a few judges spoke encouragement to those who were fine dancers, but were not yet ready to advance to the next level of competition.

The auditorium was filled to capacity with hopeful

dancers and spectators. Michael listened as the first ten were announced. His name wasn't mentioned. He grew impatient when the list reached twenty, twenty-five, thirty. Forty names passed, and no 'Michael'. Forty-five names rolled off the announcer's lips. The judge swapped pages, then continued to number forty-six, seven, eight. "Number forty-nine," the man proclaimed, "Michael Camp..."

Michael shook his head in disbelief. He didn't hear the final name, or anything else said for the next few minutes. He had made it into the competition! Somehow, wearing his tattered blue jeans and standing before the scornful judges, he had made enough of a showing to impress them. He rushed out of the auditorium, past disappointed faces, to find his aunt. "I made it!" he shouted as he bounded with new life.

Aunt Beth had been too nervous to watch, and waited outside with her hands clasped in hopeful prayer. She saw Michael's wide smile and shouted with joy as she jumped up and threw her arms around him. Even though the first round of competition didn't start until tomorrow, this seemed like a great victory. Everything that seemed to go wrong as they fought to get into the auditions was forgotten. Now he had to prepare for the real test.

The announcer instructed the crowd not to applaud for individual dancers, but to save all applause for the end. Fifty dancers prepared backstage for their moment to prove their skills to the judges of the competition. The winner of the Grand Prix would receive a full paid scholarship to Pahl School of Dance along with a thousand dollar cash prize.

With the chaos of yesterday's events behind him, Michael tried to focus on warm ups. His mind raced through the choreography Ms. Johnson had been teaching him. The contemporary dance competition was open to any style dancers felt would show off their talent. Ms. Johnson had developed this choreography during the prime of her dancing career, when her dreams were still alive. She said her dreams were now faded glory, but this choreography still teemed with possibilities. Deep down, she lived her dream through Michael, and knowing he would be performing her choreography made her dreams come to life.

A random drawing put Michael as the eleventh competitor.

Expressionless eyes greeted him as he stepped on the stage before the panel of judges. The stone faces didn't seem as foreboding now that his clothes looked like a dancer's. And he had the affirmation of yesterday's selection to encourage him. Twenty-five of the dancers from today would be moving ahead to join the dancers from four other competitions held throughout the world. One hundred would converge next month to compete in the semifinals.

Yesterday's audition wasn't public, but today they performed before a packed auditorium. Michael examined the crowd and suddenly felt weak in his legs. He turned to the sound technician and saw him nod, indicating it was show time.

Michael closed his eyes and allowed the music to carry him to the secret place where dancers live, and then began his performance. He began his dance as he bounded into the air. The knees weakened by his shaking nerves found new strength, and he remained only vaguely aware of the reaction of the crowd as they expressed their appreciation for his introduction. Gravity seemed to lose its power as he sprang from the stage, moving gracefully through the choreography as if it were bound to him through natural instinct.

Ignoring the instructions given by the host, the crowd erupted with cheers and applause. With a sense of relief, Michael returned his mind to the world around him, and the reaction of the audience almost overwhelmed him. The dancers who had given him scornful glances now showed concerned expressions, realizing the hick dancer from Wedowee had come here to compete.

Following the performances, the twenty-five semifinalists were announced. Michael Camp was among the first to be called out. As he moved from the auditorium, conversation filled the air, and excitement surged through him when he saw someone point toward him and declare him as one of the dancers to beat. He remembered the warning of his teacher that arrogance leads to certain defeat. He had to keep a level head and remain focused, but he couldn't help feeling like he was driven by an unstoppable force. Judging by the crowd's response, he stood out as one of the best dancers in the competition. It couldn't be arrogance if it was true.

The next round would bring in stiffer competition as the additional seventy-five semifinalists from other sites joined the battle for recognition. The obstacles which challenged him seemed to be no match for the invincible dancer. It felt as though destiny had already put the competition in his hands. He couldn't foresee the coming hardships that would challenge him beyond his preparations.

Chapter Nine

The response of the people of his small town surprised Michael when he and Aunt Beth returned. People kept saying he had put Wedowee on the map. Ms. Johnson took advantage of the small town excitement and petitioned for donations to pay for Michael's trip for the semifinals. She all but guaranteed a victory to potential donors as she explained the need to pay for transportation to both the semifinals and final competition. "When he wins," she would say, "everyone will know where Wedowee is and you can tell people you helped make it happen."

She also explained the need to raise enough money, so Michael could devote all his energy to training instead of reducing his chances by having to spend his practice time delivering feed. Ms. Johnson looked like a proud mother, living out her dreams of glory in Michael.

In the studio, training became merciless. Every time Michael wanted to take a day off, Ms. Johnson would say, "The competition you met is nothing compared to what you will see in the semifinals and finals. Being good is not enough. Being great is not enough. You have to show the judges something that sets you beyond the competition. That will not be possible unless you are more dedicated than your opponents."

Michael had thought he knew what it meant to work, but in the month leading up to the competition, Ms. Johnson pressed him harder than he thought possible. He had to jump higher, perform flawlessly, and make his movements flow with grace. She set goals for his jumping ability, and as he met the goal, she would raise the bar. She would make him practice each step and movement until he thought his legs and arms would detach from his body. Just when Michael felt he had mastered the move they had been working on, she would blurt out, "Don't look like you are working. Make your arms move effortlessly. Smile, and look as though you aren't putting an effort behind your jumps."

"How can I leap four feet into the air and look like I'm not putting an effort behind my jumps?" Michael complained. "How can I make my arms look like they are flowing when they are about to fall off?"

"Michael," Ms. Johnson said as she looked him in the eye, "even though dancing is physically demanding, competition is ninety-percent mental. Your arms may be screaming in pain," she turned and pointed to an imaginary panel of judges and said, "but they must think you are carefree and floating on air.

"You smile like you are moving gracefully without effort. Act like you are being carried on the wings of the wind, floating without gravity, and they will believe it. A true champion and master performer makes his audience believe he can do the impossible. And do it without effort. Your graceful motions must hide the struggles behind your efforts and give the illusion that you are beyond human limitation, so your dance is the only thing the audience sees. Your stage presence must not distract the audience from the dance. When you master the art of illusion, you master the audience. And the judges. That battle is not won on the stage," she pointed to the matt below his feet. "But right here where you and your limits battle for who will control your performance."

Michael opened his mouth, but decided not to speak. He didn't like the hard work his teacher forced him to endure, but what could he say that she would accept? If he said he was tired, she would just tell him to master his fatigue. His mind shuffled through a dozen excuses that would allow him to quit, but each argument dissipated under what he knew Ms. Johnson would say. *This is going to be a long month.*

After weeks of training, Michael returned to New York for the semifinals. At last, he could take a welcomed break from the daily labors. For the last few weeks, Michael crawled into bed aching with exhaustion each night. But he couldn't deny his endurance had improved beyond what he thought possible. Even the height of his leaps excelled beyond his expectations. When in his zone, his body seemed to take flight as he launched across the stage.

His aunt waited in the foyer as Michael stood in line to complete his registration. After inching through the line, he at last stood before the desk. A woman with short black hair took his information card, looked at it and then asked, "What choreography are you dancing to? I can't read your writing."

"Starlight." Michael smiled to himself as he thought it should be called, 'Star flight', since he seemed to spend more time in the air than on the floor.

"I haven't heard that title before," the woman said as she wrote the information on a form.

"It is something my teacher wrote. It's modern dance."

"Interesting. Be sure and deliver your music to production, and good luck in the competition."

Michael returned to the foyer to meet his aunt. As he walked, he examined the faces around him, surprised to see so many people who looked to be from different nationalities. Including the auditions, Ms. Johnson said more than twenty-five-hundred dancers had tried out for the competition around the world. Just to be in the one-hundred semifinalists was an honor in itself.

Fifty would advance to the finals in June, and only six would be awarded prizes in the final round. The top dancer would be honored with the Grand Prix.

What must it feel like to stand in front of the stage and hear the judges proclaim you as the world's top youth dancer?

He remembered how Ms. Johnson explained to only concern himself with making the finals, and to do so, he must focus on this dance, one move at a time. But it's hard to not look ahead.

"Come on Michael," Aunt Beth called out, interrupting his thoughts. "Let's get something to eat and get back to the hotel. You need to be rested for tomorrow."

Michael hardly slept, but he made sure to arrive early in the morning so he could get comfortable in his surroundings before the competition began. He liked the charged atmosphere when the place filled with excited dancers. Unlike his high school experiences, there were no bullies calling out taunts here. And no odd glances when someone discovered he danced. Everyone was a dancer in this place.

A woman introduced herself as the production coordinator, and then gave instructions and schedules. One-hundred dancers were warming up as they prepared to perform over the next three days. The top dancers would go last, on Saturday, when the largest crowd would be present. The schedule testified to Michael's low ranking, and he would be one of the first competitors. Not coming from a prestigious institution, he would have a smaller chance of getting highly ranked. It was hard to get highly ranked when not coming from a prestigious institution. *At least I'm here.*

A spot opened on the practice mat, so he decided to stretch out. "Perfect warm ups is the key to perfect dancing," Ms. Johnson often repeated to their class back in

Wedowee. "Never rush your body. Never dance cold. Never let yourself get cold."

He took everything slow, being careful not to take anything for granted on this important day. He stretched his legs, arms, back, and then worked into preparedness with progressive dance routines. After stretching out the idleness of the last two days, Michael felt strong. He moved to the open floor and began elevating his jumps, going higher as he felt his legs limbering. He spun into a few pirouettes, followed by higher and higher leaps. Now he felt ready for the competition!

Let me show you guys how the big boys jump.

After coming out of a spin, Michael launched himself high into the air, holding his pose for a long moment before preparing to land. Out of the corner of his eye, he spied a gym bag, which wasn't supposed to be on the open floor. Michael tried to avoid it, but his rapid descension made it impossible to dodge the object. His ankle buckled with an audible pop as he landed on the side of the bag, and he crumpled to the floor. Crying out in pain, he rolled into a ball, clinching his ankle. He could already feel it swelling as the coordinator rushed over and called out for someone to bring a bag of ice.

Sharp, throbbing pain started in the joint of his ankle as it sent aching shock waves up the sides of his leg, ending just below his knee. Tears stung his eyes as Michael called out, "I thought no one was supposed to put anything on the open floor! Now my only chance is gone!"

The disappointment stabbing his heart now surpassed the bolts of pain running up his leg. He had worked so hard for this moment, and now it looked out of reach.

The trainer examined him for a moment and then said, "Stand up and see if you can put weight on your foot."

With a grimace, he gripped the trainer's arm, stood on his right leg, and tried to shift his weight to his left foot. Bolts of electricity shot through his ankle, and he cried out.

The intense pain caused him to stumble, and he tried to return his balance back to his right leg. The director arrived to assess the situation.

Michael's heart sank when the trainer glanced to the director and shook his head. "It's no good," the trainer said. "He needs to ice it and see how things look when the swelling goes down."

Michael already knew things looked bad, but hearing the trainer's words made it worse. The trainer moved him to the medical room and elevated his foot, and iced it. Someone called Aunt Beth in to consent for medical treatment. Her pained eyes examined him, providing little comfort. In the distance, he could hear dancers being introduced, followed by the sound of music. He should be on that stage, not sitting in a first aid room with ice packed around his ankle.

"Why did they do that? Why did someone have to leave their stuff on the floor?" Michael cried through his clenched teeth. "It was their mistake, but now they can dance and I am out of it."

His aunt looked at him with pity as she moved close. Words were little consolation, so she stroked his hair, hoping to provide a little reassurance.

Several long minutes passed. The trainer and coordinator returned to examine the ankle. He pulled up a stool beside Michael, removed the ice, and examined the joint. Lifting the ice off the ankle gave him a needed break from the aching cold. Michael groaned when the man gripped his foot and rotated it. A look of concern etched across his face when he turned to the coordinator.

"We got ice on it pretty quick," The trainer said. "I doubt it is broken, but it wouldn't hurt to have it X-rayed. If it's not broken, it may take a day or two to determine how bad the sprain is."

The coordinator nodded. She brushed her hair behind her ear and turned to Michael. The empathy written on her face made him feel both dread and comfort. "We are going to send you for x-rays to make sure it isn't broken. Your performance is being moved to late Saturday. This will give you as much time as possible to recover. If you can dance, you will have the opportunity." She turned to the trainer before continuing, "What do you think? Any chance he could compete this weekend?"

The man frowned at the ankle, looked at Michael, then back to the woman. "It is hard to tell. It would take a miracle, but I've seen it happen before. It depends on how bad the injury and how tolerant the dancer is to pain." The man leveled his gaze to Michael. "I don't want to get your hopes up, so prepare yourself for the worst. Keep icing your ankle over the next several days and don't try to walk on it until Saturday. That will give you the best opportunity to bounce back. It is a long shot, but follow my instructions and let's hope for the best."

The trainer lifted himself from the stool and gave a reassuring squeeze on Michael's shoulder before turning to leave the room. He stopped at the door to give one parting word of advice. "Until you are ready to compete, do not put any heat on your ankle. Not even in the shower." Michael nodded and the trainer left the room, followed by the coordinator.

A nurse transported Michael to a local medical center where x-rays came back negative. At least he received one good piece of news. He propped his foot up according to the doctor's instructions and made friends with the television remote. The throbbing pain had subsided to a dull ache. This trip to New York had not gone according to plan, but he still had a slight glimmer of hope.

The milky light of dawn began to seep into the hotel window when Michael opened his eyes. He rolled over, turned off the alarm fifteen minutes before it went off, and then rolled to his back again.

Inhaling deeply, he looked at the ceiling. "Ready or not, Saturday morning is here." With a shove, he sat up and shifted to the edge of the bed. Blood flowed into his ankle, and the throbbing returned. Michael slid gently from the bed, and put his weight on his healthy right ankle. With clinched teeth, he timidly distributed his weight to his left. The ache grew as the joint compressed. He hobbled over to the bathroom to get cleaned up, then took the ice bin from the counter. Taking ginger steps, he limped down the hallway to the ice maker and hobbled back. After wrapping the bag around his tender ankle, Michael turned on the TV to pass the time. The last day of competition had arrived, and he had a few hours before he would either perform or bury his dreams of success.

There would be other years to compete, but he knew the townspeople would not be excited enough to fund another trip after this disappointment. If he had to walk away in defeat, he would be doing well to ever see New York again. To be defeated in the competition would be difficult, but at least he could concede to the fact another dancer had bested him. To be defeated by misfortune, and never have the chance to perform, is a bitter pill to swallow.

After flipping channels for an hour, most of the ice had melted. Aunt Beth emerged from the adjoining room. "How is your foot feeling?" she asked as she pulled back the bag of ice water to examine the damage.

"My foot is fine. My ankle is still sore."

"Stand up and let me see you walk." Michael eased onto his feet and limped across the floor as his aunt stroked her bottom lip. He limped back and sat down. "It doesn't look too good. Your limp is pretty bad."

Michael nodded. "Yes, but I think I can at least test it and see if I can dance today."

Aunt Beth shook her head. "I don't think so."

"I can try."

"Look at you. You can barely walk. How can you even think about competing?"

Michael's voice became pitched as he tried to present his case, "Please, Aunt Beth. I have to at least try. When I jump, I can put my weight on my right leg."

"But what if you hurt it worse? No one can dance with a bad ankle. It has only been two days and it just isn't enough time to heal." Aunt Beth's motherly tone seemed to plead with Michael to be reasonable and protect his injured ankle, but Michael would not be convinced.

"Please. Please, let me try. Everyone gave money to pay for this trip and I can't go back without at least making an effort. I'll never get this chance again. I can't walk away without at least trying." Michael looked intently at his aunt. The desperation in his voice surpassed the determination on his face. "You have to let me give it a try. I'll go back and wonder 'what would have happened if I had tried'? I will never get over it. If I try and fall flat on my face, at least I can say I did my best. I can look at Ms. Johnson and say my ankle hurt, but I still danced. Isn't that better than wondering if I could have done it? I don't want to wonder about this forever."

Michael met his aunt's gaze with pleading intensity, and the two stood in silence as the clock ticked softly in the background. Aunt Beth finally turned away as she raised her palms in the air. "Okay, but I don't think this is a good idea." She let out a sigh and turned to her room and said, "Get ready and let's head to the theater. If you ruin your ankle, I'll never forgive myself."

Michael filled another bag with ice on his way out of the hotel. When they arrived at the auditorium, he wrapped his ankle again as his aunt informed the director he would be dancing. The coordinator walked to where Michael sat.

"Are you sure you will be able to dance?" she asked as she looked down at his ankle.

"I am sure. I have been testing it and it feels fine. I will just keep it iced until it is time to warm up to be safe," he said as if the problem were nothing warranting concern. Aunt Beth raised her eyebrows as she gave a skeptical look, but thankfully didn't speak.

"Okay. There are two times available. One in an hour, and one is at the end of the program. I am assuming you will want the last performance so you have time to prepare."

Michael looked up to her and said, "Can I do it sooner? I would like to get it over with. My ankle will feel better if I do it while I am still moving around."

The woman looked skeptical. "Are you sure an hour is enough time to get warmed up and get prepared?"

"Yes."

"Well, okay." She turned to the director who had summonsed her, "Get his music ready. I hope this works out for him." The coordinator gave Michael a final look as she asked, "This is the only opportunity. Are you sure you can be warmed up in an hour?"

"I'm sure."

Michael removed the ice and began warming the ankle. He jerked back with pain as he grasped the toe of his left foot. Aunt Beth looked at him with concern, and he gave his most confident smile. She shook her head and turned to walk away. "I'll be in my seat in the auditorium. I can't watch you doing this. I don't know if I can bear to watch you on stage either."

Limping over to the bathroom, Michael poured out his ice and filled the bag with hot water. He tied it off and sat down with it wrapped around his ankle. A grimace spread across his face from the nearly unbearable heat, but he had to get warmth deep into his stiff ankle. Applying heat and stretching would be the limit of his warm ups. He couldn't take a chance on stressing his ankle with practice leaps before stepping onto the stage. Unsure if his ankle would support a jump, landing, or even the simplest of maneuvers, he decided to rest the ankle. He would have to take his chances on an untested injury.

The clock showed ten minutes before his performance. Time to wrap the ankle. Michael reached into his bag and retrieved the athletic tape. It made a ripping sound each time he looped it around his foot, then ankle, foot, then ankle. The smell of adhesive wafted through the warm-up room. It briefly displaced the ever present stale odor in the air. He stretched his clothes over the tape and smoothed it out as best as he could. Nothing more to do but wait for his turn on stage.

"Michael Camp," a voice called out, "You are up in five minutes."

Michael nodded and rose to his feet as he walked toward the stage. He tried to mask his limp, but the director looked at him, then down to his ankle. The hollow look on his face said more than words could say. He didn't believe someone unable to walk, would somehow find the ability to dance. Michael wasn't sure either.

A moment later the choreographer called out, "Position."

Darkness covered the stage when he stepped out to assume his starting position. Music began as colorful lights hit the stage, and a soft blue beam positioned on Michael. His arms flowed gracefully into the air, preparing for the beat in the music which began his routine. The deep beat of a drum sounded and Michael placed the stars into the heavens with the flow of his arms before beginning the pirouette leading into his first jump. He envisioned himself spinning his way into another world, where he could be lost in the music and the joy of dance.

Coming out of his spin, Michael launched himself high into the air. He held his pose, motionless as he sailed across the stage, then prepared to land on his weakened ankle. Pain surged up his leg, but he now felt detached from his body. It was a tool under his control, not something that would control him. For the next three minutes, the dancer pushed the world aside. It was only him—and his love for the dance. No audience, no injury, no obstacles to worry about. No longer did he concern himself with success. Love for the dance mattered. Nothing else.

His leaps were high and free as he relished the wind in his hair and the flow of his movements. The audience reacted, but they were off in the distance, peering in from another world. Their time would come, but this time belonged to him. It felt exhilarating to let go of his fears and trials for the precious few moments he snatched from the world and cherished in the dance.

The music began to proclaim the upcoming finale, and the time had come to return to the world he had left behind. He began a pirouette on his right foot, then moved his weight to his left foot, before stepping into his graceful leap which ended in the position where he began. With graceful arm movements, he retrieved the stars from the night sky and spread them on the ground before him with a bow.

Thunder erupted from the crowd hidden behind the wall of lights before him as his ankle revolted against any further use. He stood, gave a graceful bow, and then limped clumsily away from center stage.

Overwhelmed with excitement, the director hugged him as he exclaimed, "I honestly didn't think you would make it. Very well done. Very well done indeed."

On the return trip to Alabama, Michael's heart soared in the clouds. His ankle punched at him with bursts of pain, but his heart felt light with excitement. He couldn't wait to tell Ms. Johnson he had received the highest marks in the semifinal competition. Only one round to go. He wondered how hard she would push him with his ankle. It would be a challenge to nurse his ankle and train hard enough to make it into the top six on the final round. He tried to not let himself think about winning the Grand Prix, but his mind kept imagining what it must feel like to win such a prestigious award.

He knew placing in the top six would be a victory and would lead to many opportunities, but deep down he didn't want to settle for second best. Unless he could train hard, he feared even placing in the top six might be out of reach. Could it be possible to recover and get into top form in time to be at his best for the finals?

Chapter Ten

It hardly seemed like a month had gone by, but now Michael stood in line, waiting to sign in for the Grand Prix finals. A thinner crowd waited to register. Only fifty entrants. Michael remembered the first audition. The building had been overflowing with hopeful dancers, eager parents, and stone-faced judges. It felt exhilarating just to know he stood among the top fifty youth dancers in the world. What must it feel like to stand before the world as one of the top six?

"Your name?" asked the woman behind the registration table.

"Michael Camp."

He completed his registration and rejoined his aunt. During the trip, she'd said very little about the competition. Aunt Beth lived with the fear of wrong words jinxing life— including Michael's performance. He thought this was a fearful and contradictory superstition. She believed if you said something negative, bad things would happen, but if you said positive things, positive things would happen. It seemed to be a normal superstition until the time Uncle Joe watched a baseball game when the pitcher was tossing a no-hitter. When his cousin walked in the room, Uncle Joe said, "Our pitcher has a no-hitter through the seventh inning".

Aunt Beth scolded him for saying this. Apparently, acknowledging the pitcher had a no-hitter would jinx the pitcher and spoil the no-hitter. A few batters later, the pitcher gave up a hit and Aunt Beth proclaimed, "See! I told you not to say it. You jinxed the pitcher."

His aunt's law of superstition held firm unless something good was actually happening. Then acknowledging it would have the reverse affect, and the forces of good and evil would become confused and create a jinx. The thought of it all made Michael chuckle to himself. *If the forces of good and evil are so easily confused, we shouldn't be relying on them anyway.*

"How does your ankle feel?" his aunt asked, breaking Michael out of his musings.

"It feels fine. No problems at all," Michael said as he rotated his ankle to show her. In truth, it still ached when he put weight on it. Ms. Johnson had only given him a week to recover before beginning to push him again. The next phase of training had started slowly, but by the beginning of the third week, she was demanding her usual perfection from him. A month wasn't long enough to heal, and get back into good form. "Everything is perfect and nothing could possibly go wrong this time."

Aunt Beth winced at his words before countering, "Better not say that."

Michael smirked at her predictable response, and then answered, "Should I say everything is going to go wrong?"

"Don't say that either." Aunt Beth gave a look over her shoulder as if worried the spirits of fate might be listening. "Let's just not talk about these things until after the competition."

Fates must be mischievous little spirits. They have nothing better to do than to listen in on conversations and apply a list of complicated divine laws to the words spoken. Michael thought he would just trust in his training and leave his aunt to wrestle with the finicky fates.

Michael tried in vain to sleep the night before he competed. His mind raced while the clock ticked by. Sleep drifted in a few times, but it remained shallow until he finally realized morning had arrived. The alarm clock had not yet chimed when he rolled out of bed and turned it off. The pain in his ankle seemed mild, and he rotated the stiffness away before stretching out his legs. He walked into the living area of the motel suite and rehearsed his routine, substituting little hops for the jumps.

With the dance sharp in his mind, he hoped his body would follow. He did not feel as strong as he did before the injury. During practice with Ms. Johnson, his jumps hadn't been as high and his landings were a bit shaky. She would scold him, but he could not help treating his ankle with care. The fear of injury nagged at his mind. He wouldn't allow these concerns to distract him during the competition. Or so he hoped.

He looked through the curtains and saw the pale sky as it announced the coming of the sun. With the success of his last performance, the schedule now listed him as one of the last dancers. Still, he wanted to be at the auditorium early. A glance at the clock showed twenty minutes before six. Time to wake up his aunt and prepare for the day of competition.

When Michael walked in, crowds were already gathering. The dancers in the room were focused, and in their own worlds. The sound of feet shuffling and the light thump of landings echoed softly in the room. While watching them warm up, he began to feel small. These dancers were all good. As he watched them rehearsing their routines, a feeling of intimidation began to plant doubt in Michael's mind.

These are the best dancers in the world. They all went to the best schools of dance and I learned in a studio in hick town. I haven't been able to jump high for weeks. How can I compete with these guys on a bad ankle?

For the first time in the competition, Michael felt his hands trembling. Before coming to New York, he had never competed outside of Alabama. Winning at the state level had seemed easy. After finding out about the Grand Prix, his entire life had been committed to preparation, but was it enough?

In the previous round of the Grand Prix, Michael had received the highest score of anyone. Surely this meant something. Then again, all the judges knew about his ankle. Had they graded him on a curve? Did they bump up his score out of pity? In the first round, he had been picked second to last. A dark feeling began to sweep over him and he had the urge to get out of this place and fly back to Alabama.

The townspeople who had given their money came to mind. He owed it to them to push fear aside and do his best. And he owed it to Ms. Johnson.

Forget about Aunt Beth's fates and the judges, and just dance.

Hours sped by. The butterflies dancing in Michael's gut became more active as his time to perform drew near. Excitement pounded through his veins while he completed his stretches, and then he stepped onto the open floor to practice. Sweat trickled across his foot when he removed the heat wrap from his ankle. Everything felt good. Painful memories of the misplaced gym bag reminded Michael to examine the floor before making his jumps. Not wanting to stress his ankle, he saved the highest jumps for the stage.

One last step through the routine, and he would be ready for the lights.

"Michael Camp, you are on in five," the voice of the director called.

Doubt screamed in his mind as he stepped to the side of the stage, waiting for his cue to go on. Rubbery legs bounced pain around his ankle.

What is the first part of my routine? I can't remember

what to do first!

Panic shooed away rational thought.

"Position," the choreographer called.

Michael looked back for help, but the director pointed him to the stage. It was show time. *Maybe I should have picked a comedy routine.* The dancer walked onto the dark stage, feeling his knees trying to buckle underneath him. He fought back the urge to run off the stage and escape this dread. The music started, lights poured onto the stage, and he remembered to drop to one knee and place the stars into the heaven with graceful moves of his hand.

"Dance without effort," Ms. Johnson's voice echoed in his head as he saw the choreography unfold in his memory.

Michael closed his eyes and absorbed the music. He began his pirouette, anticipating the drumbeat which would launch him into his dance. The sound reverberated through his body and he spun into his first leap. His body now felt weightless, as if suspended in the air. He drifted toward the stage, holding his pose until the last possible moment before positioning himself for landing. The world faded into a distant memory, and only the dance occupied his mind. Every movement flowed gracefully into the next. His body became part of the dance, and set him from the limitations of pain, fear, and the expectations of the judges.

Entering his last series of pirouettes, Michael shifted from one foot, to the other, finally finishing on one knee as he gathered the stars from their places in the heavens, and placed them on the stage with a bow. The eruption of applause welcomed him back into this world. He bowed before the wall of lights, knowing that behind it were individuals creating the thunderous noise hammering in his ears. He rushed off the stage, grabbed a towel, and gulped down a bottle of water. Now all the hard work, pain, preparation, and struggles were behind him. The only thing remaining was to wait for the results of the judging, and to find out where he placed.

In a room off stage, the dancers gathered as the announcements began. The spokesman prepared to announce each name to the crowd, and the dancer would have to rush on stage, and wait for the others. Six dancers would be crowned and one of them would be awarded the Grand Prix.

One name rang out. The dancers could hear the muffled sound of his voice, but couldn't distinguish the words. The applause roared. The announcer called a second name, and the director rushed a dancer out of the room and onto the stage in front of the rejoicing crowd. A third name rang out. Then the fourth and fifth. The remaining dancers began to have hopeless looks in their eyes. Only one name remained. Forty-four dancers would walk away disappointed, falling short of their dreams.

As the names rolled by, Michael was determined to subdue his emotions. Some dancers were already crying, certain their hard work had been passed over. Of course he would be disappointed, but he had learned long ago not to allow love or emotions to rule his heart, for they only lead to pain.

The spokesman droned on while the fidgeting dancers waited with hollow expressions. A surge of thunderous applause shook the walls. The dancers began looking at one another, wondering about their own fates.

Every head snapped toward the door when the director emerged. "Michael Camp." Michael weaved through the room and the director began shooing him frantically toward the stage. "Hurry. Hurry onto the stage beside the others. Bow when you get there."

Michael trotted onto the stage and took a bow. The cheers erupted again as someone handed him a box. He wasn't sure which award he had received, but at least he stood among the top six. The dancers stood on the platform, absorbing the ovations of the audience, before filing off the stage. Anticipation ate at him, and he couldn't wait to look in the box. Just off stage, he eased it open to see the words, 'Grand Prix'. He had taken the top award for the competition! An open door stood before him. Now he could pursue his dream of a life as a dancer.

Michael gazed into the horizon as if trying to get a glimpse into the future. What new challenging opportunity awaited the International Grand Prix winner?

As the Grand Prix winner, Michael took home a cash prize and a full scholarship to the Pahl School of Dance, where many of the top music productions scout for new talent. Pahl had three schools of dance. One was in Knoxville, Tennessee, about forty-five minutes from Bristol where Michael's third uncle lived. Aunt Beth spoke to Uncle John, who agreed to house Michael while he attended Bristol High School and commuted to Pahl.

Michael used his prize money to buy a beat up Chevrolet truck so he could commute between Bristol and Knoxville. It looked rough, but it ran well. And Michael felt proud of his first vehicle.

Michael returned for one last visit to the studio in Wedowee to bid his teacher good-bye. Ms. Johnson was instructing the class when he walked in.

"Class, take a five minute break," the teacher said as she hurried to greet her prize student. "Congratulations again on your big win, and your scholarship! Are you ready for your move to Bristol?"

"I think so," he nodded. "I want to thank you for

helping me learn to perform. I really liked being in your classes."

"I knew you had it in you! Now I hope you see why I pushed you so hard."

Michael laughed and said, "I didn't like how hard you pushed, but I think I understand. You were right. Everything you taught me came together during the Grand Prix."

She paused, deep in thought, then smiled as she continued, "I knew the choreography was a winner. I always dreamed of performing that dance, but my injured knee changed everything." Ms. Johnson motioned for him to come with her. "Before you go, let me introduce you to our new students."

The teacher ushered Michael in front of the students. Even after all these years, it still felt awkward to be the focus of the class. It didn't matter that most were under the age of ten. He tried to look comfortable.

Ms. Johnson announced, "Students, this is our top dancer, Michael Camp. He is leaving today, but consider his example. Through hard work and determination, he climbed to the top. Last week he won the Grand Prix – one of the highest awards a student dancer can achieve." She turned to Michael and though she smiled, he saw sadness in her eyes. "He's leaving us today. Part of the prize was a scholarship to one of the top dance schools in America." She put her arm around his shoulders and gave a hug, "We are sad to lose you, but share the joy of your success. I'm certain you will go far."

Michael hadn't thought about these things in a long time. The memories brought too much pain. Here he was, homeless, and under a bridge in Manhattan.

Is this what she meant when she said I'd go far? Ms.

Johnson would be disgusted if she knew what I've become. That's why Raquel can't be allowed to know. I would be ashamed for her to see me this way.

Ache needled at his heart while he thought on Raquel. He had met her shortly after moving to Bristol. Her memory mixed joy with the pain. Their time on stage together still warmed his heart, but it hurt knowing he would never see the stage again.

Chapter Eleven

Michael remembered the first time he had seen Raquel. It was his first day at Bristol High, and he sat alone at a table in the cafeteria. She walked in and headed toward a table of giggling girls. They were looking at him, probably curious about the new guy in school. He pretended not to notice.

Raquel looked too, but she tried to be more subtle about it. Some of the girls seemed interested in getting to know him, but the boys were another story. Not being a talker, he didn't connect well to other boys. The problem worsened when they found out he danced. Bristol Tennessee isn't the best place to launch a dancing career. But it was close to Knoxville where he attended Pahl School of the Performing Arts. It would be nice to attend the New York campus, but he didn't have any relatives up north.

Pahl's first-year students were required to participate in a performing arts program in their local communities. No one joined a performance team at Pahl in their first year, yet they expected all students to gain experience on the stage. Michael thought this was a stupid rule. It forced him to join the Bristol High drama team, and still make classes in Knoxville twice a week. Pahl also had an academic program. Students with a *B* average or better in high school, and excellent evaluations at Pahl, could apply for the program. These students could transfer and complete high school on the studio campus. He counted the days until he could put in his application.

The first day in drama class at Bristol High was an unexpected disappointment. Mrs. Kahler surprised Michael with her lack of confidence in him.

"Michael, I know you've performed before, and I understand you have won some competitions, but I like to start new drama team members off slowly," Mrs. Kahler said. "So I'm partnering you with Margaret."

Won some competitions? Does she know what the Grand Prix is? How can she doubt an international champion's abilities in a lame high school play?

He should be partnered with Raquel. She was the leading lady, and with Michael's experience, he felt becoming the leading man should be a given.

Mrs. Kahler smiled and continued, "I'll be partnering you with Margaret. That should be a good match for you."

Great. One of the least experienced dancers on the team. He had already seen her practicing, and calling her a dancer stretched the meaning of the word beyond recognition. She had the grace of a wounded elk.

Michael nodded and looked over to Margaret. She looked happy. Michael gave a half-smile, then crossed his arms and slouched in the chair.

I just need to endure this junk for one year. Then I'm outa here.

Michael slipped into math class, and took a seat. He had a strategy for selecting seats in each classroom. When available, he selected a desk on the second row near the far wall. This would get him as close to obscurity as possible, avoiding the back of the room where the rowdy students congregated, and the front of the room where the teacher would likely call on him.

One thing mattered—getting through each school day so he could go to drama practice or head to Pahl. For the first two weeks, his plan to avoid detection worked. Other than a few unwelcomed attempts at conversation, life at Bristol High remained quiet.

For Michael, high school was a necessary evil. Its social sphere forced students to conform to a standard which held no value in the real world. To fit in, students had to look, talk, dress, and behave according to the accepted norm. Anyone standing out as an individual risked drawing the ridicule of those conforming to the system. He didn't fit in, and didn't want to. He longed for friends, but not those who demanded conformity.

High school bullies guarded against dissidents, demanding compliance. Michael had observed that most bullies were insecure about themselves, attempting to mask their own feelings of inadequacy by mocking others.

Few were so quick to identify nonconformists as Jeff Patterson. A cackling entourage scuttled behind Jeff, whooping like hyenas, grateful that someone other than themselves had become his source of amusement and self-glorification.

Each day, Michael pretended not to notice Jeff's wise cracks. Today, before class started, Jeff and the hyenas herded into the room. The bully's eyes found Michael.

"Hey, there's the new guy," Jeff announced with a loud voice. Michael felt everyone's eyes upon him, and wished for the bell to ring so class could start. "How come you never talk?" Jeff turned to his followers as he continued his assessment, "This guy never says a word. Have you ever heard him talk?" His companions all shook their heads. "I hear you are a dancer. Is that true?"

Flashbacks of earlier taunts flooded Michael's mind, and the mocking words of Derk echoed in his ears. *Why are the big shots always drawn to me? Why can't they just leave me alone.*

"Hey Dancer." Jeff walked in Michael's direction. "Hey Dancer, I'm talking to you. Don't act like you can't hear me."

Michael continued to look through his math book as if unaware of Jeff's bellowing voice. The bell rang, but the bully persisted.

"Hey Dancer, you ain't gonna just sit there and ignore me."

Jeff arrived at Michael's desk and forced the book

closed. Michael tried to open it, but Jeff pressed down on it with his hand. Michael stared at the large hand and Jeff's muscular arm. An eerie silence settled while the rest of the class watched the entertaining drama unfold. Snickers from the hyenas filled the room for a moment, then silence returned.

"Okay, class," the teacher announced as she hurried into the room, "Sorry I'm a couple of minutes late. Everyone take their seats so we can get started."

Jeff leaned down to Michael's ear, both hands now pressed on the book, "See you around...Dancer." He flicked Michael's pencil off the desk as he turned to walk away. Laughter from around the room praised the brave move of the jock, and he strolled triumphantly to a desk in the back of the class.

Encouraged by Jeff's example, people in math class started calling Michael by the name Dancer. The story quickly spread and soon other students began calling him by that name.

Drama class became more tolerable once Mrs. Kahler moved Michael to a better role. He learned each new role quickly, and the teacher kept moving him to new partners. She said his improvements impressed her, but he felt that other than spending more time on stage, nothing had changed. These roles weren't challenging. It would be nothing for him to take on the leading role. Plus, it would be nice to dance with Raquel since she was the only one who took drama seriously.

A couple of months after Michael joined the drama team, the opportunity he'd longed for became reality. Mrs. Kahler stood before the class with an announcement. "Class, I have some sad news. Tim's father is being transferred in his job, so he will be leaving Bristol and the drama team."

Michael perked up. *Tim is Raquel's partner—the leading man!*

She continued, "I've known about this for a few days and have put a lot of thought in replacing him. It's a very important role, and we have so many good performers on our team. It was a very hard decision, but I've decided to move Michael into that role."

"That's not fair!" Robert protested, interrupting the teacher's explanation. Michael noticed he seemed to be overbearing in the class and worried this new partnership could cause problems. Robert, or no Robert, he would not pass up this role. It was the opportunity he'd been waiting for.

While he watched the conversation unfold between Mrs. Kahler and Robert, someone slipped into the chair next to him. "Are you excited about being the new leading man?" Raquel asked.

The exchange continued between the teacher and Robert, but Michael pulled his eyes away and looked at Raquel. "He doesn't take no for an answer, does he?"

A pained expression washed over Raquel's face, and she rolled her eyes. "Tell me about it. He follows me every day, and never quits calling. I used to like the guy when we dated, but now he creeps me out."

"How long did ya'll date?"

"I've known Robert all my life. We grew up together and we kinda have always been very good friends. I broke up with him about two months ago. But he still talks about how we're meant to be together."

"What made you break up? Did he act like that?" He pointed toward the front of the room.

"No. He seemed okay until my life changed. But he can't seem to accept it."

Michael thought the statement sounded odd. How does someone's life just change? He could tell by Raquel's expression that skepticism showed on his face.

"You want to know what happened to me?" she asked.

"I guess."

"I started going to church and talking to a youth pastor. I had been pretty depressed and all. Robert got me started smoking pot about the time we started high school. We used to sneak off and smoke it together. And drink. One day at a party, he came up to me with some pills. Before I knew it, getting drunk or high was all we cared about. I did things I never thought I would do. Once I got caught shoplifting. My parents really freaked out. A friend kept inviting me to church with her. I didn't want to go, but she kept bugging me.

"One day, I started thinking about how much I hated life. I felt cheap, used, and worthless. Getting arrested really scared me. Then my friend," Raquel pointed to Margaret, "she called me and invited me to church again. I thought, what have I got to lose? So I went."

"And you found religion," Michael said.

"Kinda, but it was more than just finding religion. She introduced me to her youth pastor. I had a lot of questions. Most of the time, people just say something like, you gotta just believe. But I didn't know how to do that. Lynn, our pastor, didn't say this. He answered my questions and the way he explained things, it just made sense.

"One day, while listening to the Bible study, something just came over me. I still felt worthless. I knew I had done all those awful things, and I felt horrible inside. But when Lynn talked about forgiveness, I realized God wanted to forgive me, and take away the hurt I felt. I turned to Christ and it felt like a thousand pounds lifted off my chest. Instantly, my life changed. There had been things in my life I just couldn't stop doing, but suddenly, I didn't want those things anymore."

Michael leaned back and gave a skeptical look. "How does someone's life just change because they ask God to forgive them?"

"I don't really understand how, but mine did. It was like I became a different person. That's when my relationship with Robert fell apart. My desires changed, and he didn't like it. And like you said, he won't take no for an answer. I finally told him I couldn't handle his pressure anymore, and I broke up."

"I see why that would cause you to break up, but I don't get how saying a prayer can make someone a different person."

Raquel smiled. "It isn't the prayer that changes a person. It's God who changes a person. The Bible says that when we are born again, we become a new creation—"

"That's fine for you," Michael interrupted. "I'm not into the Bible and all. My life comes alive when I dance. But it's okay if you need the Bible. Religion is just not for me."

"No problem." Her eyes looked wounded, but he could tell Raquel tried to keep the disappointment off her face. "Hey, Michael," she continued, "Why don't you come with me to a youth study. You'll like it and who knows, maybe you will—"

"No thanks." Michael said. "Let's just stick to dancing. Who knows? Maybe we'll find everything we need on the stage."

The memories flooding through Michael's mind snagged on that final thought. The darkness under the bridge felt as cold as the blackness of his soul. *How can religion change someone? Maybe it serves as a distraction to get someone's mind off their problems. And away from bad habits. Does substituting religion in place of habits really do anything for you?*

"I just don't get it," Michael said to himself. A chilling wind curled into the cubbyhole under the bridge. He eased back down to the pad, taking care not to strike his head again. Stale odors from the blankets filled his nose when he pulled the covers over him. The effects of the drugs were nearly gone, and a hard crash took over. All energy drained away.

How does a life just change? No one can just become a different person. Religion is only a crutch—and it would take more than a crutch for me.

Soon the chills faded with his conscious mind as he slipped into sleep.

Chapter Twelve

It had been a long, trying day. Raquel looked at the clock. 9:46 p.m. The sheets felt cold when she slid under them. It seemed too early for bed, but with the long drive from Tennessee, the events of this day, and an early first day at the studio tomorrow, she wanted to be rested.

When she closed her eyes, she saw the homeless man who had washed her windshield. It wasn't just a stranger's face. It was Dancer. The sparkling blue eyes of Dancer were impossible to mistake. No one she'd ever met had eyes like his. They were mysterious and guarded, but also full of brilliance and life. She remembered the first time Dancer walked into her small town world.

It was the first day of school. She entered the lunchroom, bought her meal, and headed toward her friends. They were excitedly discussing something at the table. Their efforts to be inconspicuous were impossible not to notice. The sound of giggling whispers reached her ears long before she reached the table. Raquel sat across from her best friends, Margaret and Belle.

I wonder what's the gossip of the day? She placed her tray on the table and leaned forward to listen.

Belle turned and spoke, her voice squealing with excitement, "Have you seen the new guy, Raquel?"

"What new guy?"

"There's a new guy in school and he is cute," Belle said. She sang the last word, as she pointed across the room. "That's him over there."

Raquel looked at the table in the direction Belle pointed. A handsome boy with dark brown hair sat alone, looking at his tray as he finished his lunch. His face had a mixture of boyish charm and masculine features. Raquel felt her heart skip a beat. Something about him had a magnetic appeal. He seemed oblivious to the world around him and not bothered by sitting alone.

"What's his name?" Raquel asked as she craned her neck to get a peek over her friend's heads.

"I don't know," Belle said with a shrug, "he's in my friend's gym class and she says he's kind of quiet. All I know is he's a dancer. Our drama teacher said he is going to Pahl School of Dance and he will be joining the drama team. He's supposed to be good."

"I imagine so," Raquel said. "It's hard to get into Pahl, so he's gotta be good."

Belle looked up to the heavens and said in a dreamy voice, "Oh, I hope she partners him with me."

"Hey, I'm one of the lead dancers. She should put him with me," Raquel said in smiling protest.

"You already have a partner, so that ain't gonna happen. Unless you really screw up, and get demoted out of being a lead." Belle looked back to the new guy. Sensing eyes upon him, Dancer looked up. Three heads turned away as the girls huddled around the table and giggled.

"You all are embarrassing me. You are going to scare him off the first day." Raquel turned to her lunch plate and pretended not to be a member of the gawking party. She would wait for an opportunity to meet the dancer. If he's shy, it might be easier to get to know him in the structured environment of drama class.

Raquel smiled at the memory—and the irony. There must have been divine intervention, for a few weeks later, her leading partner moved away and Dancer became her new partner in the upcoming musical. From the first time she'd met him, she had known their relationship was meant to be. It seemed as if a voice had spoken to her heart, affirming their future together.

Even now, something deep inside continued to affirm this truth, but nothing made sense. There had been no contact for two years, and now he's homeless. He pretended not to know her. How could this still be a relationship made in heaven? Just the fact that he did not share her faith made their future incompatible. Yet, she still felt driven to hope. And to love the man who now struggled at the bottom of society.

Is this the remnants of a schoolgirl fantasy? Or is there a God-given purpose in my love for Dancer?

So many hardships and disappointments discouraged her, but it felt like a thread had been woven into her heart. The connection wouldn't break. It was hard to get to know Dancer because he kept everyone at arm's length. Each time she got too close, he withdrew.

In daily life, he had remained quiet and distant, but when he performed, Dancer came alive. Shyness may have been why Mrs. Kahler felt reluctant to put him on the stage. But the shy boy surprised everyone when he stepped into the spot light. The guy who hated being the center of attention in a classroom, became the focus of attention on stage. And he loved it. It looked as though he'd stepped into another life. One he knew how to master.

Raquel rolled over. The clock showed 10:35 p.m. "I need to sleep," she sighed. Closed eyes couldn't stop her thoughts. Memories bounced past like an avalanche. Then a fleeting memory caught in her mind. It brought warmth to her heart.

If it weren't for Dancer, I wouldn't be here in New York. He's the one who drove me to reach higher for my dream of performing with him on Broadway.

Back in drama class, at the end of rehearsals each day, Dancer often stayed and practiced alone, but as opening day for the musical drew near, Raquel decided to stay after hours to practice with him.

It had felt good to move together in precision, and

Raquel felt as if their connection ran deeper than just their love for performing arts. She wondered if Dancer felt the same connection.

They moved with grace through their routines, and Raquel looked for signs, something that would indicate Dancer's feelings for her. They had grown closer over the last few weeks. Sometimes he opened up, but other times he became withdrawn.

What is going on inside his head? she remembered asking herself.

Dancer moved with perfection through each routine without ever seeming to make a mistake. Only when learning something new, did Dancer show weakness in his performance. Many felt his drive for perfection exposed their flaws, but Dancer often complained about himself—never did he criticize the students around him. How she would love to dance with such grace. He made her want to rise above her limitations, as he seemed to do.

One day while rehearsing, as Raquel thought on how she had never seen Dancer fall, he stumbled. He tried to catch himself, but his feet tangled and he tripped toward her. Instinctively, she caught him and they stumbled backward, but didn't fall. As she held Dancer while he regained his footing, he complained under his breath, upset at his blunder.

Raquel started laughing. She laughed so hard that Dancer couldn't help laughing, too. Although his expression said he didn't quite know why. "What is so funny?" he said through a wide grin.

"I'm sorry, it just struck me as funny." She weaved her words into her laughter and said, "You are just so serious about practicing. When you fell, you acted like you failed a major audition. I can't help laughing at your reaction."

Dancer kept grinning. He always looked amused when Raquel got tickled and started snorting. Today the uncontrolled snorts began again, and Dancer smirked until she regained composure.

"Well, you might see me stumble, but you won't see me fall," Dancer said as the laughter began to fade.

"You would have fallen if I hadn't caught you," Raquel said in response. "We all need someone to catch us so we don't fall. Even you." Dancer looked deep in thought, as though not knowing how to answer. She broke the silence. "It's always good to see you happy. Your smile makes me..." She paused, unsure of whether to complete her sentence. She noticed he had not pulled away and her arm remained around him. He looked so vulnerable at the moment. She leaned forward and he met her in a soft kiss.

The kiss was brief and simple, but Raquel could feel her heart surge. Something in his eyes said he felt something for her and the gentleness in his kiss confirmed it. She could tell he searched for words, but didn't know where to begin.

Finally he spoke. "I guess we should finish rehearsing."

Raquel felt invigorated throughout the last few rehearsals. Her feet floated across the stage, and the steps flowed from deep inside. Raquel felt they were perfect partners, and their dancing beat in rhythm, matching the pulse of their hearts. Dancer hid it, but Raquel hoped his graceful movements rode on the same feelings for her.

A few days later, she waited for Dancer with the rest of the class. It was the first time Dancer had ever been late, and rehearsals couldn't start without the leading man. The drama room door opened, and someone struggled to get through. An aluminum crutch appeared, then Dancer slipped around the door. When she saw his face, horror pulsed in her chest. He looked as if he had been hit by a car.

"Oh Dancer!" Raquel cried out as she rushed toward him. "What happened to you?"

Dark purple covered the right side of his face. Dancer's right eye had swollen shut, and his lips were so bloated he could hardly talk. Bandages and a plastic boot covered his right ankle.

Taking advantage of Dancer's injury, Robert volunteered to step in and be the leading man. With only a week to go, the musical looked to be a certain disaster. Robert didn't seem bothered by the loss of their team member, but Raquel attributed it to Robert's excitement about being her partner. Once again she would be forced to work with the guy who believed their lives were meant to be together. Things were about to become unpleasant.

It was hard to pry information out of Dancer, and the only thing he would say is that his car broke down on a lonely road between Bristol and Knoxville while he drove to classes at Pahl. Four guys attacked him, and left him lying on the side of the road. He claimed not to know who they were. One of them had stomped the side of his leg.

Dancer slipped into despondency, causing Raquel to fear for his well-being. After rehearsal, she stepped to the auditorium where Dancer sat with his head buried in his hands. She sat beside him.

"You okay, Dancer?" He didn't speak or lift his head. "Michael, talk to me."

"Why can't people just leave me alone?" The muffled words dug at Raquel's heart. "All I want to do is dance. And be left alone."

Raquel moved closer, caressing his back, "It will be okay."

"No. It won't be okay!" He jerked his head up and looked at her. "Dancing is my life. If I can't perform, what's the point of it all?" Dancer looked as though he would break down, but turned away and fought back the tears. "People just won't leave me alone." He turned back and pointed to his face. "Look at me. What did I do to them?"

Raquel could feel his pain and could not hold her emotions. She wanted to be strong for Dancer, but tears slid down her cheeks. Wanting to comfort him, and herself, she wrapped her arms around him and cried. When she regained some composure, she looked in his face. "You know who did this to you, don't you?"

Dancer shrugged and looked down again.

"Dancer, tell me who did this."

"I don't know," he said in an unconvincing tone.

"You do know. Why won't you say anything? Did they threaten you?" she asked, trying to think of any reason why someone would want to hurt him. She tried to make eye contact, but Dancer shrugged and avoided her gaze.

"I'm a dancer. Just a dancer. No one wants me to be who I am." Dancer's voice almost cracked, but he held back his tears. "My life has no meaning. Life is nothing but pain."

Raquel started to speak, but Dancer cut her off. "Look at my ankle," he said as he pointed to the Velcro strapped boot protecting his foot. "I can't put weight on it. I have focused my life on performing." He dropped his elbow on his knees and buried his face in his hands. "Everyone is against me. Why do I keep trying?" he mumbled.

These words caused fear to chill Raquel. Dancer sounded so deep in despair she was concerned he might be thinking irrationally. She searched for something to say that would soothe him. "Look Dancer. I know how important dance is to you, but believe me, your life has meaning. Many people love you and really care about you. Don't place your worth in the hands of jerks. It is their lives that have no purpose."

In some ways, she understood his despair. This type of crisis is what caused her to see the worthlessness of her old life. That's when her friend began to invite her to church, and tried to teach her what hope really meant. Maybe she could do the same for him.

Unlike Dancer, she had caused her own problems. During that horrible time of her life, she'd told the youth pastor she felt out of God's reach. His words still rang in her heart.

"There's no pit so deep that God's love can't reach you,"

he had said. Then he continued, "God doesn't look at you for who you are now, but he sees what you will be when He completes your life."

Those two statements touched something deep inside her. But they didn't seem to apply to Dancer's pain. She tried to explain these things to Dancer, but she fumbled over her words, and wondered if he understood her testimony. Finally, she said, "Dancer, come with me to a special youth rally we are having on Saturday night."

"I'm not in the mood for fun and games," he said without looking up.

"It is not just fun and games. There are some really good singers coming there and my church group will be going. I want you to come with me."

Dancer grumbled at the floor, "I'm not interested in a church service. My Aunt Beth is religious and she is a confused lady. Superstition rules her life. No thanks, I don't want superstition."

"It's not like that," Raquel said. "We don't have weird superstitious beliefs. I want you to come with me." Dancer shook his head without looking up, but Raquel pressed the issue. "Please, Dancer. Michael. Please? I want you to come with me. Do it for me."

Raquel pleaded with her eyes while Dancer stared in silence. Finally, he gave in. "Ok. But I ain't getting saved. I'm just listening to the singing, and I'm only doing this for you."

Chapter Thirteen

The clock on the nightstand showed 11:23 p.m. The memories of Dancer continued to chase rest away from Raquel.

Man, I'm going to be tired in the morning. Raquel let out a long exhale and crawled out of bed. "Maybe some chamomile tea will relax my brain." A stack of boxes caught her eye, and thoughts about organizing the apartment sped through her mind. She shooed the idea away. "No, I'm not going there tonight."

After brewing the tea, she crawled into a lounge chair and sipped the hot drink. The warmth of the cup pushed the chill away. The aroma filled her lungs with each soothing sip. She leaned back into the soft cushions and closed her eyes.

"I really hope Dancer took something away from the message at the youth rally that night," she breathed over the steaming cup. "Lord, he needs hope now, more than ever."

Raquel remembered her excitement at the youth rally. These events were always fun, but it was even better with Dancer. After picking him up, Raquel drove to Calvary Church in Bristol. Dancer looked as if he felt out of place while he hobbled into the auditorium. The crowd buzzed with anticipation.

Raquel led Dancer to the section where she met up with a group from her church. "Let me introduce you to my youth leader," she said as she motioned for Dancer to follow. "Michael, this is Lynn, my youth pastor." She turned back to Dancer and said, "Lynn, this is Michael. We all know him as Dancer."

"It's great to meet you, Michael. Raquel speaks highly of you," Lynn said as he reached out his hand to shake.

Dancer looked at Lynn's hand for a moment before extending his own hand. "Good to meet you."

He moved to his seat and Raquel plopped down beside him. An energetic man came to the podium, spoke for a few minutes, and had the crowd of teenagers dance around while doing silly things. Dancer didn't participate. Apparently, he wasn't in the mood to act goofy. Raquel tried to encourage him to participate, but he remained in the pew.

A praise band took the stage and led the crowd in worship. When they stepped down, a country music singer took their place. She gave her testimony and sang several songs. The energetic speaker returned to the stage, read from his Bible, and gave a wonderful message about salvation.

The man called for those who wanted to respond while the country singer sang her final song. Raquel hoped Dancer would feel inspired, but her heart ached when he said, "What do I need to be saved from? The problem isn't me. The problem is the idiots who can't leave me alone." Dancer rested his head on his palms.

As the woman sang, Raquel saw Dancer perk up. He looked captured by the words, "I live my life by the Master's plan. So I won't be judged by mortal man. I praise my Lord each time I kneel and pray. I know he knows, I know no other way."

"At least something here makes sense," he said. "I don't want to be judged by mortal man. That's my biggest problem."

The song ended as the woman sang, "I know He knows. I know no other way."

Raquel was glad he seemed to enjoy the last of the service.

Students chattered with excitement as they began filing out. Lynn walked over and placed a hand on Dancer's shoulder, "So what do you think? Did you have fun?"

"Yeah," Dancer said, but his tone said otherwise. When Lynn started talking to him about Jesus, he said, "I am not into religion. It's fine if that's something some people need, but that's not for me."

"No problem," Lynn said. "I hope we will see you again. I think you would have a good time with our youth group."

"Okay." He didn't sound sincere, but Raquel hoped he would join the group.

Lynn motioned for a young man to come over. The boy seemed reluctant, but finally walked up. "This is Donald, one of our youth leaders."

Donald gave a sheepish smile as he said, "Hi." When he arrived, a strange look came across Dancer's face. Donald extended his hand but Dancer didn't take it.

"I believe we've met," Dancer said with sarcasm. He turned to Raquel. "Can we go now?"

Surprised, she asked, "What's wrong?"

Dancer didn't answer. He moved out of the pew and hobbled into the crowd and out of the building.

The morning of the opening day for Bristol High's musical had arrived. The once exciting musical now felt like a brooding storm. Raquel saw Dancer enter the rehearsal room, hobbling on crutches. Mrs. Kahler didn't notice, but rushed around to finish preparing for tonight's first performance. She looked more frantic than enthusiastic. The teacher looked up and saw Dancer standing in the middle of the room. Her face lit up. "Hi, Michael! How are you feeling?"

"Fine." He hobbled to where she stood. Her expression sank as she looked at him with empathy. Bruises still covered his face, but the swelling had subsided.

"I'm so sorry for what happened to you. I know you are disappointed." She thought for a moment, and swept her arm toward the cast and said, "So are we all."

Dancer nodded.

The teacher massaged her forehead and Raquel knew she felt worried about this evening. Mrs. Kahler always did this when stressed or upset.

Dancer fidgeted on his crutches as if trying to think of what to say. Mrs. Kahler gave a parting smile, but when she turned to walk away, he said, "Um, that's something I wanted to talk to you about."

The teacher turned back and raised a curious eyebrow. "Yes, Michael?"

"When I competed in the Grand Prix, I hurt my ankle, but still danced. I was thinking I could try performing tonight."

The other eyebrow rose to join the first. Her face proclaimed disbelief at the thought of Dancer walking onto the stage. Surprise softened into a warm smile. "I appreciate your willingness to help, but I don't think that will work." She looked down at his foot, and then back up to meet his eyes. "You can't even walk, and I don't think you can dance on crutches."

"It's been almost a week, and I can put some weight on my foot. It's not broken and it's beginning to feel better."

Mrs. Kahler gave her most encouraging smile. "I know you want to help—and you've worked hard on this play. I really appreciate your hard work and commitment, but there is no way you can perform tonight. Maybe you can take the lead in the next play."

Dancer started to speak, but the teacher's expression made it clear the discussion was over. Dancer nodded and turned away. Raquel's heart ached for him. It wasn't fair. If only she could take away his pain.

The drama team gathered for a final rehearsal, the

show now just five hours away. Raquel walked across the room, heading toward the auditorium where the final rehearsal would be held. "Hi Raquel," a voice called from a table across the room. She looked and saw the back of Robert's head.

Stopping for a moment, she wondered who called her name. It sounded like Robert, but he did not turn or act like he noticed her.

"Not going to speak to me?" Robert said without taking his eyes off the script. He flipped the page and continued reading.

"It's hard to talk to the back of your head," Raquel said.

Robert turned around, gave a warm smile, and said, "Hi, Raquel."

"Hi, Robert," she said, then continued to the auditorium, soon followed by the other students. *Sometimes that guy grates on my nerves.*

Dancer sat alone in the back of the auditorium, watching the final rehearsal. Raquel felt glad to see him nearby, but she could tell from his expression that Robert's presence on center stage bothered him.

Robert struggled with the routine. He couldn't get in sync with Raquel, didn't remember the lines, and stopped during each dance while he tried to remember the steps. Raquel felt a little guilty, but part of her was glad Robert couldn't step into the role on such short notice. The guy was hard to work with, and most days he smothered her with unwanted attention.

"This isn't going to work," Mrs. Kahler announced at the end of the rehearsal. "I know you are trying hard, Robert, but there just isn't enough time for you to learn this part." The teacher began massaging her forehead again as she paced around, then announced her conclusion. "Raquel, you will have to perform solo with recorded vocals. I am so sorry. This whole musical has become a disaster, but we'll just have to do the best with what we've got. It's too late to cancel or postpone."

The teacher dismissed the drama team with instructions to be at the auditorium two hours before the show. Raquel walked down from the stage to Dancer. She folded her arms and let out a quick sigh as she plopped into the chair.

"It's not fair. Those animals shouldn't have done this to you. I wish we could find out who did this."

Robert passed, but paused and looked at Dancer as Raquel made the statement. Dancer's eyes met Robert's for a moment before he continued on his way.

"I tried to get Mrs. Kahler to let me dance, but she wouldn't even consider it," Dancer said to Raquel.

"I know. I overheard. I wish you could, but you can't even walk."

"I can. I'm staying off my foot so it can be ready." Raquel gave him a suspicious look. Dancer noticed and tried to defend his statement. "I can do it. I'm sure I can. It isn't broken, and I've danced in pain before."

Raquel looked down and said, "The play won't be anything without a leading man. I've been looking forward to this day, but now I'm dreading the performance." She looked him in the eye and softly touched the bruises on his face, "I'm sorry this happened." She leaned forward and gave a gentle kiss on the cheek. "Does your face hurt when I kiss you?"

"No. It makes me feel better," Dancer said, but then looked embarrassed by his words.

Raquel placed her hand on his arm. "I have to go now. I've got to get home and back before the show." She leaned down and kissed his cheek again before walking away. She glanced back and saw Dancer struggling to his feet and heading to the double-doors in the back of the auditorium. *Maybe if I hurry, I can catch up to him before he gets to the parking lot.*

Instead of changing, Raquel snatched her satchel and

headed into the auditorium and to the back doors. Muffled voices came through the doors. Angry voices. When she placed her hand on the door, she heard Robert say, "You don't learn very easily, do you?"

With a gentle push, Raquel looked into the foyer to see Robert poking his finger in Dancer's face and saying, "We already beat the crap out of you. How much more will it take before you get it through your thick skull? Do I need to stomp the other foot? Huh?" He pushed Dancer back and said, "Next time I'm going to break it."

Both heads turned when Raquel shoved the door wide open and stepped through. "Robert? It was you?" Anger radiated from her. "What do you mean, 'Do I have to stomp the other foot?'" She stepped forward and Robert turned to face her.

Raising his palms in an innocent gesture, he said, "I tried to warn him. Besides, it wasn't just me."

"How could you do this to him? How could you do this to all of us? The whole play is ruined because of you," she screamed.

"Hey, it wasn't just me," Robert said in self-defense.

"You think that makes it okay? You attacked him with some goons, and you think that makes it okay?"

Robert pointed his finger back to Dancer. "I told him to stay in his place. He should have listened."

"What?" Raquel paused for a moment, her mind trying to grasp the words. "What are you talking about? Mrs. Kahler asked him to take the lead. That *is* his place."

"I'm not talking about the play."

A sigh escaped and she tossed her hands in the air. "Robert, what are you talking about?" She leveled her gaze and said, "If you're not jealous because Dancer bested you on stage, what are you jealous about."

Red heat spread across Robert's face and he thrust his finger toward Raquel. "He did not best me on stage. I taught him a lesson because of you." Raquel opened her mouth, but before she could speak, Robert started again. "I told him to stay away from you." He shot another glance toward Dancer. "And I meant it!"

"Who are you to tell anyone to stay away from me?"

Rage crumpled Robert's face. "Raquel, I don't want you seeing other guys. Period." He looked back toward Dancer and sneered, "Or kissing them." He pointed at Dancer and said, "I warned you, but no! You kept trying to move in and steal my girl." Shoving his finger toward Dancer to emphasize each word, he said, "Stay away from Raquel. She is mine!"

"I'm not yours," Raquel barked. "If I want to kiss Dancer, you have no right to say anything. Our relationship is over, Robert! I hate you!"

Stunned, he stared with a blank expression for a moment, then his face melted into rage. The look made her heart race, and terror gripped her when Robert stepped toward her.

Her eyes glanced to Dancer. The odd look on his face was impossible to decipher. Raquel's focus returned to Robert. "Look, I'm sorry. I shouldn't have said that."

"Raquel," he seethed. "If you ever hurt me again I'll..." Instead of finishing, he gripped her arm tightly and stared into her face. "Raquel, we have been together all our lives. We are meant to be together. You are mine." She could feel numbness in her legs as he foamed his words. "I love you Raquel." He paused for a response, then continued. "I know, deep down you love me. We belong to each other. Do you love me?"

Raquel didn't speak.

"Your words hurt me. I've done everything for you, but all you do is hurt me. The more I show love, the less people love me. You don't hate me. You need to apologize for what you said. Don't you see how much I love you?"

She stood in place, bewildered at Robert's meltdown.

"Apologize," Robert demanded. "I need to hear it.

Apologize and tell me you love me."

Raquel remained quiet.

"Apologize!" he screamed as he pulled her closer.

"Let go. You're hurting me."

A firm hand wrapped around Robert's wrist and twisted until he released Raquel. Dancer continued to twist until Robert dropped to his knees and cried out in pain. Fury exploded across Dancer's face as he raised an aluminum crutch over his head, preparing to crush Robert, who was now in a defenseless position.

"No, Dancer!" Raquel raised a hand toward the crutch and stepped forward. She looked into Dancer's eyes. Almost in a whisper, she said, "Please. Stop. Don't be like him." She touched his face and the anger dissipated from his expression. "Dancer," she said in a soft tone. "It isn't worth it."

He let Robert go, and reached down to pick up the other crutch. He gripped it and looked at Robert, who kneeled and flexed his wrist. Clenched teeth gnashed to contain the shaking rage written on Michael's face. The longer he stared at Robert, the more his hand shook with anger. For a moment, Raquel again thought he would bend the crutch over Robert's head. Then his eyes met Raquel. She could see him preparing to launch a lethal blow, and she softly shook her head. She said no words, but her pleading eyes caressed his emotions. The muscles in his jaw eased, and he allowed his grip on the crutch to follow. It lowered to the floor. For a moment, tears formed in his eyes, and Dancer turned, and hobbled out the door.

Lord, how did I get into such a mess? She fled the foyer and distanced herself from Robert. He seemed to be coming unhinged. The fear of Robert and her heartache for Dancer overwhelmed her. It had been hard to get Dancer to allow her into the world behind his walls. Now that Robert had squashed the little trust she'd fought to get into their relationship, how would Dancer respond?

Chapter Fourteen

Dancer hobbled into the rehearsal room carrying a gym bag. Heads turned to watch him. The crutches were gone, but he walked with a noticeable limp. Uncertainty raced through Raquel's mind when he sat beside her and pulled athletic tape from his bag.

"What are you doing?" Raquel asked.

A tearing sound pierced the air when he stretched a strand of tape from the roll, and pressed it to his ankle. The sound of the tape began again when he fed it behind his ankle, grabbed it with the other hand, and pulled it across his foot. He didn't say a word until he made several loops around his foot and ankle. Then he sat up and smiled, "I'm going to dance." Raquel didn't know what to say. After a pause, Dancer bent over and continued rolling the tape.

Mrs. Kahler walked into the room and stopped. A bewildered look took over her face. The teacher looked for a long moment before speaking. "What are you doing, Michael?"

Dancer tore the tape off the roll, pressed the loose end firm, and stood. He hopped a few times and smiled. "See, I told you it would be better by tonight." His mouth smiled, but his eyes pleaded with Mrs. Kahler.

The teacher's eyes darted down to his foot as she shook her head and frowned, "I can't send you on stage hurt."

"I am fine. Please. You've got to let me go onstage," Dancer begged. "Look at the crowd in the auditorium. Parents are out there, and you know how the community is always excited about Bristol High's plays. Without the main character, the play is a flop."

Mrs. Kahler scanned the students with her eyes, looked toward the door leading to the stage, and back to Dancer. She stood without speaking for a long moment. Indecision crawled across her face and frightened eyes darted around the room. Silence spanned for eons. All eyes watched the teacher.

The silence shattered with the teacher's voice. "Are you absolutely sure you are okay?"

Dancer nodded.

She looked around the room for answers, found none, then looked back to Dancer. "I'm just not sure. You were walking pretty bad earlier."

"I'm just being careful to save my strength for tonight. You've got to give me a chance. If I have trouble, I'll make my way off stage and the play won't be any worse off than it would have been without me," Dancer said as he tried to sound assured. "I don't want to let the community down," he added.

The teacher looked back toward the stage, and her hand took its place on her forehead as it tried to massage the stress away. After a quick glance at the clock, she clapped her hands twice and said, "Okay gang, fifteen minutes before the show begins. Let me do a final check on your costumes." She looked at Dancer and shook her head. "You guys are going to turn my hair gray. Okay, Michael. Get your costume ready and go onstage. But, if you have any pain, let me know and get off the stage."

Dancer gave a relieved smile.

The teacher examined his face and said, "We need to do something about those bruises. It will stand out under the lights." She turned to the floor and called out, "Does anyone have some makeup? We need to hide his bruises."

Seriousness returned to Mrs. Kahler's face, and the director in her returned. Though she shook her head as she walked, the excitement had returned to her eyes.

Raquel felt new energy in the air. With a bottle of foundation in her hand, she went to work on Dancer's face. She took a step back and curled her lip. "You look like... Like you need a little more." Half a bottle remained. She shrugged, then began shaking it out in larger quantities.

Rubbing her hands together she smeared it on his face and rubbed it smooth. After another step back, a laugh exploded from her.

"What? Does it look that bad?" Dancer asked.

"No, no. It looks fine." Then Raquel doubled over with laughter. A series of snorts echoed into the room. She regained her composure and said, "You look great!" Then let out another burst of laughter.

"What did you do to me?" Dancer rushed to a mirror. The sight of his new make-over caused a sigh to escaped from his gut. "I look like the monster of Mary Kay." His words caused a renewed round of laughter from Raquel. He turned to her. "This ain't funny." Placing his hands on his hips, Dancer said, "I don't know why you're laughing at me. I'm going to be dancing right beside you."

Laughter faded and a bright smile spread across Raquel's face. "I will be proud to stand on stage with you." Dancer smiled back and seemed more at ease. Raquel examined his face and said, "Even if you do look like the monster of Mary Kay!" She doubled over and snorted.

"I'm glad I'm here to entertain you."

"Three minutes to go. Places everyone. Places," Mrs. Kahler called out as she herded the students with a series of claps. "Michael, are you ready?"

"The monster of Mary Kay is ready," he said, and gave a playful look of scorn toward Raquel. The teacher gave a puzzled look, shrugged, then turned her attention to herding students to their places.

Raquel leaned forward and kissed his cheek. "I think you're wonderful." She took her place and the music began, queuing them onto the stage.

Mrs. Kahler looked tense, and timidly looked at the students on the stage. As Dancer and Raquel's performances were in sync, she began to look more relaxed. Other than the athletic tape's hindrance to his mobility, the dancer showed no real effects from his injury. As the scene changed, both stepped off stage to prepare for their next appearance.

"You have any aspirin?" Dancer whispered as they exited the stage, "I need to kill some of this pain—"

"Michael, you are doing great," the teacher said as she walked back to meet him. A proud smile beamed on her face. "Any pain or problems with your ankle?"

"None. I feel good," Dancer said.

"Wonderful." Mrs. Kahler clasped her hands together. "The musical is going so wonderful!" she said while hurrying back to peek onto the stage.

The musical became a big success. The play lasted for five days. Dancer tried to hide his limp offstage, but also seemed to grow stronger with each performance. Raquel felt delighted. Each time they stepped on stage, they were in perfect rhythm. The stage is where they belonged.

Unknown to her at the time, this play would be the last time they danced together.

At the start of his junior year, many changes were taking place in Dancer's life. On the first day of the new school year, Raquel saw him hurrying to class. "Dancer!" she called down the hall. She smiled as he turned to greet her.

Dancer returned her smile and said, "Hi, Raquel."

"Are you ready for the new play?" she asked as she approached. "This year's first play is supposed to be a good one."

"I'm not going to be in drama this year."

The words stabbed Raquel. She was one year behind him and drama class was where they spent the most time together. Over the summer, they had seen little of each other. He spent most of his time at Pahl. What would happen to their fragile relationship if he didn't stay with the drama team?

"Now I'm a second-year student at Pahl," he said. "I will be participating in productions in Knoxville. Raquel, this is a big step up from a high school musical. My dream is Broadway, and I've been told I'm one of their most promising students."

Raquel forced a thin smile, "I understand. I am glad you are doing well and I'm happy for you. I'm already your biggest fan."

"Thanks." His voice sounded enthusiastic, but a look of guilt etched onto his face.

Raquel fidgeted, searching for words. And searching for hope in Dancer's eyes. "What about us? Will we still be able to see each other?"

With a shrug, he said, "We will still see each other around school, right?"

Raquel looked at the floor, wondering how straightforward she should be. The five-minute warning bell rang. She raised her eyes back up. "Don't we have more than just a casual friendship? You are the only guy I really care about."

The guy she loved played with the book in his hands, and studied the floor. "Raquel, you are the most wonderful girl I have ever met. I know I should love you, I just can't."

"Does this have something to do with what happened with Robert? We can't let fear drive our lives."

Dancer shook his head as he studied Raquel's feet. "I just don't know where to start." One of his feet crawled on top of the other, then they switched positions and he continued. "Margaret once asked me about having a girlfriend and I told her I'm just a dancer and don't have a real heart." Timid eyes darted up to Raquel. He gave a weak smile, and then returned his gaze to her shoes. "I have never been loved, and don't have love to give. If I had a heart, you would be the one I would give it to, but I'm sorry. I don't have anything to give."

"You *have* been loved," Raquel said with more

conviction than she intended. "You just need to look and see it. You do have a heart. You just need to let down your defenses so the one who loves you can see it." She reached out to touch his arm. "Dancer, the problem is that you are burying your heart behind your fears of rejection. If you would allow yourself to be loved, you would find that the person who really loves you will accept the real you. But you can't experience love until you allow yourself to be vulnerable." The conversation paused while she searched for words. In a soft tone, Raquel said, "It is not your job to protect your heart. It is your job to protect the heart of the one you love—and it is her job to take care of yours."

Dancer's eyes raised off the floor. "I don't know how to do that," he said. The late bell rang, rescuing him from the conversation. With a shrug he said, "We've got to go to class."

Raquel nodded. Dancer wiped sweaty palms on his pants and walked away. Pain dug at her heart. Is this relationship meant to be? Though her heart affirmed her love, it didn't seem possible. Things became worse a short time later when Dancer found out he'd been accepted into Pahl's academic program.

Once he left Bristol High, Raquel knew the only way they could ever be together would be if she could somehow join him on stage again. She decided to visit Pahl to see how she could enroll.

Butterflies danced in Raquel's stomach as she walked into the door of Pahl. The building had a front desk, but no receptionist. She looked around the corner for someone to speak with, but the only people in sight were students walking toward a changing room.

"Can I help you?" a voice called from behind.

Turning around, Raquel saw a man dressed in a

leotard. "Um, I am looking for the registrant's office."

"You won't find one in this building. Who referred you here?"

"Oh, I wasn't referred. I'm trying to apply to come to this school."

"I am an instructor here, and I'm sorry to inform you we don't accept walk in student applications."

Raquel felt her heart sinking. "But how do I apply?"

"This is one of the top schools for the performing arts, and we only accept applications by referral from one of our partner schools." The instructor leveled his gaze and spoke in a firm tone. "Let me be honest with you. There are many aspiring dancers, but we only accept the best of the best. We are looking for specific qualities in dancers. Our partner schools only refer dancers that fit our needs, and even then, they may not be accepted. It takes a strong referral and the right kind of audition. I don't want to dash your dreams, but if you haven't been noticed by now, you probably—" the man stopped and thought for a moment. "Let's just say there are other pursuits in the performing arts that may suit you better."

The man's words cut to her heart, and she fought back the tears she felt welling up in her eyes. Trying to maintain her composure and hide the desperation in her voice, she said, "My good friend attends here and we dance together. I want to come here too. We make a good team and I know I can do it."

The man's thin eyebrows raised in apparent surprise at her comment. "Who's your friend?"

"Michael Camp."

"Ah. A very good student," the man's expression took on a pleasant look as he appeared lost in thought for a moment. "Michael is doing very well for a second-year student." He looked back to Raquel. "Michael came here as the International Grand Prix winner. If you really think you have what it takes, you can compete in the Grand Prix, or you can go to one of our referral schools. I can get you the information if you need it."

"I would like that," Raquel said as she grabbed for hope in his words. The man disappeared through a door and returned with several stapled papers.

"Here are a list of schools in Tennessee we accept referrals from. You can apply to one of those schools, and if accepted, you can try for a referral." The man's tone took on a serious demeanor. "Let me give you a piece of advice. When you apply, be ready for a hard audition. These schools are not easy to get into and you must make a good impression. No, a great impression. Even then you may not be accepted."

"Thank you," Raquel said.

The man left and she examined the list. The closest school to her home was the Knoxville School of the Performing Arts. The instructor's words made it seem as though this were a long shot, but Raquel clung to the glimmer of distant hope.

A petite girl in tights walked by and Raquel felt a twinge of jealousy. The girl looked very attractive and she wondered if the blonde girl worked with Dancer. How long would it be before another girl found Dancer's heart? She would have to dedicate herself to getting into the school in Knoxville, and get a referral. Raquel knew she would have to work harder than she had thought possible just to have a chance to get into either school. Even then, would she find the opportunity she hoped for?

Happiness with Dancer began to slip away. Now was the time to reach for a goal that would save their relationship.

Chapter Fifteen

Raquel sat wringing her hands while she waited for the judges of Knoxville School of the Performing Arts to finish evaluating her audition. Two girls and a boy sat in a cold waiting room with her. The only signs of life were the judges, and an occasional student who walked past the door's window. Chilled vinyl chairs lined the bare walls, and a table covered with magazines stood as the room's centerpiece. A forgotten poster hung by three tacks. Its message read, 'Perfect Practice Makes Perfect Performance'.

The two girls seemed just as nervous as Raquel, but the boy pulled a hand-held game out of a satchel and began playing. Surrounded by electronic sounds, he seemed lost in amusement without a care in the world.

Each girl sat up straight as the door opened. A woman with brown hair called the name of one of the girls, brushed her bangs aside with her hand, and led the girl away as the door returned with a swish and a click. Raquel felt as if she were sitting in a doctor's office, waiting to learn her diagnosis. She had been in auditions before, but this school had a different way of handling them. Instead of calling out the names of those selected, this performing arts school called each candidate in for a consultation.

The door opened again. "Raquel?" She stood as the woman flipped her hair from her eye, and gave a soft smile, "Come with me."

Trying to slow her breathing, Raquel walked back to the same room where she had auditioned. Mirrors covered the walls, making the small room appear massive. Two women and a man sat behind a table with a chair in front. The man tapped his pencil in a steady beat, oblivious to the annoyed glances of his peers. Moments ago Raquel auditioned in front of this table, but the chair now made it look more intimidating. She tried to cover herself with her arms as she sat before the staring judges.

A woman in the center of the table spoke first. "Raquel," she said in a cheery tone, "Let me start by saying you have a lot of good qualities. Your stage presence is lovely and you have good balance and flexibility. So I don't want you to take this as failure."

Raquel's heart plummeted at her words. Her eyes began to sting as she tried to blink back her emotions.

The woman continued, "I'm sorry, but you are just not ready for this school."

Raquel nodded and forced a thin smile as a tear began its journey down her cheek.

The woman gave another empathetic smile and said, "I can recommend a few good schools where you can learn the skills that can help you here. We like you and think you have potential." The woman looked to her left and right. The man stopped tapping his pencil as he nodded in unison with the other instructor, then resumed his drumming. The spokeswoman continued, "It is just that this school isn't designed to teach the basics. We are an advanced school and we would like to see you after you've developed your skills. I recommend you take classes at one of these good dance studios, develop your skills, and audition with us again." The woman stood, offered Raquel a folder, and the audition ended.

Tears trickled down and dotted her chest, but Raquel tried to look confident as she exited the room. Knowing lost time was becoming a great divide between her and Dancer, she feared it would not be possible to advance fast enough to get to Pahl before he moved away from Tennessee.

With a heavy heart, Raquel left the studio and headed to her car. An odd feeling came over her, and she turned to look at the parking lot across the street. A figure watched from a familiar car. *Robert! Why is he here?* She didn't know whether to be angry or afraid. Three times in the last week she had spotted him in the area. How many times could he have been around when she didn't realize it? Did he follow each time she left the house? Anger rose like bile in the back of her throat. *What right does Robert have to monitor my personal life?*

Raquel knew the perfect remedy after a stressful day. And after a failed audition. Shopping. Of course, her best friend Margaret would always oblige. When she returned from the mall, she saw a truck in the driveway and assumed her parents had company. A look inside the door caused Raquel's blood to run cold. Robert stood in the kitchen with her mother at the sink.

"Raquel, glad you are home," her mother, Gladys said.

"What are you doing here?" Raquel said to Robert in a cold tone.

Before Robert could answer, her mom said, "Your father's car broke down on his way home from work. Robert just happened by and gave him a ride home. Now your father has gone with a mechanic to see if they can get it going." She smiled at Robert and said, "He's such a nice young man. I invited him to visit for a spell and he insisted on helping me out in the kitchen. You are lucky to have a boyfriend like Robert. This kind is hard to find."

"He's not my boyfriend," Raquel said as she walked past.

"Would you like to stay for supper?" Gladys said to Robert.

"No, I don't want to intrude. Besides, Raquel seems like she might be a little tired."

"Oh, don't worry about Raquel," Gladys said as she waved her hand. "She is young, and she has more energy than she knows what to do with."

Ugh! He knows how to play Mr. Innocent.

Through the window, Raquel saw her father pull into the driveway and walk to the door. She stayed out of Robert's sight, but wanted to listen to see what happened to the car. After what happened to Dancer, she had her suspicions.

The door opened and her father said, "You will never believe what caused the problem. The gas tank had water in it. We had to siphon it out and refill it." He looked back out the door, "Some pranksters must have been in the area."

"I'm glad they got you working, Mr. Orren," Robert said. "When did you fill up last? A while back, I had a friend who stalled after buying cheap gas."

Looking up as if in thought, Mr. Orren said, "Now that you mention it, I did buy some gas from one of those cheap stations just outside of Bristol this morning." Robert gave a knowing smile as Mr. Orren continued, "Seems odd that it waited until this afternoon to stall the car, though. But maybe I should stay away from those stations on the edge of town."

"Robert has been helping me in the kitchen, so I've invited him to join us for dinner," Gladys said, changing the subject.

"You must be bored today," Mr. Orren said. "I thought you teenagers only cared about hanging out at the mall."

Robert smiled and said, "You guys just looked like you needed a hand today, so I thought I'd be neighborly."

"Do you and Raquel still go out at all?" Gladys said.

"Sometimes. We still hang out at school. I'm thinking about going out again. That is, if you don't object, Mr. Orren," Robert said in a voice of humility.

"Please, call me Buck. Mr. sounds too formal," he patted Robert's shoulder, "especially for friends of the family. You're always welcomed here."

Gladys shooed them into the living room where Robert could talk sports with Raquel's father. Raquel skittered out of the room toward the back of the house. When the two entered the room, Robert said, "Everything smells so good. If I remember correctly, Mrs. Orren is one of the best cooks in Bristol."

I can't listen to this sappy charade. That schmooze is such a phony. The bedroom is one place where she wouldn't have to deal with Robert. *If he's staying for supper, I'm skipping it.*

When Raquel refused to join the family at mealtime, her mother entered the bedroom. "What is your problem?" Gladys asked from the doorway, hands on her hips.

"Why did you invite him here?" she asked her mother.

"Robert? Why shouldn't we invite him to dinner? He's a nice guy."

"He's not a nice guy. He and some other guys beat up Michael. He is just putting on a show for you and dad."

"Look, Raquel. Boys fight sometimes. I can tell he really likes you, and sometimes boys get into little spats when it comes to girls. You should feel honored two boys are competing for you."

"It wasn't a little spat between boys, and this is not just competing for attention. He has been following me around." Raquel lowered her voice, and looking toward the door she said, "I'm beginning to think he's a stalker."

"Oh, please, Raquel." Gladys tossed an arm up and looked to the ceiling. "I've known Robert since he was a baby, and he's no stalker. He is a sweet boy. And besides, the only reason he came here today is because your father's car broke down. Your dad broke down in the middle of nowhere. Robert was a godsend and you should be thanking him," Gladys said.

Raquel looked to the door and said, "Speaking of that, didn't I hear Dad say they found water in the tank? The same thing happened to Michael. He broke down in the middle of nowhere because someone poured water in his tank. This seems like too much of a coincidence to me."

"Raquel! Surely you are not going to accuse Robert of

doing such a thing just because he happened to be the first one to come by. You are reading something into a good deed that isn't there." Her mother leveled her gaze and pointed her finger as she said, "Don't you go and accuse Robert of anything unless you have something other than your imagination to prove it."

"But it's not—"

"That's enough. Robert is a super nice guy. And besides, I heard your father say it was bad gas. Probably bought at the same station your friend visited when he broke down." Gladys wagged her finger and said, "Shame on you for trying to drag him through the mud. He is a sweet boy and you need to open your eyes and see it. You will never find a better man, so you better not let this opportunity pass you by."

"Mom, you don't—"

"No more," her mother interrupted again. "I am not listening to any more gossip about Robert. You are going to show him a little kindness, because that's all he has shown to you, and to us." She turned and walked back toward the living room, leaving Raquel confused. Could her mother be right? Could it be possible it's nothing more than a string of coincidences, and Robert just keeps being at the right place to cross her and her family's paths?

"Can I speak with you?" Raquel asked when she peeked into Mrs. Kahler's office at the high school drama center.

"Sure, Raquel. Come on in." The teacher's voice sounded welcoming. "What can I do for you?"

Swallowing hard, Raquel searched for words. She knew Mrs. Kahler looked forward to using her in the next musical, and she had already lost Dancer. She didn't want to disappoint her teacher, but she also knew she could not reach for her future in a high school drama center. "Um, I'm going to quit drama."

Mrs. Kahler's expression turned to shock, then drooped into disappointment. "Why? What's wrong?"

"Oh, nothing is wrong. It's just, well, I've joined a dance and theater class in Bristol. I need these classes to get into Knoxville's performing arts school. I just won't have time to take classes and stay in drama." Raquel tried to sound cheerful, but found it difficult while Mrs. Kahler had such a hurt expression on her face. She really liked Mrs. Kahler and wanted her to know her decision wasn't a rejection.

Her thoughts were interrupted by Mrs. Kahler. "You know, you only have one chance to experience high school. You are building memories with your friends that will last a lifetime. There will never be another time in your life that will create as many fond memories as these four years. Raquel," the teacher leveled her gaze, "don't throw this time away. You will regret it."

The teacher's words caused Raquel to stop and think. True, the last two years in drama were some of the happiest times of her life. She only had two more years with her friends before they went their separate ways. Then she remembered Dancer and smiled. He's the main reason the performing arts had such meaning for her. When thinking of dance, Michael came to mind. When she thought of Michael, she thought of dance and the stage. It wasn't possible to separate her love for performing from her love for Michael. In Raquel's mind, the two were one, and performing would have little meaning without him. For her, happiness would be when they could again dance on stage together.

Raquel returned from her thoughts and said, "I know, Mrs. Kahler, but I have to do this. I'm following my dream. I don't have time to wait."

"Raquel, you are young, with all the time in the world ahead of you. Don't feel like you are on some imaginary time limit. After high school, there will be many opportunities. Colleges, performing arts schools, theater. These all will be around long after you finish high school."

Searching for words, Raquel nodded to acknowledge her teachers comments, then answered, "I know these things, but I want to go to the Knoxville School of the Performing Arts. Their referral program is for youth only. The program I want to take doesn't accept students after they reach nineteen. I'm sorry, Mrs. Kahler. But this is something I have to do."

The teacher's face forced a disappointed smile as she began to nod. "Okay. It's your decision, but think about what you are missing."

As Raquel left the drama building, she felt as though she had been in a mental wrestling match. The brief conversation felt exhausting. With that task behind her, she determined to dedicate her spare time to developing her skills, and improving her dance. The next audition at Knoxville School of the Performing Arts is in three months, and she intended to be prepared.

Raquel applied every free moment of her time to dancing. Some days, she felt like her legs would not carry her, but pushed through the soreness, pain, and frustration as she fought to bring her body under control, and into each move with grace and precision. Now, she again sat in the cold room of the Knoxville School of the Performing Arts, staring at the table of magazines, while wondering her fate. Thirteen other hopefuls shared the waiting room with her, so she faced more competition than before.

For the last three months, Raquel had dedicated herself to learning the basics in a small studio in Bristol. Raquel's instructor performed in theater, ballet, and had a lot of practical advice for dancers. There were times when Raquel felt she could not measure up to the teacher's demanding standards, but after a couple of months, she could see marked improvements in her dance.

Three months earlier, she had joined the Bristol Dance Studio and explained her goals of getting accepted into Knoxville's program. She now felt closer to that goal than she had thought possible. The ungainly motions that plagued her before were fading, and now her movements flowed with grace. Or so she hoped.

The teacher had video taped her dance on three different occasions. First, when she enrolled, then six weeks later, and again at the three-month mark. When Raquel felt discouraged, the teacher showed her first two performances on a TV, and she was stunned. Raquel had thought she was a good dancer before, but seeing herself six weeks after enrolling, she realized how ungraceful she had been. This provided her with the inspiration to dedicate herself even more.

Just before coming to this audition, Raquel watched her three-month performance. She didn't look like the same person. The clumsy girl had disappeared, and she learned what it meant to dance with delicate motion.

Looking around the room, insecurity began to slip into Raquel's thoughts. Some of these girls seemed to float across the room. Even their walks were elegant and their presence seemed to cry out for an audience, but she was just a country girl from Bristol. When you think of Bristol, you think of country—not graceful dancers. She took pride in her heritage, but also realized that boots didn't train legs to move with grace. She thought back to the barn dances which used to be commonplace when she was younger. Everyone clapped while the fiddle played. In Bristol, community dances were just fun. No one cared how graceful you moved, everyone stood on the same ground. When you stomped around the barn, no one evaluated your performance, or decided whether you were good enough to dance.

"Raquel?" The voice returned her to the audition. She

stood and walked toward the same chair where her dreams had been shattered three months earlier. Two of the judges were the same, but a different man this time. This man had a scowling face and heavy eyebrows. Raquel didn't like the way he looked at her under those furrowed brows. She began to feel more uncomfortable than she felt last time. It looked like the odds were against her, and she hoped the other two judges would be enough to outvote the scowling man.

"I'm glad to see you aren't a quitter, Raquel," said the woman at the center of the judges table. "You have made a remarkable improvement over the last three months. I would go as far as to say, your performance is one of the strongest improvements I've seen in a long time. You must have had a good teacher." The other woman nodded but the man did not hint at an expression. The woman turned to him and asked, "What do you think, Mr. Bellowski?"

The man arched up as though just realizing his reason for being present. He said, "I thought your audition showed great promise. With a lot of hard work, I think you could do well." The man had a strong East-European accent. When he spoke, his brows raised into a warm expression and his voice sounded pleasant and strong. This surprised Raquel because she expected him to sound gruff and speak through his frown.

The woman spoke again as the man returned to his furrowed posture, "Mr. Bellowski has been an international dancer and performer for more than twenty years. We are excited to have him join us as an instructor. Our school," she turned to Raquel, "and students like you, will greatly benefit from his expertise. You will learn a lot from his wealth of experience."

Raquel straightened up. Did this woman just say that she would be learning from Mr. Bellowski? Could she be into the school?

The woman gave a kind smile as she said, "Welcome to

the Knoxville School of the Performing Arts."

Raquel put her hand over her mouth as her body began to shake. Tears filled her eyes again, but this time for the right reason. She struggled to regain her composure as she grappled for words. The only words that came to mind were, "Thank you."

"We look forward to having you as our student. Our assistant will show you to the registrars office. You and your parents will need to fill out the registration forms and you'll be assigned to a program. Go with the registrar and she will get you the forms."

As Raquel followed the woman, everything seemed surreal. She couldn't believe it finally happened, and couldn't wait to tell Dancer.

The news Dancer shared dashed the thrill of her own success. He had been offered a position on Broadway. Once he finished taking finals, he would leave for New York. Each time she expected to draw closer to Dancer, she remained a step behind him. Now she would have to make it all the way to Broadway before they could reunite. And that would take a miracle.

Three failed auditions at Pahl seemed to put any hope of reaching Broadway to rest. But Raquel's miracle arrived unexpectedly. The dream of reaching New York had been buried with her hopes of reuniting with Dancer. Her requests for auditions went unanswered, and Raquel resolved herself to accepting the fact she would be a local performer.

For the last two weeks, she had performed at the Laurel Theater in Knoxville. With ten performances completed, she could now relax with this latest show behind her. After three years of daily training and repetitious work in the studio, it felt rewarding to see all the boring routines pay off on the stage. Dancing on stage is exciting, but after ten straight nights of performing, the studio looked welcoming.

As she began warming up on the mat, her instructor called, "Raquel." Mr. Bellowski scurried over. "Great job. Your performance this week was top notch."

"Thanks, Mr. Bellowski."

"There are some people up front who wish to see you. One is Joseph Rodney. He is a Broadway talent agent." The instructor placed a hand on Raquel's shoulder. "They want to schedule you for an audition." A proud smile burst forth on Mr. Bellowski's face. "This could be a great opportunity for you!"

The words of Mr. Bellowski caught her by surprise. Cats began fighting in Raquel's stomach and she rose on legs of spaghetti. Not having time to prepare for an interview, she wondered what to say to make a good first impression. As she walked with her instructor, Raquel's mind tried to think of what to expect and how to answer questions. It would be better to have time to prepare, but today it wasn't an option.

Mr. Bellowski led her to a conference room, then returned to the floor. Looking in the room, she could see people waiting around a table. Raquel wiped the moisture off her forehead. She whispered, "Lord, give me the words to say," and walked into the room.

That interview led her to Manhattan. After a trip to New York for an audition, a producer named Marcus offered her a position as a secondary dancer. The worst part about leaving Bristol had been hiding her plans from Robert. He sensed something going on, and pried for information. Knowing he watched her every move, she designed a plan of diversion. The morning she left, she made plans to meet Robert at a cafe in Bristol. While he waited, she left town. Though she knew he sat at a table on the other side of town, she still watched her rear-view mirror all the way to New

York. Now she was actually on Broadway, far from the stalker, and living out her dream. Or at least part of her dream.

At last, Raquel began to feel drowsy. She sipped her Camomile tea. Now room temperature, the tea no longer seemed satisfying. The clock showed 2:21 a.m. "Oh, goodness! How am I going to get up in the morning?" With a sigh, she stood, gulp down the last swallow of lukewarm tea, and placed the cup on the table.

For years she had wondered why Dancer never called, and why his phone had been disconnected. The reason now made sense. He's homeless. But then again, Dancer being homeless didn't make sense. He left to become a Broadway performer, so how did he end up washing windows off Broadway?

Sleepy fingers found the light switch. With a click, the lights went off, and she slid under the covers. The sheets were cold again. Now, she needed to find out what happened to Dancer.

Chapter Sixteen

A chilly wind swept across Raquel's neck when she stepped out of the Belasco Theater. She adjusted her scarf and pulled the coat tighter against her body. Cold and snow were common back in Bristol, but its winters didn't prepare her for this New York wind. And it wasn't even winter yet. The light began its separation from the evening sky. Her legs were tired from a long day of rehearsals, but this evening, she committed herself to looking for Dancer.

Each day Raquel looked down West 54th street, but never saw Dancer among the panhandlers and window washers. She walked down 7th avenue toward Central Park. As night began to fall, the sidewalks became less crowded. She examined each face as she strolled six blocks to the park entrance. Raquel walked past horse drawn carriages, carrying lovers on romantic rides under the bright city lights.

The park still bustled with pedestrians as they enjoyed cool walks in the park. Passing the Heckscher Playground, Raquel continued deeper into the park where the crowds thinned to a few stragglers. She'd heard that many of New York's homeless used Central Park as a rest stop, but so far, she only saw park visitors. It seemed like this park went on forever. Even if Dancer was here somewhere, the chances of finding him were slim. When she neared Turtle Pond, she saw a group of men who looked homeless, but the dim light concealed their faces.

A park bench in front of Turtle Pond made a good resting place. Raquel watched the shadows dance on the surface of the water. After all this walking, she still wasn't halfway through the park. A group of men sitting at a picnic table kept looking her way. The feeling of being alone made her uncomfortable. Time to walk back to Broadway. When darkness fell, Central Park seemed like a different place. Few pedestrians now moved about the paved walkways, and Raquel began to feel foolish for staying here after the crowds dispersed.

Unseen eyes seemed to watch her from the shadows. Now feeling paranoid, Raquel left the bench and paced quickly toward the walkway. She looked back and felt relieved to see that the men remained at the picnic table. She turned around and her heart stopped. A man stood before her. She stepped to the side, but he stepped in front of her. Two other men stood behind him.

"Excuse me," she said as she tried to push past.

The man gripped her arm firmly as he said, "What's a pretty little lady like you doing here alone?"

"I'm meeting a friend here, so let me go." She tried to appear forceful, but her voice sounded like a plea.

"I bet you're looking for a good man," he said. Without warning, another man grabbed her, and the third man ripped her purse from her arm. A hand pressed hard against her mouth and strong arms lifted her from her feet. The men were dragging her toward a thick patch of trees and shrubs.

Oh, God, no!

The ground slammed into her back. The attacker had her pinned. Raquel heard her heart pulsing in her ears, and excited snickers from the men. "It looks like we are the only friends you ha—"

The man's words were cut short by a commotion. In the faint light she saw a fourth shadow struggling with the men as they shouted and fought. Raquel struggled to regain her footing as the fight continued. She wanted to run, but her petrified legs wouldn't cooperate. The sounds of something hitting flesh echoed in the quiet night, mingled with profanity and protests.

In a moment, the shouting stopped and silence returned to the cold night air. A shadow approached and her heart screamed in terror. She gasped as a hand gripped her coat and pulled her upwards.

"What are you doing in the middle of the park, alone, at night?" The voice sounded harsh and angry. "Are you some kind of a fool?"

When they emerged from the woods, two of the men were gone and the third sat on hands and knees, while gagging. "Is he okay?"

"He's fine. He's just thinking about his painful lesson, but why should you care?" the stranger said. Raquel realized she recognized the voice.

They approached the walkway. Raquel turned to try to get a glimpse of the man's face. "Dancer?" she said as she tried to see his eyes. The man didn't speak, but hurried his pace, and pulled her toward the main walkway by her coat.

He stopped when they reached the road, then said, "This is 79th Street Transverse. Walk that way," he pointed down the road. "Keep going until you leave the park. Turn left on Central Park West and follow it all the way to Broadway." He held his finger up in a scolding posture. "Never come into the park at night alone. This isn't Brist—." He stopped his words and regrouped. "This isn't a small town, and big cities have an ugly side you don't want to see. I would advise you to not walk alone at night. Period."

"Dancer, I need to talk to you," Raquel said when he finished his instructions.

"You need to leave the park," he said and pointed in the direction she needed to go.

"But I—"

"GO!" he interrupted. She stood for a moment and he shouted loud enough to frighten her, "You. Need. To. Leave. The. Park. NOW!" His shouts made her heart race and her fingers tingle. She turned and made a hurried retreat in the direction the man pointed.

Michael watched her until she turned the corner and disappeared from view. He walked back down to where he fought her assailants and found the man who had been on his knees had staggered to his feet. Michael shoved him backward, causing him to tumble to the ground as he pleaded for mercy. He walked past the man and picked up Raquel's purse.

Plopping onto the park bench, he sorted through the bag. Looked at her cell phone, returned it. A quick dig around produced a wallet. Inside were two twenties, a ten, and three ones. He stuffed the bills in his pocket and pushed the wallet back into the purse.

Not wanting anyone to see him with a purse, Michael stuffed it under his tattered coat, and headed toward his supplier. This would be enough money to buy several hits. Drugs no longer produced a high. The addiction only served to get him close to a feeling of normality. Life now consisted of surviving between highs. Michael longed for the time when he controlled his life, but now this worthless substance controlled him. The challenge would now be to keep Raquel from discovering the truth of what he'd become.

Chapter Seventeen

Michael leaned on the wall outside the Belasco Theater. He had Raquel's purse tucked under his ripped jacket, trying to hide it from public view. A man in a long black coat walked in his direction. When the man turned toward the theater's door, Michael pushed off the wall and approached him. They made eye contact, and the man looked away while hurrying his pace, trying to reach the door before Michael could get near him.

"Excuse me."

The man didn't respond, but stared ahead and reached for the door.

"I don't want money," Michael called after him. "I just want to know if you can give this purse to someone for me?"

The words froze the man as he pulled the door open. He looked toward Michael and Michael reached under his coat and pulled out Raquel's brown leather purse and held it out by its strap.

With a puzzled expression, the man let go of the door and turned to face him. His eyes followed the strap down to the purse, then shifted to Michael's face. "What are you doing with a lady's purse?" His voice sounded accusatory.

"It belongs to Raquel Orren. She's a dancer but I'm not sure which theater she's in." Michael held the strap out toward the man. "It has her cell phone in it." He felt uncomfortable as the man stared at him and tried to come up with a reason for having it. "She left it in Central Park last night."

Reaching out a hand, the man in the black coat took the strap. "How did you know where to find her?" Michael didn't answer but turned to walk away. The man followed for a few steps, then said, "What's your name?"

"She will know who it's from," Michael said as he retreated down the sidewalk.

"Your name wouldn't happen to be Michael Camp, would it?" the man called as he took a few more steps down the sidewalk.

After hearing his name, Michael picked up his pace and hurried away from the theater. He could hear footsteps behind him, so he broke into a sprint. Time to get away from this place.

How did he know my name?

His mind raced as he sorted through the names and faces from the past. He didn't remember meeting this man, but somehow this stranger knew his name. He hoped it wasn't a detective. If it is an investigator, the law must know the things he'd been doing. From now on, he would try to stay out of public view as much as possible.

With the exhaustion she felt, Raquel was glad rehearsals had ended. She thought her school in Knoxville had been demanding, but Broadway made that look like a walk in the park. Her late night in Central Park made her fatigue worse. Tonight she would have to get plenty of rest. She changed clothes and started to leave the theater, but the reporter she'd met on her first day stepped out to intercept her.

"Raquel, do you remember me? We met in the hall of the new Broadway office," Richard Barnhouse called out when Raquel approached.

"I remember," she answered with a cold tone.

"Can I speak to you for a moment?"

"I'm really tired and need to get home. Sorry," she said and pushed past the reporter.

"Can I at least give you your purse?" Raquel stopped and turned. Richard had a satisfied look as he held the bag high for her to see.

"Where did you find it?"

"A homeless man gave it to me. He said you would want it—and your cell phone back." Raquel walked over and reached out to grab it, but Richard pulled it back. "First, can I talk to you?"

"Please give me my purse," she said in a firm tone. Richard held it out again and she pulled it. She glared at him when he didn't immediately release the strap, and he gave a knowing smile, then let it go. After rifling through it, Raquel let out a relieved sigh. "Thank God. My keys, wallet, and credit cards are here. The only thing missing is the cash."

"How did Michael end up with your purse?" the reporter asked.

"How did you find him so fast?"

Holding his palms up, Richard said, "Hey, I'm a seasoned newshound. I can sniff out a good story from a mile away. He didn't tell me how he came by it." When Raquel looked toward the ground, he pressed for details. "Did he steal it from you?"

"No, he didn't!" she protested. "He recovered it from someone who snatched it from me."

"Have you got a few minutes to talk to me?" He seemed rebuked by the look she gave and added, "Or should I fill in the gaps with my own assumptions?"

Raquel's mind raced as she thought through the situation. If the reporter exposed Dancer, he would be humiliated before all of New York, and word would likely travel back home where Raquel's friends still asked about him. She had evaded their questions, not knowing what to say.

Raquel knew Richard didn't have much to go on. If Dancer had talked to him, there would be no need to probe for more information. Looking up to meet his eyes, Raquel said, "I don't have any information on him, now please excuse me. It has been a long day and I have to get some rest." She hurried away as she put on her coat and pushed through the door and out of the theater.

"Not even a—" the door closed behind her.

Richard Barnhouse lowered his voice, finishing his sentence under his breath, "thank you?" This story might be difficult to nail down, but Richard realized it had the potential of becoming big news.

I don't go away that easy. I'll break this story with or without you, Raquel.

Michael stuffed his hand into his pocket, pulling out the remaining cash. He counted out three dollar bills. Not even enough to get a bite to eat. The drugs bought earlier were gone, and the hard crashing began. Hunger gripped his stomach, but his drug craving felt like an elephant sat on his chest. Relief wouldn't come until he satisfied his body's demands. Michael forced himself into motion, and wandered toward the nearby residential streets.

An apartment building caught his interest. He entered and wandered down the halls. Without knowing what to look for, he hoped opportunity would present itself. It did. The sound of jingling keys drew his attention. A mother with her two kids locked the door to their apartment. Michael fumbled with a nearby vending machine, attempting to look occupied. The woman hurried her children away, testifying she understood he didn't belong here.

A moment later, he stood in front of the apartment door, looking back and forth to insure no one remained in the hallway. Two quick steps back, and he rammed his shoulder into the door with a jarring thump. The frame splintered. He rushed inside and began rummaging through drawers and cabinets, looking for anything of value. In the back of a clothes drawer, he found small pieces of jewelry and some coins. These were shoved into his pockets while he continued his search.

What a waste of time. This woman doesn't have anything worth taking.

"Who is in there?"

He froze. The door creaked open, followed by the sound of a man's voice.

"Hello?" the man called out as Michael retreated into the hall corner, next to the bathroom. He could hear the man drawing closer. "She hasn't been gone ten minutes and someone has already cleaned her out," the man said to himself and flipped on the light, unaware the burglar hid nearby.

From where Michael stood, he could see an older man who looked to be in his mid-seventies. His thinning white hair made a vain attempt to cover his freckled scalp. The man walked to the window and looked out. Seeing nothing that caught his interest, he turned, and saw Michael in the corner.

"Oh, my God!" the man cried as he rushed for the door.

Michael leaped out and pursued the fleeing man. The neighbor rushed into the hall and pushed open his apartment door, but before he could slam it closed, Michael forced his foot into the doorway. The man pushed the door hard against Michael's foot, but his strength couldn't compete with the burglar. With a hard push, Michael burst through the door, sending the man sprawling backward onto the floor.

"Help!" he cried out.

"Shut up!" Michael demanded in a forceful whisper.

"Help!" he shouted louder.

Michael knew he had to silence the man before anyone heard his cries. He pushed the door closed and tackled the man, who was climbing back to his feet. Michael put his hand over the man's mouth as he said, "Shut up, old man."

The man jerked his head to the side as he cried, "Help! Somebody call the police!"

Michael drew back a fist and struck the man hard. He lay silent for a moment, but regained his bearings and cried out again. Another hard blow and the man fell silent. Michael climbed to his feet and rushed to the door. Looking through the peephole, he didn't see anyone in the apartment hallway. He stood motionless, listening for the sounds of anyone responding to the man's cries, but didn't hear anything. Looking back at the man lying on the floor, Michael had a sinking feeling in the pit of his stomach.

What have I become? My addictions have turned me into a monster. Michael pressed his palms into his eyes. *I'm not living my life. I'm being driven by something I can't control!*

He knelt beside the old man and checked his breathing. At least the man was alive. Rising to his feet, Michael began to search the room for valuables. He rummaged through the drawers, stuffing anything of worth into his bulging pockets. Then he pulled the mattress up.

Bingo.

Michael grabbed an envelope, flipped through a wad of bills, and crammed them into his pocket. This would cover him for a while. He stuffed his coat with food from the refrigerator and took a final look around the apartment.

Softly, he leaned against the door and listened for any sound of people. After hearing none, he peeked into the hall, then slipped out of the man's apartment. With a quick pace, he walked down the hallway toward the stairs. Now he just needed to reach his supplier and get some relief from these horrid cravings.

Raquel began to feel comfortable in her new

environment. She found it easier to walk to the theater from her apartment, than to fight the one-way streets and heavy congestion. It's a seven-block walk from West 54th street to the Belasco Theater on 47th, but the refreshing walk took ten minutes at a brisk pace. Some days she walked past Broadway en route to the theater to see if Dancer worked in the area. It had now been three weeks since she'd last seen him.

While strolling down the Broadway sidewalk, she examined each bearded face she passed until arriving at 44th street. Disappointment weighed on her as she turned the corner and walked toward the Theater. Her spirits were lifted when she saw the bright smile of her fellow dancer, Tedra Madaih.

Over the last few weeks she had grown closer to Tedra. Though they came from different cultures, Raquel found she had a lot in common with her fellow dancer. Tedra's father was from India, but her mother grew up in New York. Her friend barely stood five-feet tall. The petite woman had a dark complexion, and long black hair that reflected the stage lights. Most of the time she kept her hair in French braids and pinned to the back of her head. High cheeks gave her face a lovely, delicate look, and thick brows accentuated her dark eyes.

"Hi, Raquel!" Tedra said with her usual bubbly voice while rushing over to give a warm hug.

"Hi, Tedra!" Raquel received the embrace.

"We are having a get-together tonight at church. Want to come?"

"Well, I don't know. I had some things I wanted to do tonight"

"Come on, it will be fun. I really want you to meet my family," Tedra said and placed both hands over her heart, looking as if her happiness depended upon the answer.

Tedra's pleading eyes and hopeful expression compelled Raquel. She didn't want to disappoint her friend.

The truth is that she wanted to look for Dancer tonight, but since three weeks of searching hadn't paid off, what would it matter if she missed one night? "Oh, okay."

A joyful expression filled Tedra's face. "Oh, I'm so glad. We'll have so much fun." Her white teeth seemed to glow against her dark complexion. "I've been telling everyone all about you, and I can't wait for you to meet them." A mischievous look formed on her face. "I told my mom you're from Tennessee and you eat grits. She wants you to tell her what a grit is."

Raquel gave a playful roll of her eyes, and laughed with her friend.

Southern life is always good for humor, and is fascinating to these people who have never stepped outside of the city lights. "Well, I'm glad I can at least be a source of amusement."

Perhaps a change of pace would do her good. The obsession of finding Dancer deprived her of any type of social life, increasing her feelings of loneliness. With her drained emotions, she needed something to charge her, and provide the strength to continue searching for the missing piece of her heart.

Chapter Eighteen

Raquel walked out of the studio and began her trek back to the apartment off 54th street. The November snow continued falling, brightening the trees, and causing the road to pile up with slush. Winter had arrived early this year. Even for New York standards.

When passing the corner of 47th, she saw a man with a squeegee, cleaning windows in the gray slushy snow. A closer examination didn't help. The man had a beard, but most of New York's homeless did. The washer scraped, sprayed, and squeegeed each window, rushed to the driver, then headed to the next car.

She stopped and watched as the man cleaned four windows before the light turned green. He walked toward the intersection and waited for the light to turn red again. Sensing eyes upon him, the scruffy man turned to see Raquel standing at the corner of a building, and his eyes widened with recognition.

"Dancer." She smiled and walked toward him.

No answer. Instead, he spun to face traffic. The light turned red and he began his work again. He stuffed a couple of ones in his pocket and rushed to a second car. Raquel walked closer. The light turned green and the line of cars started moving. Dancer didn't return to the street corner, but began walking up the sidewalk, away from Raquel.

"Dancer," she called and hurried to catch up. "Michael!" Still no answer. When she drew closer to him, she said, "I want to thank you for returning my purse. And for protecting me in the park."

"I think you have the wrong person," he said, keeping his back to her.

"Michael, I need to talk to you."

"You need to go away and leave me alone," he snapped,

still facing away from her.

Raquel hurried to get closer. "Please don't push me away. I just want to talk. It doesn't matter to me if you've hit hard times. I just want to see you."

Dancer reached the corner of the far end of the street. He shot a sideways glance and said, "I think you are mistaking me for someone else," then he turned the corner and hurried away.

Raquel stood and watched as he walked to the end of the next block and rounded another corner. A long exhale escaped her lungs as he disappeared from view. Why wouldn't he at least talk to her? Feeling rejected, Raquel continued her walk home. The snow seemed colder now. She thought she should just forget about him, but her heart wouldn't cooperate. How could she have peace without at least knowing what had happened to Dancer?

Raquel finished showering and drying her hair. Too tired to go out again—but she had promised Tedra. After a hard week of rehearsals and late nights, Raquel felt drained and in need of rest. A knock on the door announced her friend's arrival. *Why did I agree to go with Tedra tonight. I don't feel like exerting myself. And putting on a happy face—for people I don't even know.*

"Not tonight," she sighed. Raquel would just tell her friend they could go together another time. The bolt made a swish and a click, then Tedra's smiling face came into view. "Hey, Tedra."

Her friend's face beamed, and she clasped her hands over her heart. "Hey, Raquel! I'm *so* excited about tonight. I can't wait for you to meet my friends at church. You're *just* going to love it."

"Tedra, I don't..." A sinking feeling came over Raquel. How could she disappoint her friend. Excitement beamed from every part of her. Raquel looked back to the warm bed, then turned back to the door. "I don't think you know how excited I am to go out with you." *What are these words coming out of my mouth?* She hid her dread behind a smile, grabbed a coat, and slipped out the door.

The milky sky gave a dim glow as the sun slid from view while Raquel and Tedra walked along 110th Street. They cut across to 111th and an older building came into view. When they arrived, Raquel saw a humble sign over an entrance announcing, *Welcome to the Church at Central Park*. Aging white paint coated the old brick structure. Dark red trim covered the windows and door. The church connected into a long line of buildings running the length of the block.

"This is it," Tedra said, her face glowing with anticipation. "The building isn't fancy, but I think you will really like the people."

Dread filled her, but she followed Tedra through the door. The moment the door opened, savory aromas gripped Raquel, causing her stomach to rumble. She hadn't felt hungry before this moment, but the smell of food tantalized her appetite. Raquel saw a handful of people sprinkled through the room. Years of wear and scuffs from the metal chairs marred the hardwood floor. An acoustic guitar leaned against a white painted podium. Chips in the handmade stand indicated it had many years of wear behind it. Raquel felt awkward as eyes around the room looked to see the new visitor. A black man in a white shirt began walking toward them. He had the darkest skin Raquel had ever seen.

Tedra gripped Raquel's arm with a gentle squeeze and said, "Here comes our pastor." The man walked up and his face seemed to glow when his smile burst forth. "Kenyon, this is my friend Raquel. She's the one I've been telling you about." She turned to Raquel and said, "Raquel, this is our pastor, Kenyon Pamella."

Kenyon reached out his hand. "Raquel, it is so good to

meet you. Thank you for coming to spend your Friday evening with us."

Raquel extended her hand. His accent indicated he wasn't American born. His English sounded proper and his dialect indicated he might be from Africa. His firm grip and comforting smile warmed her. In spite of the warmth of this place, Raquel still felt apprehensive.

"It is good to meet you," she said, forcing a smile.

Tedra introduced Raquel to her family and friends, and the people tried to make her feel welcomed. Everyone seemed friendly enough, but with all the strange churches and cultures surrounding Central Park, she had the fear of walking into an evening of odd rituals.

Kenyon stepped behind the podium to announce the order of the evening's events. Dinner waited. Afterward, they would sing, and enjoy a brief study. The pastor gave thanks for the food, then the chairs scraped the floor as people stood and headed to the food in the back of the room.

A hand touched her shoulder from behind. She turned to see a smiling woman. "Visitors go first. You and Tedra head to the front of the line."

Raquel felt a little sheepish, but Tedra led the way with eagerness. In some ways the table reminded her of the potluck church dinners she had back home, but some of the food looked like ethnic samples of the culture surrounding Manhattan.

"You've *got* to try these things," Tedra said, pointing to something which looked like a turnover. Its layer of yellow bread told her this would be a new experience. "The pastor's wife makes them. It is some sort of meat pie, or turnover. I don't know what you call it, but it is *good!*" She took the liberty to plop one onto Raquel's plate. She gave a delighted smile and said, "Be glad we are in the front of the line. These are the first to go."

Raquel played it safe with her food selection. She didn't want to chance offending someone in the church. After tasting the meat turnover, she said, "Wow! You are right, these are very good." She saw a woman across the room wearing a flowery hat look up and smile. The satisfied gleam in her eye indicated she must be the pastor's wife, and the maker of the turnovers.

Feeling satisfied with the meal and the friendly conversation of the people in the small church, Raquel now felt glad to be here. She hoped the remainder of the evening would be as pleasant.

It wasn't long before people finished their meals and conversations filled the room. The sound of a guitar interrupted the room's chatter. A heavy man with a gray beard began strumming a hymn. The man's tattoos matched his gruff appearance, but his voice carried a peaceful melody that caught Raquel by surprise. As he sang, others joined in. He sang a variety of songs, most of which she didn't know.

"I have a new song I want to teach you," the rugged man said to the congregation. "I just heard this song the other day and fell in love with the words. I think you will too." He strummed for a moment and began, "You May Doubt, What I believe...." The words resonated with Raquel as she realized their familiarity. She knew this song. She raised her voice with the chorus:

I live my life
By the Master's plan
So I won't be judged
By mortal man
I praise my Lord
Each time I kneel and pray
I know he knows
I know no other way

Suddenly, she felt warm and at home. Raquel was six hundred miles from Bristol, in a culture mixed with people from around the world and different walks of life, but in a moment, these people did not seem very different from her. It's amazing how people from different cultures can feel connected by a simple song.

She remembered a friend who once went on a mission trip to Russia. He told a story about taking a walk down the road one evening. As he walked, he hummed the tune to 'How Great Thou Art'. He passed an older Russian man who stopped in front of him and began humming the same tune. The old man could not speak English, and her friend couldn't speak Russian. They stood for a few seconds, humming the song. The man smiled and pointed heavenward, and walked away. Two people were separated by language and culture, but connected by a common faith expressed through a simple song.

This wasn't Russia, but at times Raquel felt as lonely as someone living in a foreign country. Yet a single song connected her to a group of people, and made her feel at home, among friends. She did not want this hour to end.

The music concluded, and Kenyon stepped up to the podium. Echoes of the guitar seemed to hang in the air. The preacher began reading from Psalm 139. He talked about how God fashioned our days for us before we were born, and he was leading us down the path designed by the Lord for our good. "Quit resisting God!" Kenyon called out with conviction. "He created the works beforehand that we should walk in them. Stop leading yourself, listen for His call, and walk by His leading hand."

Contemplating these words, Raquel's mind wandered back to the time when she first met Dancer. Something deep inside affirmed her love for him. Against all odds, she'd made it to Broadway where she knew they would cross paths again. Since the time she met the dancer, it felt like she had followed a path ordained by the Lord. Obstacles and hardships frustrated her, but events always seemed to drive her forward.

Now she had come to New York, her path had crossed Dancer's, but everything seemed to be falling apart. Was he just a tool to get her to Broadway, but this is where their relationship ended? Her mind told her she should just forget Dancer, but something deep inside kept telling her to keep hoping. Yet, each time she met him, he rejected her and treated her with hostility. Confused, Raquel didn't know which path to take from here.

Is he just an image from the past? Or does he play a role in my life in the future?

The voice of Kenyon pulled her out of her thoughts when he asked if anyone wanted to come forward for prayer. She felt compelled to go forward, but Raquel pushed her feelings down, knowing it would take too long to explain her situation at the end of a service. A few people made their way to the front and one asked for the whole church to pray for a sick relative.

Preparing to close the service, Kenyon gave a final word, "Don't forget the new month midnight prayer. For those of you who are new, we meet the first Saturday night each month to pray for the city and the people around us for the next month. Those who can make it that late hour are welcomed. Visitors are also welcomed. Let's unite in prayer and seek the Lord for our church, its members, and stand in the gap for the lost culture of Manhattan."

A feeling of heaviness weighed on Raquel as the evening came to an end, and people began filing out. She should have prayed for Dancer.

Many thanked her for coming to their church as they wandered toward the door.

"What do you think? Want to come again?" Tedra asked with a cheerful smile.

"I enjoyed being here."

"Ready to head back?" Tedra asked. Raquel nodded and the two arose.

Kenyon shook their hands, and thanked them for coming as they headed out into the crisp November air. After taking a few steps from the door, Raquel said, "You go on. I need to ask the pastor a question." Tedra insisted on waiting and Raquel eased back through the door.

Kenyon gave a surprised look when Raquel came back into the building. "Can I talk to you?" she said.

"Certainly," the preacher answered as he led her toward the front row of chairs.

Raquel spent the next ten minutes summarizing her relationship with Dancer, his difficult life back in Tennessee, and his reaction to her since coming to New York. She looked up to Kenyon, "I don't know what to do? I still feel a connection to him. I still feel like there is something I need to do, but I just don't know what that is. How can I reach out to him when he pushes me away? He won't talk to me, and I don't even know what happened to him." She looked up, "What can I do?"

Kenyon listened, nodded, and then let out a slow exhale. "Sometimes we don't know what to do. There are times when our only calling is to keep walking in the direction God is leading—even if it doesn't make sense or we don't see results."

"I feel like I'm being directed to him, but what can I do if he won't even speak to me?"

The preacher stared up and stroked his chin, lost in thought for a moment. After a contemplative pause, he said, "You know, the Bible tells an interesting story which may help you. There was a day when Jesus told his disciples to get into a boat and go to the other side of the sea. He commanded them to go with the promise that he would meet them. A strong windstorm blew against the boat and the twelve men rowed hard against the current while Jesus stood on a mountain and watched them for nine hours. You know they had to be weary, but they did not give up. He knew what they could endure and in his own time, he then came to them on the water, got in the boat and he took them to the other side."

Raquel looked up to Kenyon, who smiled as if the story had a profound point to ponder. "What does this have to do with Michael?"

"Well, it shows us that sometimes life doesn't make sense. We don't know why the Lord sent these men to row fruitlessly against the wind. Perhaps he meant to test their faith and see if they would obey. If you look closely, you will see faith and obedience is all Jesus asked of these men." Kenyon leveled his gaze and Raquel could see a calm intensity in his eyes. "Raquel, faithfulness and obedience belongs to you. Success—whatever it may be, belongs to God alone. The results are not up to you. The only thing you must do is walk where he leads, and trust in the Lord for the results."

"What if I don't see results?"

A confident smile spread across his face, and he spoke in a comforting tone. This man had a calm assurance, unlike anyone she had ever met. "It doesn't matter," he said. "You don't even know what the results will be. You don't know what God is doing. In fact, we know so little and our point of view is so restricted, we don't have the right to doubt God's plan. Don't ask the Lord to bless your plans. Seek him alone, and walk in the works he established for you to walk in. He may ask you to row against the wind, but that's okay. Row with faithfulness and obedience. Even if you're weary."

"I wish I had your confidence," she said.

Kenyon looked Raquel in the eye as he lowered his voice to a soft tone. "You know, few people will ever experience Jesus getting into the boat. Most will give up in frustration when they get tired and discouraged. They get discouraged because they are putting their trust in their efforts instead of realizing our labors only show obedience and faithfulness. Our trust must be in God, who comes in his own time and accomplishes his plan through our labors. It's his works, not ours, that produce success. Our labors don't produce God's work until the time he decides to enter into the work and produce fruit through our labor.

"The only way to see the miracle of God's hand is to

stay faithful until the end. And you can't know where the path is until you seek the Lord. His word is a lamp unto our feet and a light to our path. We have to be near him and walk in his word in order to see the path and know where we are to walk. Sometimes the only part of the path we can see is the next step, but not necessarily where the step will lead. We walk as we learn to trust him. Only when we quit demanding answers and start seeking his guidance will we find the confidence to truly walk by faith." He paused for a moment, then asked, "Does this make sense to you?"

Raquel nodded. "Yes, but I just don't know. It seems like I'm walking in circles. In my heart, I feel like the Lord has brought our paths together, but it seems like nothing changes. I keep hoping, and then having those hopes dashed." She looked into Kenyon's dark eyes. "Michael is rowing in a different direction. How do I know when to keep rowing, and when to get out of the boat and let him go?"

"I'll have to be honest with you, Raquel. There are no cookie cutter answers. There have been times in my own life when I find myself going through the same circumstances again and again. I'm tempted to throw my hands up and cry out, 'Why does this keep happening?'"

"Exactly! That's what I'm feeling now. Each time I think this is behind me, it's like God throws me right back into the problem again," Raquel said.

"Right. I used to ask God 'Why' all the time. Then one day it was as if God pulled the blinders off my eyes. Suddenly I saw the Lord taking me through the same things until I learned the lesson he was trying to teach me, or realize something God was trying to show me."

"So how do you know what God is teaching you?"

A slow smile spread on Kenyon's face again. "We pray for God to open our eyes. Instead of saying, 'Why, God', we must learn to say, 'What, God.' Ask God to open your eyes and show you what he is trying to do. In your life, in Michael's life, or in both of your lives."

"I wish he would just show me," Raquel said.

"In some ways, that would be nice, but as the Proverbs say, the secret counsel of God is with those who seek him. If life came easy, we would take it for granted, and we would put ourselves on God's level. But when we learn to depend on him, we also learn to seek him on a deeper level. Then we see life from an eternal perspective."

Raquel nodded thoughtfully, then Kenyon continued. "When God is doing something big in our lives, we often mistake it as coincidences. The truth is, God often repeats things in our life so we don't miss it."

"What do you mean?"

"Look at how God used events in the Old Testament. He used real people and real circumstances, but guided their lives in patterns that we can see looking back. But at the time, only those who looked to the Lord understood. Historical events in the Old Testament repeated so when God revealed his plan in the New Testament, those whose hearts were open could see it."

"I never thought of it that way."

"God doesn't change, so we see similar things in our own lives. Situations may change, but patterns repeat. That's why I catch myself asking why this keeps happening. Now I try to remember to ask God what he is trying to show me. It's not easy to see unless we prepare our hearts to seek him."

"I think I understand now." She looked at her watch. "I've got to go. Tedra is waiting for me, but you've really helped me.

"Can I pray with you?" Raquel nodded again, and Kenyon dropped to one knee as he bowed and prayed for her direction, guidance, wisdom, and understanding.

Raquel left the building to join Tedra, and felt uplifted during their walk back from the church. There must be a reason why she felt burdened for Dancer. She just hoped she would have the endurance to press on and prayed she would see the Lord do something to redeem the fallen dancer.

Chapter Nineteen

Bright sunshine greeted Raquel when she walked out the door of her apartment. It had been another long week of rehearsals, but today belonged to her. She wished for her best friend from back home. It would be a lonely day off without someone to share it with. But at least she didn't have to spend the day in grueling practices.

Central Park lay before her. It reminded her of the park near her home in Tennessee. She missed home. *After a quick walk in the park, I'll head to the shopping district.*

Families gathered in the park, and seeing the kids running around caused her to miss her brother and sister. *How can I be so homesick after only a few weeks? I need to—*

"Could you use a little company?" The voice startled her out of thought. It was her agent, Joseph Rodney.

"Oh, hi!" She could feel herself brighten into a smile. "It's good to see a familiar face."

"Sorry I couldn't give you a tour sooner. Do you have time for me to show you around now?" Joseph's warm smile made her feel at home.

"Now would be a great time. I have all day, and nothing to do."

"You do now. I'm not sure all day will be enough, but it's a good start." Joseph held up his elbow and Raquel slipped her arm through. The two strolled into the park. "No rehearsals today?"

"Nope. My first full day off in a week."

Extending his free arm, he shook his sleeve to reveal his watch and checked the time. "Let me show you a few of my favorite spots in the park, and then we'll cut across to 5th avenue. There's a wonderful little cafe where we can have brunch. After that, we can tour the shops and see a few sights."

Michael sat on a park bench, lost in thought. He watched as a small boy tried hard to contribute to a backyard football game. Though he was always open, the bigger kids never threw him the ball. Without realizing it, tears began forming in Michael's eyes. Not until he felt a tear chilling on his cheek, did he realize his deep felt emotions. He wiped it away.

The young boy reminded him of the only true friend he'd ever known, and the pain that swirled around those memories like a whirlwind. How long had it been? Fifteen or sixteen years? Why was he crying over a childhood friend he lost when he was six? Or could it be because he lost his friend, Tommy, on the same day he lost his mother?

Michael could still see his mother backing out of the driveway of his uncle's house. He just stood under the porch light, watching Uncle James yelling at his mom's car as she pulled away. She didn't wave or look back. No cards. No phone calls. No letters. Did he ever cross her mind?

With grimy hands, he wiped the cold tears from his stinging cheeks. *Am I so worthless that not even my mother can love me?* He cursed the pain. Cursed the deception of love. And cursed the trail of rejection and failure from that day until now. Why are some people so happy, while his life is filled with emptiness and heartache?

Kenyon locked the church doors and began his walk home. When he needed a quiet place to study, he took a stroll to this building where he could be alone. He stepped back to examine the aging white structure.

It is a hole in the wall, but it always feels like home. By New York standards, it's humble, but back home it would look like a mansion.

Life's good. Kenyon relished the peace that flowed from his heart after spending several hours in Bible study and prayer. He felt the Lord speak to him, and it renewed him with strength. Even hard times can be endured with joy when walking with the Lord. As he strolled toward home, the sight of a hotdog vendor reminded him he'd missed lunch. The thought of a large frank made his stomach rumble with anticipation. He fished in his pocket for cash.

Four dollars and a handful of coins. It's probably just enough to grab a bite before heading home.

"I'll have a dog loaded with relish and a touch of mustard," Kenyon said to the vendor. "Oh, and a bottle of water."

Steam rolled out of the wheeled cart when the man pulled open a lid and dug for a frank in the hot water. Placing it on a bun, he slathered it with relish, then pointed to a tray with a yellow and red bottle. "Ketchup and mustard are there." The man handed over the items and said, "That will be five-fifty."

Kenyon handed over four crinkled ones and began counting out his change. Reaching in his pocket for more change, he shrugged and said, "I'm a nickel short."

"I need five-fifty," the man insisted.

"Can I scrape off five cents worth of relish?" Kenyon said with a tone of humor. The man gave a cold stare as he waited for the money. "Can I owe you a nickel? I come by this way almost daily. I will be glad to bring back a nickel the next time I walk by."

"Mister, does this look like a charity?" the man said, waving a hand over the cart.

Kenyon gave a pleading smile, "I'm not asking for charity, just a little grace. I promise I'll keep a spare nickel in my pocket and make sure you get it when I come back through."

The man continued to stare without expression, making Kenyon feel uneasy. He could return the water, but he needed something to wash it down. Just as he had given up hope and started to offer the water back, the man spoke. "Take your hotdog and get out of here."

"Thank you very much. I promise to get you the rest of the money," Kenyon said with a relieved smile.

"Forget the nickel. This one is on the house—but just this once." The man held up his finger for emphasis.

Kenyon gathered his food and drink, then gave a friendly wave. Thinking it would be soothing to watch kids playing in the park, he decided to cross the street and relax on a park bench. When he neared the bench, a figure came into view. The disheveled man sat with his legs curled under him. He watched the kids playing while massaging his cold feet.

Looking down at the hotdog and water in his hands, Kenyon felt his heart constrict. It had been a long time between meals. "Lord, I am starving. Please don't ask me to give away my food." The preacher heard no audible voice, but he knew he was being drawn to give away his food to the man shivering on the bench. His stomach rumbled as the aroma of the frank tickled his senses. "I don't have anymore money and I'm so hungry I have the shakes," Kenyon spoke out loud. He stood for a moment wrestling with his heart and hunger. "Okay, Lord," he said, and then swallowed his mouth's anticipation.

After speaking the words, Kenyon had the feeling of being watched. Turning to the side, he saw an aging woman wrinkling her nose, while observing his odd conversation from under her hooded coat. She looked at Kenyon, looked to his right, then to his left as if to say, "Who do you think you are talking to?"

"How are you today," he said with a smile. The woman shrugged and shuffled off without answering. *Just another crazy, huh?* Kenyon turned back to the park and walked toward the bench.

"How are you?" he said as a greeting, and sat beside

the man.

The vagrant looked over and nodded to acknowledge the question, but didn't answer.

"I thought you looked hungry, so I brought you a bite to eat." Kenyon offered the food, but the man just looked at it with skepticism. "Go on, take it," Kenyon encouraged as he stretched out both hands.

The homeless man reached out with caution, and took the hotdog and water. "Thanks." He spoke to Kenyon, but his voice sounded disengaged. He devoured the food with vigor, and Kenyon wished he had enough money to buy him another one.

"My name is Kenyon. What's your name?" he asked, offering a handshake. The vagrant didn't respond. Instead he stared off in the direction where kids played football in the park. Kenyon sat, watching a group of boys tackling each other in the snow. After observing the game for a few minutes, he looked to the man and said, "Looks like they are having lots of fun, doesn't it?"

The man nodded, but didn't take his eyes away from the park. He seemed lost in thought.

Realizing the homeless man wasn't open to conversation, Kenyon decided to head home. Standing up, he patted the man on the shoulder. "It was good to meet you. Maybe we will cross paths again."

The man in tattered clothing nodded without speaking and Kenyon stepped away.

He stopped and turned back to the man on the bench, "I am a pastor of The Church at Central Park. We welcome..." Kenyon paused. He nearly said 'people like you' but realized it sounded condescending. He reconsidered his words and said, "Everyone is welcomed and people just come as they are. If you are in the area of 111th Street, please come and visit."

He stared silently ahead and Kenyon wondered if he stared through a drug stupor, or was just disinterested.

"The Lord sent you a meal to show He loves you. I pray he will send you to us, and you will experience His love." After a silent moment, Kenyon said, "Good-bye," and began walking toward his apartment. *Lord, why did you send me to someone who doesn't seem willing, or capable of responding?*

Though he felt discouraged after his encounter with the unresponsive man, Kenyon had the feeling this would not be the last time their paths crossed. His heart told him the Lord was working according to His own plan, and to keep praying for this man.

The sun began its descent from the New York sky. Days were brief this time of year and Raquel hated to see her day off fading from view. It had been fun touring Manhattan with Joseph. Another hour and bitter cold would begin howling through the dark air. They walked down 5th Avenue beside Central Park.

"Let's take a ride," Joseph said, motioning to a horse and carriage.

A break from walking would help her tired legs, but she didn't know how to respond. She'd wanted to ride on one of these since arriving in New York. "I don't really have the money for a ride."

"Don't worry about that." Joseph turned to the driver, spoke a few words, and pulled out his wallet. He walked to the side of the carriage and lifted a welcoming arm. "Step aboard, my lady."

Lunch and dinner had been on Joseph, so she felt sheepish about doing something else that would cost him. But since he had already paid, she couldn't say no. She took his extended hand for support and climbed onto the carriage seat. Joseph followed. The evening air grew more chilly, so she was glad Joseph sat close beside her.

The ride felt magical. After dark, the lights around the park provided a beautiful view. Somehow, the cold night air made the carriage seem cozy. Sensing eyes on her, she looked at Joseph. The corners of his mouth lifted into a smile. The carriage passed under a lamp, causing light to splash across his face. She couldn't help noticing his deep green eyes. His smooth face looked no more than thirty, if that, but a dusting of gray sprinkled his black hair. *He looks very handsome.* She returned his smile and looked back toward the lighted trees.

"It's a beautiful view," she said.

"Yes it is. And it's beautiful outside the carriage, too."

Raquel could feel her neck flush. She didn't know how to respond to the compliment. Thankfully, the darkness hid her blushing face. She felt a little uncomfortable, but she also welcomed the attention. It was wonderful to be treated like a princess.

Thoughts of Dancer emerged, but Raquel forced him out of her mind. This wasn't a day for feeling pain. She had to admit her day with Joseph had been one of the best days she'd had in New York. Maybe this is what love is meant to be. Had the Lord brought Joseph into her life? For years, she'd held on to her love for Dancer, hoping their relationship would blossom. She would always pray for Dancer and count him as a special friend, but perhaps the time had come to let go, and allow her feelings for him to drift into the past.

Chapter Twenty

When Raquel stepped out of her apartment into the December cold, she discovered snow had again fallen overnight. The cutting wind announced the approaching Christmas holidays, and seemed to join in her excitement of her new experiences on Broadway. These first two months had flown by.

With the storm long gone, bright sunlight now peeked from behind puffs of clouds. Even native New Yorkers complained about the bitter winter this year. Though the cold felt biting, the view looked spectacular. Central park looked like a bride draped in white.

It's great to finally have a day off. And a better day for a walk in the snow.

Gray slush splashed when she stepped into the street and headed toward the park. The crunch of fresh snow under her feet announced her arrival at the entrance of Central Park. It beckoned like a call from another world. Raquel could almost forget she stood in the middle of one of the most populated places in America. This park wasn't quite like Bristol, but she had grown to cherish her strolls here. She could find a little solitude amid the crowd of others seeking escape from the city.

It had taken awhile to get accustomed to a place where it's nearly impossible to be completely alone. This park provided a zone of solitude so she could find quietness to pray, and each day she set time aside to lift up Dancer. It had been two months without results, but she believed there had to be a reason why her heart felt burdened for him.

Children built snowmen and snow forts, and occasionally an icy projectile would pass by when she wandered through someone's battlefield. Couples walked past, holding hands through padded gloves. It reminded Raquel of the longing in her heart for a close relationship.

How ironic to feel loneliness while drifting along Manhattan's flow of people. Some of the men who danced on Broadway had asked her out, but she could find no real connection with them. In her loneliness, she wanted to push Dancer out of her mind and into the past, but despite her efforts, her heart wouldn't let go. Perhaps her growing relationship with Joseph would help her escape from the grip Dancer had on her heart.

The first time she'd met Michael in Bristol, her heart danced. Something inside affirmed their lives were meant to be together. For years she'd held onto this as though it were a message from heaven, but now she struggled with her doubts. *He's a hard man to get to know.* On stage, he opened up and their relationship blossomed, but off stage he surrounded himself behind a hard shell. He had obviously been wounded deeply in his past, but details were sketchy.

A man in a tattered coat with a frayed beard drew her eyes. Her breath paused but then his face came into view. It wasn't Dancer. She felt silly at the thought. *Am I the only person who gets excited to see a man in a filthy jacket?* A prayer arose from her heart. *Lord, if this is truly your plan, open the door to his heart. I can't get in unless you break through his defenses. I don't know who hurt him in the past, but touch his life, and show him that love produces more than just pain.*

The setting sun announced the day's end. *It's not even six o'clock. Why are winter days so short?*

On the way to her apartment, Raquel peeked down every street, looking for window washers. Slushy days provided many dirty windows for Manhattan's homeless to clean, but no sign of Dancer.

Throughout the day, many vagrants crossed her path. Each of the homeless men had a story behind their descent to the streets, and she wondered what tales they kept from those around them. Could Dancer be on one of the streets nearby working for donations? What she would give to know his story. Is this hope, or just foolish thinking? Maybe his voice is something from the past, but he had no future. At least not in her life. Still wishing things could be different, she fought to convince her heart of this harsh truth. Raquel grew tired of bouncing between hope and despair for him. It's time to let go. After fumbling for her keys, she unlocked the apartment door, and left her day off behind.

A chill walked over her. It felt like the cold Manhattan air had followed her into the apartment. She wrapped herself in a blanket, visited the kitchen, and sat in front of the television with a cup of hot tea. She flipped the channels, searching through the garbage on TV, looking for something of interest.

A face on the TV caught her eye. Richard Barnhouse. There had been a lot of talk about his upcoming behind-the-scenes story of Broadway. Her heart jumped with excitement when he began his presentation.

"Today we are presenting a behind the scenes look at Broadway, and I am going to conclude with an inside story about a fallen dancer—a former Grand Prix winner who now fights for survival among New York's homeless," Barnhouse announced, his face drooping into dramatized sadness.

Raquel felt sick at the pit of her stomach, but stayed glued to the television, waiting to hear the inside story. Richard interviewed several prominent dancers and showed the rehearsals and the backstage preparations that go into Broadway productions. At the end of the backstage look, he interviewed a dancer Raquel had never seen. "Do you remember a performer named Michael Camp?" Richard asked a young, blond-haired man.

"Yes," the man said. He wiped his face with a towel, and draped it over his neck. "I used to work with him. He was a leading actor until he started missing rehearsals and acting weird."

"What happened when he kept missing rehearsals?"

"Our producer gave him, oh, about a dozen chances." He grabbed both ends of the towel with each hand. He studied the ceiling, trying to recall the details. "Finally, one day he fired him. We couldn't depend on Michael and it was getting too close to opening day."

"What did you think of Michael Camp?"

"He kept to himself but seemed like a good guy. He was one of the hardest working people I know. And he could outperform just about anyone. But he changed. I don't know what happened. He just started missing rehearsals, and before you knew it, he was gone."

The broadcast showed footage of Richard trying to interview Michael, but he just walked away. It ended with Richard standing beside a road and pointing to a bridge. "We followed him and located his home." The camera zoomed to a bridge where Michael could be seen climbing into a crevasse. Richard said, "As you can see, success on Broadway doesn't always mean success in life. One of America's most promising dancers now resides under the Henderson Mill bridge as he lives hand and mouth on the streets of Manhattan."

Raquel stared at the television screen for several moments, but the reporter's words faded behind the thoughts screaming in her head. *Leave it to a reporter to find a negative slant to an inside Broadway story.* Pushing her brown hair out of her eyes and behind her ear, she let out a long exhale. Cats began fighting in her stomach. *I guess this shouldn't be a shock. Good news doesn't draw much attention, but bad news sells.*

Her heart ached at the thought of Michael being made into a spectacle. She knew Richard Barnhouse had been sniffing around for information about Dancer, but she had hoped he wouldn't find anything worth reporting.

Sudden resolve shot through her. *He's at the Henderson Mill Bridge.*

She pulled on her boots, buttoned and buckled her coat, then stepped out of the apartment into the night air. A blast of cold wind stung her face and found gaps in her clothing, causing her body to shake with the chill. She would need to take the car tonight.

Lord, please let me find him. Please let him talk to me.

A few minutes later, she parked her car on the curb of Henderson Mill Street. Raquel stepped out, and looked into the dark shadows under the bridge. Why hadn't she brought a flashlight? With caution, she eased toward the shadows and called, "Dancer?" No reply. She walked under the bridge, straining to see into the crevasses, and called his name again. "Dancer? Are you here? Michael?" Still no answer.

Her boots fought for traction as she began climbing the slanted concrete, attempting to reach the shelter where the cameras showed him living. Sucking in the freezing air made her chest hurt, but she panted to the top of the concrete hill. "Dancer," she whispered. Distant light seeped into the shadows, and soon her eyes adjusted enough to see an empty nest in the cubbyhole. Someone definitely lived here.

Fighting to remain on her sliding feet, Raquel descended to the road, taking careful steps between stumbles, until flat ground came to her rescue. Dancer always seemed more active at night, so she wondered how long before he returned. Raquel knew she couldn't wait here all evening and decided to give him until eleven to show up.

She passed her time waiting by alternating between sitting in the car and pacing in the cold. After a long wait, she paced back to the car and looked at the clock. Just past eleven. Rehearsals will come early in the morning, so it's time to head back. When preparing to leave, she saw a figure walking down the sidewalk in the distance. She watched the person drawing near and hoped it was Dancer. The figure approached and Raquel shivered. Is it the cold, or the memory of being attacked in the park.

The figure stopped as he approached, apparently wondering why a car waited under the bridge. He began walking again, but with caution. He craned his neck, trying to look for any activity under the bridge. Raquel decided to call out his name, thinking it would ease his concern.

"Dancer," she called.

He froze in his tracks.

After he stood for a few moments without moving, she called again, "Dancer. It's me, Raquel."

Looking down, he shook his head and began walking toward the bridge. He walked past her and stepped toward the slope leading to his nest under the bridge. "Dancer," she said, instinctively reaching for his arm. He pulled away as he attempted to evade her. "Michael, I'm not leaving until I at least talk to you."

He paused. "Why are you here? And how did you know where to find me?"

Raquel didn't know what to say. She didn't want to tell him about the news broadcast, but couldn't think of any reasonable answer to his question. She shrugged, then said, "Dancer, I just wanted to see you. And talk to you. Can you please just give me a few minutes?"

"Why don't you just leave me alone? You have your life, and I have mine. You've made it to Broadway. Your world is over there." Dancer pointed in the direction he had come from. "But my world is here." His arms spread out as if to show the wonders of his residence. "Live your life. Be happy. But stay away from the mean streets of Manhattan."

"That's just it," she said. "I can't go and live my life as if you don't exist. You are a part of my life."

"No!" Dancer snapped. "I am no longer a part of your life. *Or* normal society. I have fallen out and you need to realize things have changed. I have changed. Look, it will be easier on both of us if you drive away and forget I exist. I don't belong in your world, so please, just go."

"That's not true."

"Just go!" he shouted and pointed to her car.

Her heart pounded at his sudden outburst of anger, and she fought the urge to run to her car. Her head told her to run, but her heart ached to stay. Summoning her courage, Raquel held her ground. "No. I'm not going until I can talk to you. I can't just walk away."

Dancer gave an exasperated sigh. "Okay then," he plopped down on the cold slope, "start talking."

Raquel sat beside Dancer, an awkward silence between them. He showed his annoyance through occasional sighs as Raquel's mind raced for something to say. "Do you remember Margaret?"

"Margaret?"

"Your first dance partner at Bristol High."

Dancer nodded, "My second dance partner. I remember her."

"She is my best friend and asks about you every time I talk to her."

Looking down at the ground, he shifted uncomfortably. "So did you tell her how big of a loser I turned out to be?"

"I told her I've seen you in passing, but you've been too busy. I told her you were working off Broadway." Dancer's face brightened into a smile, but he quickly wiped it away. "You know you aren't a loser, right?" Raquel's question was more of a statement.

Dancer leaned back on the concrete, staring up at the shadow of the bridge above them. He let out a long exhale and gathered his thoughts. "You know, I have been fighting battles my entire life. I had to deal with my mother abandoning me. I was kicked from house to house, because no one wanted me. I've been bullied and mocked, but I fought my way to the top against what seemed like insurmountable odds." He turned to look at Raquel, "The one enemy I could not overcome is right here." Dancer pointed his finger at his heart. "This is the only enemy I can't beat." He swept his arm outward as he continued, "My enemies gnashed at me, attacked me, and tried to take me down, but they couldn't. But my inner demons turned out to be the real enemy. I could beat anything that attacked from out there, but I cannot stand against what is in here."

Raquel touched his arm. "I'm so sorry, Dancer. I—"

Before she could continue, he cut her off. "I thought I was invincible. Nothing stood in my way and I thought I stood on top of the world. Look around." Dancer raised his arms and scanned the area with his eyes. "I'm now in the gutters of society—the bottom of the world." Turning to face Raquel again, he continued, "I once said you would see me stumble, but you would never see me fall." Raising his palms, he said, "I guess you can see I've fallen. And hard. It was a long drop from Broadway to the gutters." He forced a thin smile, "Thank you, Raquel. Thanks for not telling your friends I'm a bum."

"I don't want to see you humiliated. I still believe you have a future," Raquel said.

The fallen dancer's eyes dropped to the ground and he shook his head in rebuke. "No. As you can see, the song's over for me. I told you three or four years ago that dancers aren't real people, and we don't have real hearts. If you could see my life, you would see it's true. I'm a man without a heart."

"That isn't true. True dance comes from the heart. The problem is that you need a new heart. Do you remember the day you went with me to the youth night?" He nodded and Raquel continued. "Do you remember the speaker saying, 'all things are new, the old things pass away when the Lord gives a new life?' The new life starts with a new heart."

"Look, Raquel. I know you mean well, but I don't want to hear that Jesus stuff. It works for you and I'm glad for you, but it isn't for me. God could never forgive me for the things I've done."

"Yes. He can. God can forgive anyone, and will forgive you. All he wants is your life. Then He will give you a new life and you'll become a new creation—with a new heart."

Dancer leveled his gaze to meet Raquel's eyes, "Since you mentioned the night of the youth rally, let me tell you something. Do you remember when I was attacked before the high school drama play?"

Raquel nodded.

"And you worried about my depression? You insisted that I go with you to youth night. At the rally, do you remember when your pastor introduced me to one of the youth leaders in your church?"

She remembered the day like it was yesterday. The sweet spirit she felt, plus the joy of having Dancer at church with her, and hearing music that spoke to her heart - it all kept this memory fresh in her mind. "Yes."

"You had asked me what happened when I was attacked, but I never told you." Dancer dropped his head between his knees. "You might as well know the whole story. It started when driving from Bristol to Knoxville to attend dance classes at Pahl.

"I still remember. It was Thursday afternoon, and only a few days before opening night. I looked forward to a week of performing before live crowds. None of my shows in Alabama were performed in front of such a large audience, but Bristol residence sure loved their school plays."

A few minutes into my drive, the truck began to sputter, and then the engine stalled. The gas gauge showed a full tank and it wasn't overheated. Pulling to the side of the road, I got out and lifted the hood. I don't know anything about cars, so I checked for loose cables and tried to crank again. The truck did nothing but sputter. After several attempts, I decided to walk toward the convenience store I'd passed a mile or so back to call for help.

While I walked, an older car rambled toward me and pulled off the road. At first I thought someone stopped to be helpful, but dread filled me when Jeff Patterson, the school bully, opened the door. I'm not sure if you remember, but he's the one who mocked me relentlessly. He's the one who first called me Dancer. Jeff meant it as a taunt, but everyone started calling me by that nickname.

When he pulled over, he said, "Get in the car, Dancer, and I'll give you a ride." His tone sounded friendly, but I didn't trust him.

"No thanks," I said, "I am meeting someone at the store." I meant to point to the store, but I realized there was nothing in the direction of my finger, but empty road.

"Don't be an idiot, get in and take a ride."

"I need the exercise, but thanks anyway."

A door opened on the passenger side and Robert Jones stepped out. My heart raced. Now I knew this wasn't just a chance encounter. Robert had threatened me several times, but he became furious when you kissed me in rehearsals. He warned me to stay away from you, but that wasn't possible since we were dance partners. After the kiss, I saw revenge in his eyes.

When he stepped out of the car, he pointed an angry finger at me and said, "That's fine, we can settle this here."

The bully's friends stood with him, so fighting wasn't a good option. I started walking down the road, hoping they wouldn't follow. The bully also climbed out of the car, followed by two of his cronies. They were carrying sticks. Jeff jogged past me and put out his hand, forcing me to stop. Robert hurried to catch up.

"Didn't I warn you?" Robert's expression melted into a look of rage. He poked a finger in my chest. "I told you to stay away from Raquel."

I stepped to the side and tried to walk toward the store,

but Jeff, the bully, jumped in front of me. "Oh, no. You aren't going anywhere." He placed a firm palm against my chest. I could feel the other two guys taking positions behind me.

My heart raced and I glanced around, trying to assess the situation.

"You said you were going to teach the man a lesson, now is the time to do it." Jeff spoke to Robert, but his eyes never left me. "Don't back down now."

Robert stepped forward with balled fists. Someone shoved me from behind and I stumbled toward Robert. Before I caught my balance, a fist pounded hard off the side of my head. The blow stunned me for a moment, but I managed to step out of the path of Robert and regain my bearings. Robert swung his fists wildly, but kept missing. I knew I had to fight, so I prepared to counterpunch, but something hit hard on the back of my head. The sound of a wooden rod echoed in my ears.

My eyes lost focus and I dropped to the ground. Blows began arriving from every direction. It felt like all four guys were hitting and kicking me. I struggled to get to my feet when a kick erupted into my face. I don't remember falling. I just remember laying flat on my back. My arms wouldn't cooperate, and everything began fading from view.

I don't know how long I was out, but I remember hearing voices and laughter. I forced open my eyes, and Robert's face came into view.

"Didn't I try to warn you? You brought this on yourself." He turned to his companions, and they egged him on. Robert seemed to relish in the glory of his victory. He held his arms out and said, "Life deals hard lessons. If you can't hang with the big boys, you should have stayed off the field."

Everyone laughed as if he were a comedian.

Leaning close to my ear, Robert said, "Do you know how to hunt down a buck? They think they're so smart, but the dumb animals follow the same path. Just figure out where they want to go, and you can hunt those bad boys down with ease." His lips curled into a satisfied grin. "Dancy boy, you're so predictable. You think you're somebody, but you're a nobody. No-bod-y." He emphasized every syllable.

Pushing my head hard against the ground, Robert said, "If you tell anyone about our little meeting, something might happen to Raquel." He hissed in my ear, "If I can't have her, nobody can. I'll handle Raquel, and I'll make sure you get more than a roadside whipping." I felt his hand lift off my head. "Here is a final lesson for you." He looked behind me and said, "Don't let him move."

I rolled over to my side, but hands pressed down on me to keep me from getting up. I watched Robert walk to my feet and wondered what he had in mind. He placed a carefully aimed stomp into the side of my right ankle. I screamed while they laughed.

"Class is dismissed," Robert declared, and then walked toward the car.

The cackling cronies ran to the car, revved it to life, and peeled away, slinging rocks over me as a final insult.

"Next time don't use water for gas," Robert called out the window when the car looped around, heading back to Bristol. The laughing faded with the sound of the car as it sped away. I tried to stagger to my feet, but the exploding pain in my ankle wouldn't bear my weight.

I wiped the flowing blood from my lips. I could feel the swelling. All I could do is lay back on the shoulder. Luckily, someone came by and helped me.

Michael turned toward Raquel. "My life has been filled with pain like this. Every time something good happens, disaster is right behind it."

"Oh, Michael. I'm so sorry." Raquel pulled close to his

arm. "I didn't—"

Michael interrupted her. "Wait. There's more. When we were at the youth rally, you introduced me to your youth pastor. He introduced me to a youth leader. Do you remember how he acted reluctant to come over?"

Nodding her head, Raquel said, "I do remember the rally, and you meeting the guys from our church."

"Lynn introduced me to the youth leader. He had to motion him over several times. When he came up, he offered me his hand. I refused to shake and said, 'I think we've met.'" Michael turned to look at Raquel. "Well, that youth leader was one of the four guys. He, and the others, hit me with sticks, kicked me, and he held me while Robert stomped my leg."

Raquel felt the air squeeze out of her and she gasped to retrieve it. "Michael, I'm so sorry." Her hand drew up to her mouth. "Are you sure you aren't mistaken?"

"There is no doubt. That's why he didn't want to come when your pastor tried to introduce me. He would not even look me in the eye. Did this man have a new heart?" He looked at Raquel, but before she could speak, he continued. "If this is the new life your God gives, I want nothing to do with it. Let's face it, if your God exists, he hates me, and my feelings are the same toward him."

"Don't say that!" Raquel snapped. "You don't mean it. God doesn't hate you, he loves you."

"Love?" He gave a scornful laugh. "What kind of love does he show? Does he send those preachers who scream at me saying, 'You're going to hell'? I can't walk down the sidewalk without someone shouting damnation at me from a bullhorn. Then saying I now have no excuse for rejecting God's love." Michael looked at the ground and his tone softened as he reflected on the pain of his life. "If God loved me, would he rip me away from my mother?" His eyes raised, and he looked Raquel in the face. "I haven't seen my mother since I was six. Not once has she ever called to check on me, or even wish me a happy birthday. Would a loving God create a mother who hated her son?"

Tears began stinging Raquel's eyes. Her heart ached so much for his pain, it felt like her own. Wiping the cold stream running down her cheek, she looked ahead and her mind raced. This is why Dancer resisted people. All these years she wondered why he pushed people away who wanted to care for him, and now it made sense.

Dancer turned his eyes from Raquel to stare in the distance. "Did he love me through the bullies who mocked and attacked me? The truth is, God has always hated me, and I fought my way to the top against his hand." His head dropped and he said, "But in the end, his wrath was too strong for me. He finally destroyed my life. Who do you think created the demons that haunt me?" His eyes lifted and he said, "The God who hates me knows I hate him. He won't forgive because he doesn't love me. I don't see anything in anyone's life that proves the love of God. I only see hypocrisy and hatred."

"Is this what you see in my life?" Raquel asked in a soft trembling voice. She felt another tear trickle across her cheek and wiped it away.

Staring toward the horizon, Dancer seemed lost in his thoughts for a few moments. "No. But you are just a good person. It isn't God's love. It is your kindness I see."

"Kindness comes from the love of God. Not everyone who claims the name of God has actually experienced the love of God. The only real evidence that someone knows the Lord is by the love they show." Raquel felt the weight of his words and wished she could lift the burden off his back. "Dancer, the Lord loves you and wants to make your life new."

Dancer laughed and shook his head. "Yeah? Then why has all this happened to me?"

Raquel shrugged. She didn't know how to answer his question. His life had been a traumatic one and it is true, often life isn't fair. "Maybe you are going through these things so you can one day touch others who may go through similar hardships."

"Why doesn't God just get rid of all the suffering in the world, instead of making people suffer so they can tell someone else suffering is okay?"

"I don't know. Maybe it is to make people see the meaninglessness of life outside of His love? Maybe He will make up for all the pain and restore what you have lost in ways better than you expected. What he will give is better than anything you've lost."

Waving off Raquel with his hand, he said, "I don't know why I'm still talking about this? I said I don't want to talk about Jesus." He rose from the concrete, "Well, I have a busy day at the office tomorrow, so I better go find a hole to crawl into. I'm sure you have an early day, too."

Dancer rose to his feet and began his walk up to the bridge.

"Good-bye," Raquel called.

He raised his hand in a wave without turning or slowing his pace. She watched him until he faded into the shadow of the bridge before climbing into her car and burying her face in her hands, crying as she prayed for him. She refused to believe his fate ended on the streets of New York. Why did the nagging hope keep telling her their lives would be together? How could this be? This wasn't the direction she thought life would take them.

Is it possible this man, filled with bitterness, angry at God and the world, could find peace and rise from the ashes of a destroyed life?

Chapter Twenty-One

Another day of rehearsals ended, and Raquel exited the dance studio, shivering as she stepped into the evening breeze. With a hurried pace, she made her way toward Central Park for her daily escape from the city. Clumps of snow fell, adding to the white blanket already draped across Manhattan, and Christmas music called out to pedestrians from every retail store around Central Park. She had already seen more snow in the last couple of months in New York than she had seen in the last four years in Bristol.

A stroll through the park provided a breathtaking view. Ice skaters flowed with grace across the rink. She watched starry-eyed lovers walking with warm hearts in the cold snow. Raquel had tried to move on with her life, but hope for Dancer kept drifting into her heart. He didn't understand he held her heart, but his remained behind the walls he'd erected. Love was becoming painful.

With Christmas only two weeks away, Manhattan felt lonelier than ever. Her family was six hundred miles away, and Dancer might as well be a million miles away. Tedra remained her closest friend, but had begun a new dating relationship that often crowded Raquel out of the picture.

Raquel's heart ached. What she would give to be walking with Dancer right now. Maybe she should be thinking of Joseph. He was stable, successful, and actually wanted to be with her. Why was it hard to retrieve her heart from someone who didn't want it, and give it to someone who did? A cold stream trickled down her cheek. She wiped her thoughts away with the tear.

The daily walk along Park drive neared its end. It was less than two miles to make a full loop around this portion of the walkway. Though she felt tired, Raquel decided to take a trip to the Henderson Mill Bridge. This time of day it's hard to find Dancer, but maybe she would have the good fortune of finding him there this evening. She put bags of trail mix and dried fruit in the car. Since finding him, Raquel always left nonperishable food for him under the bridge.

The car pulled to the curb and she climbed up the slick concrete, struggling to the crevasse where Dancer slept. Her heart sank.

Where is his stuff? His place is empty!

Tears stung her face and heart. *He's gone.* Not just for the evening, but he had moved away. She sat on the ledge and buried her head in her hands, tears seeping through her fingers and running in cold streams down her arms. The only option now is to pray.

On the edge of the crevasse, Raquel sat and poured her heart out until her shivering became unbearable. For a moment she studied the bags of food, then decided to place them into the space where his bed once laid. Maybe he would return to get it.

Hunger pangs poked at Michael's stomach. When did he have his last meal? It was time to get something besides drugs into his body. Darkness had fallen, and he prowled for something to sustain him. Night gave enough cover to move without drawing attention, and tonight he would focus on one of the streets he'd scoped out earlier.

Michael visited a hotel parking lot off 108th street, and browsed among the car windows while doing a walk through, looking for cash or something small and valuable. After identifying his targets, he could return and make a fast hit and run.

A car with a wallet on the dash. Not smart. A few cars with change, but nothing with a big score. There is one with a strap on the passenger's floorboard. Possibly a purse tucked under the seat.

Voices carried across the lot from a motel room. He froze and retreated from sight. People prepared to leave and cut off the room lights, indicating no one remained behind.

This will be a good target.

Michael watched until the couple climbed into their car and drove away, then made his way toward their hotel room. It looked like the perfect location, in the corner of the hotel, with no lights illuminating the walkway. After approaching the door, he saw an overhead light fixture, but apparently no one paid attention to the burned out bulb. The adjoining room was also dark, so if he acted quickly, he would probably not draw any attention during his entry.

Ramming the door with his shoulder, Michael burst into the room. The beat of his heart pounded in his ears. Listening for sounds, he stood motionless. No people outside. No voices inside the room. All clear. The room lit up with the flip of a switch. A quick rummage through the room netted a music player and a watch, then he turned to the closet. The suitcases contained nothing of value. This break-in wasn't paying off.

With caution, he eased open the door and looked out. There were a few people walking around, so he waited until they wandered out of the area. Moving to the adjoining room, he slammed through the door, hoping the occupants were not inside sleeping.

No sounds. Good.

A flip of the switch, the room lit up, and he rushed to the closet. Two suitcases were on the floor. One had a lock. Dumping the contents of the unlocked suitcase, he rummaged through its items, but didn't find anything of value.

Michael turned his attention to the locked suitcase. He

took it to the bathroom and slammed it onto the hard tiled floor. The seam bulged, but didn't open. He slammed it again. And again. And again. A final hard jolt broke the lock free, sending its contents flying around the room. In an adrenaline inspired rush, he sorted through the items and found another watch, a necklace, and a small wallet. The wallet contained a stack of bills. He pocketed the items and left the room.

Passing the cars he'd scoped out earlier, he thought about doing a smash and grab to finish off the night, but decided against it.

No point in pushing my luck tonight. I have enough for my meals and some hits. Maybe even enough for the week.

During his trip back, a small café caught his attention. The outdoor tables were empty, so he took a seat and devoured a couple of burgers and a large fry. The cold night air chased customers inside, so he had the outdoor seating to himself. Hunger dissipated as he stuffed down two juicy hamburgers. He wiped his hands, and held up the saturated napkin.

What's the deal? Only one napkin! Are these too valuable to give more than one per customer?

He tossed the napkin toward the trash, but missed. After shaking off his dripping hands, he wiped them on his pants, and his mouth on his coat sleeve. With his stomach now full, Michael headed toward the other side of Central Park to find his supplier.

Cold stung his face and numbing pain hammered at his feet with each step. His shoes offered little protection against the cold when they were dry, but as the snow worked into the holes and melted, he wondered if these shoes were better than nothing.

His legs became sticks. His feet could no longer feel the ground. The frigid temperatures made his body ache, numbing out his other senses.

Fighting to stay on his feet, Michael stumbled down

111th street. If he could get to his supplier, a couple of hits would numb the pain. It would kill both the pain in his feet, and the pain in his heart. He might even freeze to death without realizing it, but what did it matter, as long as he couldn't feel anything. Unable to feel his feet, he looked down, lost his balance, and fell on the hard sidewalk. With considerable effort, he struggled back to his feet.

The sound of faint music reached his ears. It came from a building just ahead. He pressed forward through the cold. The singing grew louder near the end of a white brick building. The music came from behind the door he now stood before, and he stopped to listen. The song sounded familiar. The voices of the congregation seeped out of the building, and a familiar melody gripped him.

I live my life, By the Master's plan.
So I won't be judged By mortal man.

"It's *that* song!" he said to himself.

The irony struck Michael. Just a few days ago, he had talked about the youth rally with Raquel. Now he heard a song from that night. It was the only thing he liked about that evening. Thoughts of the youth night swirled in his head. Raquel begging him to go, and him agreeing to do it just for her.

"I'll go, but I ain't getting saved," he remembered saying. Feeling a smile ease onto his face, his mind returned to the memory of that service nearly four years earlier. Students danced around, doing crazy things, but he couldn't get into the silliness. He wondered what kind of weird things were going on inside this building. *I never thought I'd hear this song again. I hobbled into the church that day, and now I'm hobbling again, barely able to walk.*

The irony of the thought made him chuckle. Is it really funny, or is his mind delirious from the cold? Maybe it's a sign. For a moment, he felt like the words were welcoming him home. A safe feeling ran through him when the next line rang out.

I praise my Lord, Each time I kneel and pray
I know he knows, I know no other way.

"Maybe I'll just step in long enough to get the feeling back into my frozen feet," he said to himself. A gentle push eased the door open. All eyes turned to see him in the doorway, and the feeling of safety blew away like the wind. Feeling like an animal at a zoo, he retreated from the door and stepped back into the snow.

A moment later the door swung open and he saw the preacher he'd met at the park. It was Kenyon. "Friend, come inside." The preacher waved his hand toward the building.

Michael stood for a moment, unsure if he wanted to be paraded in front of the church.

"You look cold. At least come inside and get warmed up," he said with a warm smile. "I'm getting cold out here without a coat, so I know you must be cold. Come inside. You can leave anytime you wish."

Climbing the three stairs leading to the door challenged his uncooperative legs. He tottered as Kenyon pulled the door closed, cutting off the stinging cold.

"Come over here beside me," Kenyon whispered in a hushed tone.

Michael knew he smelled bad, but Kenyon acted as though he were an old friend, and part of the congregation. As the service continued, Michael's feet went from numb, to aching with pain, and soon began to feel warm again. The church sang a variety of songs, some even he liked. Kenyon preached something about the love of God and lives becoming new, but Michael couldn't concentrate. His mind could only think about getting to his meth supplier. The hard crash bore down on him, and the weight on his chest felt like it would crush him.

The service ended with Kenyon inviting anyone who wanted a new life to give their old life to Jesus, but Michael thought how absurd it sounded. Few things in life were certain, but one thing Michael knew—Jesus didn't want his screwed up life. He couldn't stand himself, much less would this holy God be able to tolerate something as unholy as a stinking drug addict.

People began filing out, and most of them came by to greet Michael. A few even hugged the homeless man in rags. He wanted to get away from this place as fast as possible, but part of him felt drawn here. An odd feeling tugged on a chord deep inside.

Kenyon walked back from the pulpit and spoke to Michael. "I am so glad you came."

Michael had to admit, the man's personality seemed genuine. He had met people who smiled with safety-pin grins, while they plastered fake smiles on insincere faces. Preachers and politicians were masters of the safety-pin grin, but something about this preacher went deeper than face value.

"It's cold outside. Do you need a ride somewhere? I don't have a car, but I can arrange someone to take you," the preacher said.

"I'm okay," Michael answered.

"Can I ask your name?"

"Just call me, dirt-bag."

"Well, now. Unless your parents were dust bunnies, I don't think you would have a name like dirt-bag." The corners of Kenyon's mouth turned up. His eyes seemed to smile, too.

Michael couldn't keep himself from smiling, but he quickly wiped it away. *I kind of like this guy, he has a quick wit.* "I don't give my name to strangers."

"I don't like calling anyone something degrading, so can I call you DB for short?" Michael gave an amused smile, and Kenyon continued, "I can see you aren't feeling very good about yourself right now. You know, DB, there is more to life? Most people don't know this, but I was a street thug when I came to New York. I spent some time in jail for petty crimes. And those were the one's where I got caught. I was serving a life-sentence, one small conviction at a time.

"One day a man told me God wanted to give me a new life, and the only thing he wanted from me was to surrender my old life." Kenyon smiled and seemed to drift back in his mind, "I thought it sounded like a good deal. I would give my life, which had been corrupted by crime and sorrow, and receive a new life where I could start over—with all things new. What a deal!"

"Thanks for the sermon," Michael said, "but that won't work for me. Even God can't forgive the things I've done."

"You don't understand." Kenyon leveled his gaze on Michael. "It doesn't matter what you've done. God doesn't fix your old life, He puts it to death and buries it. Then you are raised as a new creation, where all the old stuff has passed away—it's buried. And now everything is new."

"God hates everything about me, and the trail of disaster behind me is proof. He doesn't love monsters like me."

"Have you murdered any preachers?"

"No. But I have thought about it a time or two." Michael grinned at his own words.

"Well," Kenyon said, grappling for words, "the Apostle Paul was once a preacher killer. He hunted down Christians, arrested them, had them killed, and yet, God forgave him and used him to write two-thirds of the New Testament."

"Look, preacher," Michael said, "I know you are trying to help me, but this religion stuff isn't for me."

"Is the life you are living the life you want?"

"I've got to go. Thanks for giving me a break from the cold."

Michael rose to his feet and pushed out the door, heading into the night. He wanted to escape this preacher. Now to find the only real source of relief he knew of. He patted his pocket, making sure he still had the cash for his drugs, then set off across Central Park to reach his supplier.

Kenyon walked out and watched Michael as he faded into the darkness.

Lord, that is twice we have crossed paths. Please show him what you are doing. Please show me how to reach out to him.

The homeless man hurried away, but Kenyon had the feeling this would not be the end of their relationship.

Chapter Twenty-Two

The closing curtain fell in the Belasco Theater. A thunderous applause marked the end of a flawless performance of *The Nutcracker*. Although Raquel's part had been secondary, it felt exhilarating to stand on a Broadway stage and see the enthusiasm of a large crowd. To her, this production made Christmas come alive with excitement. She put all her heart into her minor role.

One day, I'm going to be a principle dancer.

To gain a principle position, she knew she had to treat every task as though it were the most important position on the stage. In some ways it was. If even a snowflake gave a poor performance, the entire stage would suffer.

"Raquel," Tedra called with a song in her voice. She always sang her words when in a teasing mood. "There's something backstage for you."

Tedra rushed over and tugged on Raquel's arm, and bounced over to a table with Raquel in tow. She stood by a bouquet of two dozen roses. Raquel saw a card with her name and a heart. She took the card and looked up to Tedra, whose face beamed with excitement.

"Who is it from?" Tedra's hands clasped together. She looked like a kid at Christmas.

Unable to suppress her own smile, Raquel said, "Girl. Don't you ever get tired? You're bouncing like a ballerina before the play, but I'm exhausted."

"Open it. Open it."

She already suspected who had sent it. Raquel slid the small card out of the pink envelope and read it. *To the angel whose beauty lights up the stage.* She felt her face flush. Tedra noticed.

"Who is it? Is it Joseph? It is, isn't it?" She bounced with excitement. "I know it is! He really likes you!"

Another taped note hung from the green paper around the roses. *I had to get with Marcus after the play, but I'll be at the coffee shop if you guys want to meet me.*

"Raquel! You're killing me," Tedra said. "What does it say?"

The hand of Tedra reached out, and Raquel let go of the card. She jerked the note to her eyes and started bouncing again.

"I knew it, I knew it! Joseph is smitten." Tedra waved a hand at Raquel. "Snowflake girl, you have got a man. And he is a keeper." She strung out the word *keeper*, for emphasis. A bright smile appeared and she put a hand on Raquel's shoulder. "Don't get embarrassed. This is a good thing."

"I know. It's just happening so fast. Plus I'm not sure. Things were supposed to be different. I kind of expected to reunite with..." Raquel fumbled for words. "Well, I don't know." She felt foolish for wanting a homeless man over a Broadway agent.

"You mean the bum? If I were you, I'd set my sights a little higher." She put her arm around Raquel. "I know you really care about him, but, you can't make someone change. Keep praying for him, but don't anchor your life on someone who doesn't care about himself. Or you."

"I know. You're right. It's just that a part of me won't let go."

Tedra waved her hand. "Perfectly normal. Broken hearts never quite mend. But you can't build your life on a broken foundation. Let that place in your heart pray for him, and then let him go. He's in the Lord's hands. Not yours."

Raquel nodded. She knew Tedra was right. It was time to move on and let go of the past. Maybe the Lord will redeem him, but one thing appeared certain-they were taking different paths, and the time had come to turn her focus to a new direction.

Tedra stepped in front of Raquel and grasped both of her hands. "I know what. I'll call my sweetheart, we'll get changed, then head out for a cup of coffee." Raquel nodded and Tedra began bouncing again. A laugh escaped from Raquel. Partly because she felt embarrassed, and partly because her friend looked so giddy with excitement.

Tedra's right. Today begins my new life. It's time to let go of the past, and reach for the future.

The clock showed ten-thirty in the evening when Raquel and Tedra stepped out of the theater. It had been a tiring day, but it's hard to come down from the excitement of performing on stage. They had one more show before breaking for Christmas. After tomorrow's Christmas eve performance, they would have three days off. Then they would rehearse and perform again for the next week starting on New Year's Eve.

Raquel already had her car packed. She had been planning to stay in New York during Christmas, but after learning there would be no rehearsals for three days, she decided to go home for the holiday. They walked to the 8th avenue coffee shop where Joseph and Tedra's boyfriend would meet them. After ordering a caramel brulee, Raquel joined Joseph by the window. They talked and watched the thinning crowds of cars and pedestrians.

Performing on Broadway had been fun, but she looked forward to spending Christmas in Bristol. It would be exciting to tell everyone about the sights and sounds of New York. Her family would not believe a place like Central Park existed in the heart of Manhattan. She had always pictured New York as a concrete jungle without trees or parks. At eight-hundred and forty-three acres, it's bigger than most farms in Bristol. To Raquel, Central Park is what made New York feel like home—or as close to it as she could get north of the Tennessee border.

Raquel's thoughts were interrupted by a scruffy man shuffling past the window. He glanced inside, and their eyes met.

"It's Dancer!" she shouted. She jumped to her feet and started for the door. Raquel darted back, and laid a hand on Joseph's arm. "Joseph, I'll be right back." Without stopping for a response, she rushed to Tedra, who waited at the counter for her overpriced coffee. "Tedra, I'm going outside to talk to Dancer."

"Wait," Tedra said, but Raquel bolted out the door.

Up the 8th avenue sidewalk, she saw a man in ragged clothing, and ran to catch up.

"Dancer!" she called. He didn't answer, but continued ambling up the sidewalk. When she caught up, she said, "Where have you been? I came to visit you, but you aren't on Henderson Mill anymore."

"You told everyone where I lived, and people and news reporters wouldn't give me a moment of peace," he said, and picked up his pace. "Don't follow me this time. I don't need the publicity."

Rushing ahead of him, Raquel stopped and put a hand on his arm and tried to look him in the eye. He dodged her look, but she tilted her head to look him in the face. "I'm so sorry this happened, but you've got to believe me. I didn't tell anyone where you were."

"Yeah, right. After you came, the whole world followed right behind you."

He started to walk again, but Raquel pulled his sleeve to make him face her.

"I didn't want to tell you because I thought it would upset you, plus I didn't know people would be coming. I found you because a reporter showed the Henderson Mill bridge on the news. The news report showed me where you were. I never talked to any reporters or told anyone where you lived."

"Good," he said as he turned, and began walking again. Raquel hurried to match his pace.

"How have you been?" she asked.

"Oh, wonderful. My limousine broke down. That's why I'm walking." The sarcasm in his words sank into Raquel's heart like a dagger.

"I've been worried about you," she said. His eyes were fixed straight ahead and he didn't answer. "I pray for you every day. I just want you to know that people really care about you. I care about you."

Dancer stopped and looked Raquel in the eye. "Look, I know you mean well. And I appreciate your concern, but I am at the bottom, and I'm not coming up. All I can do is drag you, and everyone else down with me. Live your life and forget about me. I'll be okay," he said. He tried to look sincere, but Raquel wasn't buying it. He read her expression. "Really. I'm okay."

"Maybe I don't want to live my life without you." Dancer looked at the curb, but Raquel thought she saw something in his face. "Think back to our days at Bristol High. When we danced onstage, those were the happiest days of my life. Do you ever miss those days?"

Dancer shrugged.

"I know you haven't forgotten. Do you remember how we stepped all over each other's feet the first time we tried to dance the *Southern Fried Musical?*" Raquel could see a thin smile form behind the frayed whiskers on his face. He brushed it aside.

"I don't know. That was a long time ago."

The look in his eyes said he remembered, and it still held a place of fondness in his heart.

"Come on," she said, pulling his arm. "Let's step through the dance again. I know you still remember the song." She tugged on his arm as she sang a tune.

"I don't want to dance." He looked around.

"What's the matter? Afraid one of your buddies might

see you dancing with a Broadway girl?" She pulled him along, striding through the steps of their old musical. "You aren't ashamed to stoop down to my level, are you?"

"Yeah, right."

She pulled him through the steps. He reluctantly followed along, but those memories seemed to ignite something in his eyes. An ache filled her heart when Raquel thought about all he had lost. She pushed aside the heartache and focused on the warm memories of dancing with him on stage.

"Okay. One dance, then I need to get off to work," he said with a sly smile.

The two dancers performed on the wet, salted sidewalk, and he let himself be drawn into the dance with Raquel. He hasn't forgotten. Visions of the old Michael resurfaced, and it became clear that for a moment, he allowed the world around him to disappear. They were on stage in Bristol, reliving the faded memories.

Late night walkers stopped to watch the Broadway girl dancing on 8th Street with a tattered homeless man.

"Hey, that's the homeless dancer from TV." A man pointed at him. "Isn't this the guy living under the bridge?"

The voice jolted Dancer. His grace disappeared and he became a lumbering homeless man again. "I'm sorry," he said to Raquel while turning from the crowd and ducking his head. Shielding his face with an arm, he hurried up the street to escape the attention.

Raquel let out an exasperated sigh while watching him disappear into the night. "Dancer," she whispered, "you've got to let go of your past mistakes. Reach up. You don't have to live in failure."

Chapter Twenty-Three

New York, like every major city, has its share of homeless and downtrodden. Each of these men and women has a story behind them—life stories built upon hardship and personal choices. Often, one poor choice leads to a lifetime of consequences.

Vashan's trouble began this way. In college, he had a promising future, but the partying lifestyle pushed his ambitions to the side. Friday night binges rolled into Saturday, and soon the craving for a drink demanded his constant attention.

Though some people around him expressed concern over his excessive drinking, Vashan was able to keep it under check so it didn't interfere with his business life. When college was behind him, his career budded. The demands of corporate America, married life, and the responsibility of a new child added to his stress, causing him to seek an escape from daily life through the bottle. For years, he'd told himself he deserved relief, but as he became dependent on the bottle, it became harder to deal with the stress.

It became difficult to get up at six in the morning with the effects of the previous night's liquor still pounding in his head. He started arriving late for work, then his absenteeism began to mount. When his company put him on a final warning, he quit drinking for a month, but stress continued to build. He didn't know how to handle life outside the bottle. Cleaning up never lasted, for each stressful moment sent his mind hunting for the liquor. Sooner or later, he would follow his thoughts to the drink.

His employer showed patience, but as the whiskey took over his life, it became impossible for Vashan to be dependable. Eventually, he was fired. Two years later, steady jobs continued to evade him. When the bills mounted, he downgraded his apartment, but still struggled to survive. Now two months behind on rent, his family became neglected and needy. Vashan cared about them, but the liquor took its portion first, then his wife and son got what little remained.

Vowing to quit, he joined a support group. Each time he felt tempted, accountability partners rallied to his aid. This worked for nearly two months, but it had been a stressful week. The hard work and a demanding boss wasn't worth the minimum wage. Unable to cope, he stormed out of the warehouse and went home.

After a fight with his wife over quitting another job, he reached the breaking point, and turned to the only way he knew to escape the stress. Dipping into the bill money, he scraped together enough cash to buy his booze and began drowning his troubles away.

Darkness fell, but Vashan was in no hurry to get back into the battleground of his apartment. Stumbling down the icy alley, Vashan carried his brown sack with his bottle of whiskey. It felt mostly empty, but his eyes wouldn't focus. He shook it.

"Sounds like I'm running low. Better get some more."

Unable to find any sense of balance, his feet lagged behind, and he lurched forward and tumbled to the ground. Clumsy fingers lost the bottle when Vashan hit the pavement. His legs slipped on the ice as he kicked to get them under him, but he couldn't find traction. Panting from the effort, Vashan decided to take a rest and warm himself with a little whiskey.

Trying to focus his eyes, he lifted his head from the pavement and stretched his neck to see to the left and right. Nothing looked like a bag. He arched back and saw a brown fuzzy image about the size of the bag. He reached for it, but it rested just beyond his fingertips.

Digging his heels in the ice, he kicked hard while

pushing off with his hands. The cold stung his fingers, but he kept pushing against the frozen pavement and toward the brown blotch. He reached out his fingers and touched it. It crinkled, and his fumbling fingers pushed it out of reach again. Kicking harder, he reached upward, being more careful this time. He pulled the bag toward him and pulled out the bottle. He shook it to gauge how much remained.

Sounds like about three or four swallows.

Cold fingers turned up the bottle, and he chugged down four swallows, then five, six. He lost count, but he gulped until the bottle emptied. When he shook it again and didn't hear the sound of liquid, he tossed the bottle to the side. It clanked off the ice and he could hear it sliding off into the night. He expected to hear it shatter, but it just sang as it skidded away.

"Now to get to my feet," he said, and tried to curl his knees under him.

Vashan grabbed his knees, and pulled his body to a sitting position. He struggled to get his feet under him, but he sprawled backward, hitting hard on the ground. He rolled over and felt the ice stinging his face and fingers. Pushing himself up, he put one foot under him before his hands and feet shot outward, causing him to bounce face first off the hard, ice coated alley. He grumbled and rubbed his lip. The taste of blood seeped into his mouth.

After several hard hits on his face, Vashan decided to roll onto his back, and try again to get up from a sitting position. Vashan struggled to get his feet under him until exhaustion set in. His head throbbed with pain, and fingers ached from the icy temperatures. As he lay still, his thin jacket couldn't fight off the frigid air. The temperature had slipped into the teens. His body vibrated, trying in vain to shake off the cold. Too bad he didn't own a thicker coat. Without the strength to fight to his feet, Vashan lay helplessly, hoping someone would walk down this alley at two in the morning.

The shivering in his body grew more violent, and Vashan began to have a strange, distant feeling. He felt as though his body remained somewhere behind him, but he couldn't look back to see. His eyes and his head were fixed straight ahead. A figure moved just out of view. It remained in a shadow, just to his left. Though his eyes could only look straight ahead, through the corner of his vision he could detect something terrifying—eyes without pity.

Before him, his wife came into view. Tears streaked her cheeks. His five-year-old son looked up beside her.

"Don't cry mommy," the boy said.

A group of men walked in the door, and began to carry boxes of clothes out of the apartment. They returned and pushed his wife and son out the door, bolting it behind them. She took an armload of clothes in one hand and grabbed the boy's hand in the other. Vashan found himself on a bench with a bottle in hand. His neck freed to move and he felt relieved the heartless eyes were no longer beside him. He saw his wife approaching, and she tossed him a shirt.

"It's all that's left." She stared hopelessly into the distance, then began walking away.

"Where are you going?" Vashan asked.

A heavy weight seemed to force him backward and he no longer sat on the bench. Frozen to the ground, he fought to move. Fear shot through Vashan as he tried to free his arms. He tried to look around him, but again, he could only stare forward. Walls seemed to be around him, but he could see faces above. They were looking down at him. His wife and son looked down, without expression. Terror filled his mind.

"Help me!" he cried.

They didn't respond.

A voice just out of view said, "He was a good man." His wife winced at the words.

Why did she wince? Doesn't she think I'm a good

person?

Vashan cried out again, louder than before, but they seemed unaware of his voice. A lid began to close and light disappeared. He screamed frantically, terrified of the thick darkness which iced his soul.

Ahead he saw a distant light. It came closer and he began to feel hopeful, but the merciless eyes came into view. The shadowy figure moved out of his line of sight, but he could see it raise an arm, pointing ahead. His head could move again, but Vashan's eyes were glued to a dreadful throne now in view. A judge sat on the throne. The very sight of him sent panic through Vashan's body.

Terrified, he couldn't bear to look at the judge on the throne. Men and women lamented before it. He began to feel their terror as if it were his own. Heavy fear crushed down on him, seeping into his soul. Vashan began to quake, feeling the agony of those in despair before the judge. He felt their legs collapsing below them, under the weight of the pressing terror, as fear took away their strength.

People lined up ahead of him and crowds around the throne room came into view. Their faces changed while voices spoke. Sometimes they showed sorrow, other times the faces were hard as stone. Pangs of terror pulsated through Vashan. Looking at each man and woman in line ahead of him, he felt their agony and regret.

The closer they stepped to the throne, the more they began to weep. The man in front of him began shaking with such fear, he could barely stand. Terror began to fill every fiber of Vashan's being as an unseen force drove him closer to the throne.

"Oh, God. Save me. Jesus, save me!"

No one could hear him cry. He tried to stop walking, and though his legs had no strength, he could not prevent them from taking their place in line.

A voice cried to his left where the merciless eyes continued to glare at him, "The wicked shall not stand in the judgment."

He stared at the scene before the throne to see another collapse, unable to stand.

"But I'm not wicked," Vashan cried. "I'm not wicked."

His life flashed through his memory. His understanding dawned, and every thought and action of his life testified against him. Even his good deeds declared his self-centered motives. His kind acts had no other motivation than to make himself feel good. Nothing in his life seemed good, and he understood he was about to stand before that throne without a defense. There wasn't anything to show the judge as a merit to his credit.

"Nothing in my life is good," he wept, and tried in vain to cover his face. Even with his hands over his eyes, he could still see the throne before him.

"The wicked shall not stand in the judgment," the voice kept calling out, reminding each person of their fate at the throne.

Trembling, the man in front of him walked up to the throne. His legs began to shake as he walked and the voice thundered down. The shaking grew into violent tremors until he collapsed. Vashan strained to hear the words, but could not understand what the judge said to the man now lying in a heap at the base of the white throne.

"You will understand the voice when you are before the throne," the shadow beside him called out.

"I don't want to stand before that throne!" Vashan cried with a loud voice. His turn arrived and an unseen force drove him forward. "Have mercy on me!" he screamed. "Oh, God. Have mercy on me!"

A strong hand gripped him, snatching him away from the shadow with the merciless eyes. He couldn't see who spoke to him, but he heard a voice in his ear. "Go sit on the bench against the wall surrounding the park at 79th. A man will ask you if you're a thirty-two."

"What does that mean? What do I say to him?" Vashan

asked. "What happens after that?"

The voice faded, but the thought resonated in his mind, *He will tell you how to find mercy.*

Vashan opened his eyes to find himself in a hospital room. Uncontrolled weeping took over, and through his tears, he thanked the Lord for taking him out of that place of horror. He ran a hand over his face and said, "I've got to find the park bench at 79th."

Chapter Twenty-Four

Fear and excitement raced through Raquel's heart when she crossed into Virginia, heading toward the Tennessee state line. Excitement over seeing her family and friends, but fear over the possibility of having to face Robert. Now only a few hours from Bristol, she began to fidget with the memories of the man she'd escaped from.

The words he told Michael still rang in her ears, "Something might happen to Raquel. If I can't have her, nobody can."

Not long ago, she looked at Robert as nothing more than a blow-hard and not someone to be concerned with. After piecing Michael's testimony together with what she already knew about Robert, it all made sense. *How could I have been so blind?*

She knew he was a stalker, but had convinced herself that he was just a pushy person who couldn't take no for an answer. She never took his threats seriously, but now she thought he was someone to fear. He had tried to control her, manipulate her, and make himself the center of her life. But never did she fear he would actually harm her. Even after seeing his outbursts of anger, she had still deceived herself into explaining it away as childish behavior.

Before sneaking out of Bristol and heading for New York, Robert was relentless. Love notes and flowers from him appeared in her locked car—even when she attended dance school in Knoxville. A relationship with him was like petting a moody dog. If you kept petting, he acted happy, but the moment you stopped, he growled and threatened to bite. Robert is like having a friendly enemy.

Agreeing to date him again after high school turned out to be a big mistake. Dancer seemed to have dropped off the earth, and Robert nearly drove her crazy with his efforts to win her back. To have some semblance of peace, Raquel decided to adopt the proverb, *Hold your friends close, and your enemies closer.* She hoped to have peace by pacifying him. Instead, his obsession continued to escalate.

She thought back on the events leading up to one of their many breakups. One day, she went shopping with her best friend, Margaret, hoping to have a Robert-free day. The phone call after leaving the mall still lingered in her memory.

Raquel had walked Margaret to her car, before getting into her own. Sliding behind the wheel, she heard her cell phone ring. Heat began rising from her neck into her face, and she felt her jaw tighten. *It's Robert. And he knew exactly when I got into my car.*

The thought of ignoring it crossed her mind, but she knew he would keep calling until she answered. She thought about turning it off, but then remembered Robert's rage the last time he couldn't contact her. He became insanely jealous and tried to maintain a short leash. He would certainly be in control, sooner or later. Resistance was futile. As much as she would like to ignore him for a day, Raquel knew it would only make her life miserable the next day, when she had to face his red, bulging eyes, and watch the veins stretching out of his neck.

She picked up the phone, "Hello, Robert."

"Who was the guy I saw you talking to?"

What? Not even a hello? "What guy?"

"Don't play stupid with me. The one you met up with. How many guys did you meet today?"

Her mind raced to think about any men she encountered. "I didn't meet up with any guys. Margaret is the only person I was with."

"You are a liar!" he shouted. "I saw you talking with a guy in the mall!"

Clinching the steering wheel, Raquel let out a long exhale. She remembered Margaret talking with a friend from drama class. *She was the one flirting, not me.* "This is ridiculous, Robert. That was Rod. You know, Rod from our old drama class. You know him just as well as I do."

"I don't care who it is. Why are you meeting up with him at the mall?"

Raquel didn't attempt to hide her annoyance. "Come on, Robert. He works at the mall and he just said, 'Hi'. What's wrong with that?"

Robert seethed into the phone, "Look, Raquel. I don't want you talking to other guys. Understand?"

"You look, Robert! You don't own me and if I want to say 'hi' to an old classmate, you have no right to call me on the phone, screaming in my ear!" Robert started to speak, but Raquel interrupted. She could feel her temper running out of control, but she made no attempt to stifle it. "Another thing. I am sick of you following me around, spying on me, and watching me. You promise the stalking will end each time I agree to go out with you, but it keeps getting worse. The last two years have been the worst years of my life. It's over, Robert. I don't want to see you anymore! Don't call me or contact me again!" She disconnected the phone without giving him another chance to speak.

After hanging up, she headed straight for home. A feeling of dread hit Raquel when she pulled into her driveway. Robert's truck was already there, and he was in the yard playing with Stewart and Johanna on the rope swing under the old oak tree. He played with her little brother and sister as if nothing happened. Not a care in the world. She slammed the car door and stomped into the house without giving Robert a glance. Her mother worked in the kitchen preparing for supper. "Mom," Raquel said, "I've got to talk to you."

"I already know," her mother said.

Taken back, Raquel asked, "What do you mean?"

"Robert told me all about it. He said you would probably be upset and to tell you he's sorry. It was a big misunderstanding," her mother said.

"What misunderstanding is this?" Raquel asked, crossing her arms, and already anticipating a skewed interpretation of today's conversation.

"He said he saw you talking to another guy and asked you who it was. You apparently assumed he was prying and got angry. Raquel, he was just curious, but he trusts you. So you shouldn't be so defensive and misunderstand his intentions."

Yep. Poor ol' Robert. Even when he said the most awful things, he could retell it in a way that made himself sound like a victim, and me look like an overly sensitive basket case.

Breaking up was short lived. Being with Robert was hard, but breaking away became nightmarish. He never relented. He never tired. He never stopped pursuing. Each time she came out of the Knoxville studio, he waited somewhere in the area, watching. But when she complained, he could always prove he worked on a construction site miles away. Either he could be in two places at once, or he knew how to manipulate others into lying for him. Or maybe he convinced them that he ran errands nearby.

Raquel thought about the day she had relented after breaking up with the stalker yet again. For weeks he had called, left notes, manipulated her family, and pursued her through every area of her life. She stepped out of the Knoxville studio into the bright Tennessee sun. She squinted in the light, trying to see if she could detect Robert's truck in the area. Walking to the back of the building, she had a familiar odd feeling of being watched, but saw nothing out of the ordinary.

Until she escaped to New York, she always knew that though Robert and his truck were not in sight, odds were, he was out there, somewhere, watching her. His behavior grew more obsessive each day, and she considered getting a restraining order. She feared her family wouldn't understand, knowing they only saw Robert on his best behavior. Raquel also feared it might push Robert over the edge.

If he could just give me a little space, I could take his behavior.

She thought on how most of her spare time focused on keeping Robert pacified. Walking around the shrub hedge which decorated the center of the lot, she rushed to her car door, unlocked it and slipped behind the wheel, scanning the area surrounding her.

"Glad you finally decided to show up."

Raquel gasped and jerked around to see Robert's innocent grin. Being distracted by looking for something outside the car, she never looked inside her vehicle. "Robert, you scared the crap out of me! What are you doing in my car?"

"You left it unlocked, so I thought I would take a seat and see if you wanted a little company," Robert said in a humble tone.

"That isn't true, I know I locked it, and how dare you break into my car. Why can't you just let me have one day to myself?" She placed both hands on the steering wheel and lowered her head. "Just one day would be nice."

Robert's eyes grew intense and his voice took on a serious tone, "Our families have been friends since we were kids. As far back as I can remember, I knew we were made for each other. Raquel, I know we are meant to be together. If you will look, you'll see it too." His eyes saddened and the corners of his mouth drooped. "Raquel, when you left me, it hurt me. I never got the chance to show you what was in my heart." Robert patted his chest softly. He continued in a hushed voice, "Raquel. Just give our love a chance. You will be happy with me, if you just let me into your heart."

"Get out of my car!" she shouted. "Get out of my car," Raquel repeated and pointed toward the passenger window. Robert sat without moving, a hurt look remaining in his expression. "Robert, you have no right to hunt me down, break in my car, and force your will on me. I am tired of this. I am going to get a restraining order on you." Anger swept across Robert's face. The storm brewing behind his eyes caused Raquel to realize she pushed the wrong buttons. Softening her voice, she said, "Please, Robert. Just get out of the car so I can go home."

Relief replaced fear when he opened the door and stepped out, but the chills returned when he stuck his head back into the car and said, "I would recommend you not do anything you might regret. You wouldn't want anything to happen to your little brother or sister. If they get into trouble, I might not make it in time to save them."

"I know you wouldn't hurt those kids," she said, but the dreadful look in his eyes made her doubt. Surely he wouldn't try to hurt her family, or would he? As Robert's behavior grew more bizarre, she wondered if he was losing touch with reality.

"Oh, I wouldn't think of hurting them. I'm just saying accidents happen, and I would hate for something to happen when I'm not there. Who would protect them?" His eyes continued to show his anger, even while a warm smile returned to his face, causing Raquel to shutter at the eerie expression. The door slammed and Robert strolled away, leaving Raquel's heart racing.

She cranked the car and gripped the wheel with her trembling fingers. Did he have the capability to do harm to those kids?

The memory of that day sent a chill across her. And now she was going back to Bristol, where he would likely try to get together again. *Like a fool, I convinced myself he was just being manipulative. To keep the peace, I took him back. I'm such an idiot.*

The exit for Chilhowie passed her line of vision. In forty minutes she would be home. *Oh, God, please don't let Robert be waiting for me.*

How many times had she come home to find Robert waiting when she pulled into the driveway? He loved to sit in the porch swing that faced out to the field. His back was to the door, yet he could still monitor it like a centurion. It's here that Robert nearly discovered her plan to escape to New York.

Joseph and another man had seen her performing in Knoxville, and visited the studio to interview her. In a moment, everything she had dreamed of seemed to fall into place. With excitement, she rushed home to tell her parents that she was being flown to New York for an audition.

Her excitement turned into dread when she came home to see Robert's red truck in the driveway. She couldn't allow him to discover her plans to move to New York.

When she saw his truck, it reminded her of the need to be cautious about what she said to others. Robert seemed to hear all conversations, even when it didn't seem possible. If she didn't want him to know her plans, she would have to be quiet about this audition until he wasn't nearby.

Robert's truck occupied her space, so Raquel parked in the yard. He sat on the swing with her little sister, facing away from the front door. The chattering voice of Johanna could be heard from across the yard. She felt certain Robert must have seen or heard her pull up, but he seemed lost in the swinging conversation with her little sister.

Maybe I got lucky, and he didn't notice. That would be a first.

She walked up the stairs and watched the porch swing rocking twenty feet away. Robert seemed engrossed in Johanna's talk about a kitty as the swing's chains creaked.

Just as Raquel's hand contacted the doorknob, Robert said, "Raquel! Hello."

She jumped at the sudden sound of her name, and could feel her face growing flush. "Why do you always do that?"

He shifted sideways to look at her. "What? Greet you? I like to say hello to those I care about."

"You know what I'm talking about," Raquel said. "Is this a game with you? In a room, on a porch, wherever, you make sure your back is to me, and you always say something, while pretending to be preoccupied."

"I'm sorry. I usually am preoccupied, but I just have the ability to notice whatever is going on around me." Robert gave an innocent smile. "In the future, I'll try to remember to face you before saying 'Hi.'"

Raquel rolled her eyes and pushed through the front door. Another one of Robert's mind games. It's his way of letting her know he always watched, even if she didn't think he could see.

Oh, I left my organizer in the car. I don't want the all-seeing-eye to find that.

She trotted to the car and retrieved it. In the few moments it took to jog to the car, Johanna was already going inside, leaving Robert standing on the porch alone, waiting on Raquel.

"I need to talk to you." Robert's voice echoed with restrained agitation.

"I really have a lot to—"

Robert gripped her arm tightly and cut off her words. "I'd better not *ever* see you roll your eyes at me again. You understand?" Robert's eyes blazed as he spoke through clinched teeth. His words spewed from a flaming volcano. Pain throbbed as he squeezed her arm.

Unable to keep pain and fear from showing on her face, Raquel worried her expression might encourage his rage. He drew his face near hers, and she could feel his hot breath.

Her pulse beat in the skin under the hand clamping her arm. Fear kept her gaze frozen upon him, though she wanted to turn away from his angry eyes.

"Do. You. Under. Stand?"

Raquel nodded.

Robert's eyes lowered to the organizer and he wrapped his fingers around it. Raquel held on, knowing it contained more information about her life and plans than she wanted Robert to know. They battled over the organizer as he pulled and she gripped it with both hands.

"What is in here that you don't want me to see?"

"Nothing. But can't I have a little privacy?" She hoped her voice sounded more confident than she felt.

Incensed at her defiance, his eyes furrowed and his rage began to build again. "Let me just look at it," he demanded.

"No, Robert."

His lips curled into a sneer, but they were interrupted by the sound of the front door opening. In an instant, Robert's rage disappeared and a different man stood before Raquel. A warm smile appeared on his face, and his eyes showed nothing but loving-kindness.

"Don't forget to pencil me into your busy schedule," he said in a sweet voice as he gently pushed the organizer back toward Raquel. He gave her an affectionate rub as he opened the door wider, letting his sweetheart into the house. "See you in a bit," Robert sang as her father stepped onto the porch and gave a knowing smile, thinking he had interrupted a romantic moment. "Hi, Mr. Orren. What do you think about this week's Tennessee game? Do you think the Vols can take Florida?"

Voices faded behind the closing door. Raquel rushed away from the scene, wanting to get as much distance as possible between her and Robert.

Raquel's thoughts were drawn back into the present when the sign for I-381 passed overhead. "Crap! There's my exit."

Darting her eyes to the lanes beside her, she saw a gap and cut across to get into the left merging lanes for Interstate-381. A horn blared its protest. "Watch the road girl," she said out loud. "Watch the road." A glance in the rear view mirror gave her a shot of relief. *No blue lights. Don't want a ticket for my illegal lane change.*

Fifteen or twenty minutes from home!

I wonder if he's still angry over me standing him up at the cafe?

Raquel had remained tight-lipped about her move when near Robert. His keen perception told him something was going on, so she had claimed to be going to audition for a play in Richmond, Virginia. Knowing he would be keeping a close eye on her, she made plans to meet him for breakfast in Bristol the morning she left. Moe's cafe was far from the interstate, insuring their paths wouldn't cross. His plans would be focused on the meeting, and by the time he realized she wasn't coming, she would be halfway to New York.

Lying about her plans caused her to feel the weight of her guilt, but she didn't know any other way to escape from Robert's iron fist. If given the opportunity, Robert would ensure he remained in control. Cutting off all contact and taking steps to eliminate the opportunity for him to follow her seemed like the only way to keep him from manipulating her life. The day before leaving for New York, she'd changed the number of her cell phone.

Raquel turned down the road leading to her house and felt relief when her house came into view. "No red truck! No Robert!"

Now if she can just keep Robert from finding out she had returned to Bristol until after she left for New York again.

Kenyon wrapped his coat around him, and called out to his wife, "I'm going for a walk in the park, Honey." He stepped out of his apartment. A familiar drawing tugged at his heart, calling him to the park. This is where he had his quiet time and he always felt like he connected to the Lord in prayer, walking among the trees. Crossing Central Park West, he entered what looked like a snow covered wonderland.

"Oh, crap!" Michael said to himself, "it's the preacher man." He darted into the trees, trying to avoid being spotted. *I hope he didn't see me. That Bible thumper keeps following me and trying to force his Jesus stuff down my throat.*

He crossed the park near 86th street, and headed for the east side where he would be far from the pastor. Emerging from the thicket, Michael saw a group of three ladies at a diner. They were chattering with excitement, preparing to go separate ways. Two walked south and one walked north on 5th Avenue. Michael followed the woman walking alone, staying near the trees to avoid being seen, and waiting for an opportunity to make his move. 5th Avenue shoppers usually had money, and the purse hanging from her shoulder had captured his attention.

The woman walked four blocks before turning down 94th street. This looked like Michael's opportunity to make a move. Running softly across 5th avenue, he entered the road behind the woman. No people in sight. Breaking into a sprint, he caught the woman by surprise, knocking her to the ground, then ripping the purse from her grip.

Stunned, the woman sat silent for a moment as

Michael ran back toward Central Park. When he turned the corner onto 5th avenue, he heard the woman beginning to scream, but it was too late. No one would catch him now. He crossed over and disappeared into the thick trees.

To play it safe, Michael didn't quit running until he reached the ball fields in the center of the park. He sat among the trees and place the purse on his lap, hoping to find enough cash to sustain his habit for another few days. It felt like eyes were watching him. There wasn't anyone visible in the area, but he had a strong feeling of being watched. It might be someone who saw him steal the purse.

It's not safe to stay here.

To escape the area and the watching eyes, he cut across the ball fields. He emerged from the trees and found himself before a dark face.

"Hello DB," Kenyon said.

Michael looked down to the purse and Kenyon's eyes followed. Both men looked up and connected in an awkward stare. Michael didn't know what to do.

How did the preacher follow me here? This man keeps chasing me, and somehow knows where I'm going. Maybe God IS talking to him, directing him to catch me. Michael shrugged and handed the purse to Kenyon.

"I'm sorry," he said. Ashamed and disappointed, Michael turned to walk away. All his efforts had been in vain.

"Where is the owner of this purse?" Kenyon called.

"Somewhere near the cafe across 5th avenue." Michael disappeared into the woods, frustrated with his lost opportunity to find a little cash. "I wish this preacher would just leave me alone," he said under his breath, putting distance between himself and Kenyon.

He hoped this would be the last encounter he would have with the preacher, but if things continued the way they had been going, he knew their paths would cross again.

Chapter Twenty-Five

Raquel pulled the car into her parent's driveway. For a moment, she sat in the car, soaking in the view of the snow covered Bristol landscape. When she opened the door, a comforting chill washed over her. It felt like Christmas had arrived at last. Thoughts of both Dancer and Robert skipped through her mind. The irony struck her. She had avoided Robert, and Dancer had avoided her. Both were on a mission to reach out to someone who didn't want to be reached.

There is one difference. I want Michael to regain control over his life, but Robert wants to be the one in control of mine. Stalking is to cage someone, but outreach is trying to set someone free.

One thought worried her. Would her lies to Robert come home to roost? Or could being away for a few months have changed Robert's mind about having ownership over her.

"Raquel is home!" Johanna hollered while running toward the gravel driveway.

"Hey, Johanna!" Raquel said, stepping out and giving her little sister a hug.

"I'll be right down," her ten-year-old brother, Stewart, called from the housetop.

"Stewart? What are you doing on the roof? You are going to slip on the snow and break your neck," Raquel shouted up to him.

"I *am* being careful," he said with annoyance, as if Raquel's concern was unwarranted. Stewart had strings connected to a large black garbage bag and tied like a harness under his arms.

"Stewart, what are you doing?"

"I'm making a parachute."

Johanna looked a Raquel and said, "He has been playing with plastic army men. The paratroopers gave him the idea."

"No way!" Raquel said, pointing her finger up at Stewart. "You are not jumping off the house with that bag."

"It will work," Stewart insisted. "It's as big on me as the parachutes are on the army men."

"No, no, no." Raquel shook her finger while walking toward the end of the house where Stewart headed. "You'd better not jump off the roof. It won't work."

"Yes it will." Stewart moved to the end of the house with the most open space so he could have room to drift down. "Watch," he said, then launched himself into the air.

The homemade chute didn't open. The last thing Raquel saw was the bag flapping in the wind, and Stewart disappeared from sight, followed by a wet thump, and sounds of groaning coming from the side of the house.

"Stewart!" she cried. With snow crunching under her feet, she ran around the corner.

Her little brother rolled in the snow and pitiful sounds emerged from his mouth. Raquel scooped him up and dashed for the front door.

This little monster is getting heavy.

When Raquel burst through the door, her mother looked up and saw Stewart being carried. "What happened!" her mother shouted. She tossed a cleaning rag aside, and followed behind Raquel as she rushed to the living-room couch.

"The little twerp jumped from the house. He thought it would work like a parachute," Raquel said, pointing to the tangle of string and plastic.

"You sure are stupid," Johanna said, pointing a condemning finger down at her brother.

"Be quiet Johanna. Run along now," her mother said, shooing her away from the couch. Returning her attention to Stewart, she asked, "Where does it hurt?"

"I think I'm okay," Stewart said, regaining his breath. Raquel felt relieved to see the wheezing had stopped. He had knocked the wind out of himself with the hard landing, but now recovered his bearings. Stewart sat up, inventoried his parts, and gave an unsure smile. "I wonder what I did wrong? It should have worked."

"It's a trash bag, not a parachute, you turkey," Raquel said with a wag of the finger and a condescending smile.

"Don't ever do that again. You scared the heck out of me!" her mother shouted.

Raquel smiled while her mother gave Stewart a tongue-lashing. It's good to be home, and good to see little had changed since her departure. This was going to be a wonderful Christmas!

Kenyon stepped out of the Tip Top shoes with his new winter boots and a fresh pack of socks. Excited about his new purchase, he headed toward home. Money had been tight, as usual, but Kenyon had managed to save enough to buy a pair of new boots. The old boots on his feet were looking worn and stained by the dirty slush that gathered on the streets after each snow. The boots looked nice and were supposed to be good for keeping feet warm and dry. He tucked the box under his arm and began his trek home.

Cutting across the street toward the park, Kenyon decided to try out his boots on the walk home. He sat on the bench and began to unbuckle his old ones. His eyes were drawn to a park bench about fifty yards away. There, DB sat, feet curled under him as he tried to recover from a walk through the snow.

"Oh, no, Lord. Please, no. I saved for a long time to get these boots."

Kenyon again found himself wrestling with the burden of his heart, knowing he was being called to meet another need in DB's life. For a moment, he thought about giving his old boots, but he knew this wasn't what he needed to do.

A long sigh escaped, and Kenyon looked at the box of new boots and thought, *Maybe its just in my head.* "Lord, if these are for DB, have them be his size. If he doesn't wear nine and a half, these babies are mine."

Suddenly feeling paranoid, Kenyon looked around and saw an old woman wrinkling her nose at him. The same woman he encountered the last time he prayed out loud. He chuckled and said, "I wasn't talking to myself. I'm talking to the Lord."

The woman looked at his boots with a puzzled expression and back to Kenyon. He shook his head. "Not the boots," he pointed skyward. "Him."

After glancing at the sky and seeing nothing, she wrinkled her nose again, adjusted her scarf, and hurried away.

Kenyon walked over and plopped down on the bench beside the homeless man. "Hey, DB." The homeless man looked at him and his eyes widened. "I have a question for you, what size shoe do you wear?"

DB gave a puzzled look. "What?"

"What size shoe do you wear?"

He shrugged and said, "nine-and-a-half, why?"

Kenyon gave a pained smile when he looked at the shoe size—nine-and-a-half, narrow. His smile brightened, "Wide or narrow?"

"Narrow."

Holding up the box, he gave a final affectionate look at his new boots. *Good-bye my little darlings. It was a short affair, but it has been nice knowing you.* "I felt burdened to meet a need in your life and I want to give you these boots," he said and slid the box close to DB. He looked at the socks, "I imagine you could use a fresh pair of socks, too." He placed the three-pack of black socks on top of the box.

DB looked down at the boots, then back up to Kenyon.

"Why are you doing this?"

"I have to confess, it wasn't my idea," he said to the man. "This is a gift from the Lord. He knows what you need, and this is his expression of love to you."

Slowly he nodded and said, "Thank you. I can barely tolerate the snow."

He looked guilty for taking this hand out. Kenyon smiled. *Funny how DB seems to feel worse about taking a gift than stealing a purse.*

The wet shoes came off, followed by the saturated socks. When DB tossed them on the bench, the socks made a splat. Kenyon noticed his feet looked almost blue from the cold. The vagrant slipped on a fresh pair of socks, and then the boots. He stood and walked around a few steps.

"My feet already feel warmer." Kenyon could see his whiskers rise at the corners of his mouth. "I really appreciate this."

"No problem," Kenyon said with a smile.

"Hey, man. I'm sorry about the other day. The purse, and all."

"Don't apologize to me," he said and pointed upward. "The Lord is the one you need to ask forgiveness from. You know He's ready to forgive, because the Lord sent me to you with new boots."

DB smiled, then turned somber. "Did you find the woman?"

"You mean the owner of the purse? Yeah. I just followed the police lights. She was shaken, but glad to have the purse," Kenyon said. "Do me a favor, don't leave me with stolen goods again. A black man walking down the road with a stolen purse is not a good scenario. Good thing I didn't have a beard."

After an embarrassed laugh, DB said, "I suppose you're right. It won't happen again."

"Enjoy your boots," Kenyon said, and rose from the bench. He pressed a friendly hand on the man's shoulder.

"I'll be looking for you to come back to church, DB. I'll keep a seat open for you."

"Thanks."

"Oh." Kenyon reached into his pocket. "Here is my card. If you need me, call my number anytime—day or night." He handed the card to the man and headed home, wondering how to explain to his wife how he managed to spend his money and come home empty handed.

Michael determined to change his life. He promised the Lord he would not rob or steal again. And committed himself to quitting meth. He just hoped he had the strength to fight off these urges.

Chapter Twenty-Six

Michael cleaned a window, received a tip, and walked to the stoplight. Cars rolled through the intersection, their drivers hurrying to many destinations. He wasn't sure how much he'd made, but it wasn't looking good. Trembling hands pulled out the crinkled bills, then reached back in for the change. Sorted out his money.

"Only nine dollars," he grumbled, and shoved the money back into his pocket. This whole day seemed depressing. It's the day after Christmas, and the biggest tip of the day is a dollar. *Where is Santa when you need him?*

He'd been scraping windows all morning but no one seemed to be in a Christmas spirit. At least not toward a homeless man. Hunger pangs hammered at his stomach, while he fought the foreboding feeling that had lingered over him since the drugs began receding from his bloodstream. He fought through the crash, trying to keep his mind off of getting a fix. Though it felt like his chest caved in, he determined to keep his life on the straight and narrow.

There is enough for a bite to eat, so he would put his attention there. If he got water and the lowest priced burgers, he could probably squeeze out two meals.

Kenyon trotted across the park with excitement. His friends and family had pooled their money for a Christmas present and given him a two-hundred dollar gift certificate for New York Stylish Coats. The coat he owned looked rough, and he was delighted to be able to get something new for himself.

The Lord is good!

He had given up his shoes, and the Lord had returned the blessing in double. The shoes were a little over a hundred dollars and now he had two-hundred. With his meager income, he could never afford this much for a coat. Nor could his family. So when his family, friends, and congregation pooled their money together, it was quite a surprise. Never would he have dreamed of getting such an expensive gift.

Inside the store, he flipped through the coats, and found the one he wanted. "Wow, what a beautiful coat." It's a Bogner Madoc ski jacket. Weather proof, warm, and very stylish. He loved the cheerful yellow color and the black stripe gave it a sleek look.

"This is the one!" He flipped the tag over and felt the breath squeeze out of him. "A thousand dollars?" Disappointed, he pushed the jacket back into the rack. *Who can afford a thousand dollar coat?*

A Goretex coat caught his eye. The size on the tag was medium. He stretched out the coat sleeve, and held it against his arm, then slipped it on and looked at himself in a mirror. "Yep, it looks like a thirty-two inch sleeve."

It's weatherproof and still looked nice. It wasn't the sleek style of a Bogner, but is still one of the nicest jackets he'd ever purchased.

Happy with his buy, Kenyon left the store, turned the corner of 79th Street, and began his trek toward Central Park. He waited for the light to change at the crosswalk at 5th Avenue when he spotted a man on the bench shivering in a thin windbreaker.

"Oh, no!" he said out loud. "Lord..." he stopped and looked up. "I already know." Looking at the coat he said, "He has a size thirty-two sleeve, right?" Feeling paranoid again, Kenyon looked to his right. There stood the same woman with the wrinkled nose. She pointed up to the sky and Kenyon nodded with a smile and pointed up as well. "Yep. I'm talking to Him again."

The light changed and the woman scurried across the street, putting distance between herself, and the man talking to the sky. *That woman is everywhere.* Kenyon walked over to the shivering man in the worn windbreaker.

"Hi. Would you happen to wear a thirty-two sleeve?"

The man's tired face turned toward Kenyon, then his eyes lit up. He looked heavenward and said, "Thank you, Lord!" Looking back to Kenyon, Vashan said, "How do I stand in the judgment?"

"What?" Kenyon asked, surprised by the odd question.

The man held up a Bible and pointed to the first Psalm. "I found the words that I heard. They're right here. I need you to tell me how to find mercy, so I can stand in the judgment."

Michael sat on a bench near the Wollman outdoor ice skating rink in Central Park. Though the other benches were full, no one wanted to sit next to the ratty-looking homeless man. He admired the skaters gliding on the smooth surface. One lady was teaching a young boy a difficult routine. When the child stumbled, he looked defeated, but his teacher lifted his chin. The two were out of earshot, but Michael could see her encouraging the young student. After a brief word, the lad seemed to renew with confidence.

For a moment, he missed his old teacher, Ms. Johnson. Since leaving Alabama, she'd hardly crossed his mind. *What is she doing now?* When he left, she expressed confidence he would go far. Chances are, she had no idea how far down he would go. Seeing the child renewed with confidence caused Michael to realize how valuable her assurance had been for him. Too bad she couldn't coach him through this addiction. But then, no one can do this.

I wonder where Raquel is? Wonder if she's in New York.

Nah, probably went home.

A hopeless feeling washed over him. He looked around and saw happy faces everywhere. Only he sat alone, without family or friends. Or a home. Mothers shared themselves with sons and daughters. Something he never had. Never would. An ache pulsed through him, and he realized he couldn't watch this any longer. He rose from the bench. Time to find another distraction. One that's not so painful.

He ambled away from the rink, longing for something to occupy his mind. It had been four days since He'd taken a hit of meth. Though being drug free seemed to make a difference, his body buckled under the strain. Despite the sinking feeling in his chest, he felt good about his progress. How long had it been since he'd known life without numbing the pain?

Excited children rushed by, enjoying their days of Christmas break. He tromped through the snow, past the pond of ice skaters enjoying the winter. Their graceful motions reminded Michael of dancing. How he missed his days on the stage. That longing feeling needled at his heart, reminding him of the never ending regret of the fateful decision that changed his life.

A year after coming to Broadway, Michael got a break in his career. Many days of pushing through pain and long hours of rehearsing were paying off. He had just signed a contract, and joined the staff to perform at the Majestic Theater. He was to star in *The Return of the Phantom*.

A smile eased onto his face, but then sorrow dug at his heart when he thought about the first time he walked on the stage of the Majestic. On stage, he looked upward to the seating. The place where he stood seemed like the center of the world. There wasn't a bad seat in the house. He felt small, and a sense of awe at the sixteen hundred seats surrounding him. A proud feeling filled his heart. He stood on a platform coveted by all performers.

Michael was cast for the leading role of Viscount Raoul

de Chagny, but his goal was to win the crowning role of Erik, the Phantom. When beginning rehearsals for his new role, he felt grateful Pahl had prepared him through years of hard work. Superior coaching and training prepared him to take advantage of opportunities, and allowed him to sail beyond his previous leading role. Many dream about it, but few landed on this coveted stage.

Michael began rehearsals with three other new actors, and quickly realized this would be more demanding than anything he'd experienced before. New cast members were given a crash course in the play that required extended hours of rehearsals. Long after the seasoned cast members left for the evening, the four new actors rehearsed lines, sang their parts, and performed late into the evening.

His producer demanded perfection, and said relief would not come until each word, movement, and song was so ingrained into their nature that they would be able to perform it in their sleep. At times Michael thought he was already doing this.

Though the new actors were struggling through demanding schedules, one of his fellow actors, Alec, always seemed cheerful and energetic. After two weeks, Michael had to force his aching body out of sleep, and drag himself to the stage, barely able to get rolling. It was an hour into the daily routine before he felt alert, but Alec bounced with excitement and life each morning. Alec was full of energy when rehearsals started, and still filled with exuberance when the day ended. Michael admired this amazing man.

What I would give to have that kind of energy.

His performance was becoming second nature by the third week, but exhaustion dragged Michael down, while Alec remained unaffected by the grueling schedule. Michael finally asked his fellow actor where he found such energy after long days of work?

Alec invited him to his car to talk. Along the way, he bragged that he worked, danced, and partied after work without ever tiring. He then explained his source of energy. "Here is my wonder drug." He held up a bag filled with smaller zip lock bags. "This is the secret of my success." Alec explained that he had more energy than he ever thought possible.

"What is it?" Michael asked.

"Ice."

"Ice? I thought that was something you put in tea?" Michael said with a hint of skepticism.

"You know, Ice. Meth. It's an energy drug. Sleep in a bag," Alec said. "If you take a hit off one of these, you will be running like the wind."

Alec went on to explain how he had been taking it for months with no real side effects. He looked like such a good performer, and he seemed happy and carefree, so Michael decided to give it a try. The first couple of months everything was perfect. He had limitless energy, and the drug made him feel on top of the world. A few months into his use, the energy began to fade. He took more of the drug to get that feeling, but it was never quite the same. At times he would crash and sleep for days at a time. He called in sick when he crashed, but as his absences increased in frequency, he was put on probation, then fired from the production.

It seemed odd, but being fired didn't bother Michael nearly as much as running out of drugs. Six months into his drug use, meth dominated everything about his life, and nothing mattered except getting his next fix. His utilities were turned off, he was evicted, and his life on the streets began. Each day was the same. Find the money to get enough food to survive, and a daily supply of meth. If money remained tight and he could only afford one or the other, meth always took priority.

When the effects of the drug wore off, he fell into a pit of despair. It wasn't a minor depression. It felt like an iron safe was on his chest and about to crush his heart.

This is how Michael felt today, and had been feeling for the last several days. Though he still felt the weight of depression, the crushing feeling had eased up slightly. Even with his depression, he felt better than he had felt in years. His energy dragged, but he still felt good for a homeless wash-up.

I have the strength to beat this thing!

Raquel had enjoyed Christmas with her family. It felt good to be home in Bristol for Christmas, but the time had flown by. Her best friend, Margaret, joined the family for dinner the day after Christmas. Yesterday had been a noisy celebration as her little brother and sister tore through packages and played with their presents. Today she enjoyed a relaxing meal at the lunch table. Margaret and Raquel's family seemed excited to hear about the new world Raquel had discovered off Broadway. They were amazed at her descriptions of Central Park, thinking that New York consisted only of concrete and asphalt. Raquel thought everyone's ideas of New York were silly, but she remembered her own expectations of New York before arriving on Broadway.

People in New York think that southern life is filled with spitting tobacco and chasing each other with shotguns. In the south, people think New York is filled with rude people, and thugs chasing each other with knives.

Raquel smiled to herself. *Such different cultures, yet so similar.*

The phone started ringing, and her mom rose from the table to answer it. She turned to Raquel and said, "It's Robert. Should I tell him you're here?"

Raquel felt a scowl etch across her face. *I think you already did.* "No, I'm not here. Tell him I stepped out," she said, and headed toward the door.

Her mother gave a disappointed frown as she walked by, and then spoke in the phone.

Robert is a keen observer. Though he often misinterpreted clues, he rarely missed one. Raquel wouldn't have been surprised if Robert had found her new number and called her in New York, but all had been quiet since she moved to Manhattan. Now, she didn't have to face him and could ignore his calls if he did get her number. Manhattan is a big place with millions of people. There's no way he would be able to find her in the sea of humanity once she got back to New York. Tomorrow she'd return to Manhattan, so she only had a few more hours to evade him before she slipped beyond his reach again.

Chapter Twenty-Seven

Michael decided to distract his mind with food. Walking up to a burger stand, he ordered a meal and dug the dollars out of his pocket. He paid for his food and walked to a bench to eat alone. He counted his remaining money. A dollar and some change. Without warning, he found his mind drawn to the substance in the ziplock bag and began craving a hit.

"No!" he shouted to himself and tried to think about other things. *I'll go back in the park. Maybe something there will take my mind off my... No, I don't even want to think it.*

He shoveled down the rest of his food while walking toward the park. Michael dropped the wrapper in a trash bin and hurried his pace. Walking didn't help. Cravings attacked his mind like hornets. People stared when he grabbed his hair, trying to wrestle the thoughts out of his head. Scooping up a handful of snow, he rubbed the cold powder on his face. "Snap out of it!" he yelled to himself.

Something caught his attention. School aged kids were performing an outdoor play. It might have been a church, he couldn't tell. *Maybe this will get my mind off... I'll just watch for a minute.*

Kids were singing Christmas carols and telling the story of baby Jesus being born in a manger. One child looked terrified. The child looked seven, maybe eight. The lady directing the play tried in vain to order him into the scene. The boy shook his head at first, but when the teacher insisted, he sat down and curled up behind his knees. Michael wanted to come to his rescue. Just as he'd done for his friend Kenneth when they were children.

It had been the first play Michael participated in. When he joined Ms. Johnson's class, he was six years old. Because he was shy, the teacher didn't think Michael would do well on stage, so she put him in a minor role. The play, Guys and Dolls, reminded him of Tommy. He loved it. One of the boys, Marty, had the lead role of Sky Masterson. But each night when Michael got home, he would pretend to be Sky, and one of his pillows was Sarah Brown.

He'd turn the music up loud, sing the songs and perform with Sarah until Aunt Beth made him go to bed. Of course, he learned his role as a crapshooter, too. But that wasn't any fun. There were only three boys in Ms. Johnson's class, so most of the leading boy roles were played by girls. Michael thought he should have had one of those roles.

Since the studio was not near his house, Michael rode the bus from school to Ms. Johnson's class, and his aunt would pick him up each night. Every day, the school bully picked on the three boys on the bus. The bully's fans followed him off the bus. They often stood between the dancers and the studio, threatening to beat them to a pulp.

It had been a daily routine, but one day, Marty seemed to think he really was Sky, and bet the house he could beat the bully. He'd had enough and stood up to the challenge. The results weren't pretty. Sky took a beating. When Michael tried to intervene, the followers of the bully turned on him too. His punishment wasn't as bad as Marty's. Michael managed to land a good right hook on the thug's jaw, but it had no effect. It just made him angrier. But at least he escaped with only a black eye.

The next afternoon, Michael took his seat behind Kenneth. One of the girls from Ms. Johnson's class, Susie Anne, moved to sit with him. "Is your eye okay?" She tried to touch it, but Michael flinched and pulled back.

"It's okay if you don't touch it." He looked around. "Where is Marty?" Susie Anne shrugged. Looking around again, he made eye contact with the bully. The behemoth pointed at Michael's eye and snickered.

The towering giant walked up to resume his daily

taunts. "Look at him," he howled, "I stood there and let him hit me in the face." He turned his face to the left and right to give the audience a good look, "Do you see any marks on my face?" He walked up and leaned over, "You hit like a girl. Want to hit me again?" The bus driver turned to order him back to his seat. He pranced down the aisle, continuing his taunts. "Look, I'm Michael. I'm going to hit you," He imitated a girlie punch before dramatizing the effects, "Oooh! That tickles." Michael looked out the window, ignoring the hooping laughter. "Hey girlie boy, where is Tinkerbelle?"

That was his nickname for Marty. The kids on the bus whooped at the comment, but Michael tried to block them out.

The three dancers were relieved to see Ms. Johnson had decided to meet them at the corner. She glared at the bully and his friends with a daggered stare. They scurried away like roaches. The dancers walked in the comfort of Ms. Johnson's shadow. They dressed and took their positions in the room with mirrored walls. The teacher called everyone together. Her face drooped and her eyes looked tired.

"I have some bad news," she said. All eyes were glued on her face, and hanging on every word. "Marty has dropped out of the play." The students looked about, whispers filling the air. "I am hoping he will return in the future, but for now, Kenneth, you will be taking the lead role."

Kenneth looked like he'd been shot. His face turned pale and he looked to his classmates as though one of them possessed his courage.

Ms. Johnson tried to reassure him, "It's okay, Kenneth. You have two weeks and I will help you along."

Kenneth's new role terrified him. He didn't like singing, but Ms. Johnson said it was important to have the lead characters performing songs live. The show would not be exciting without dancers singing the songs, but Kenneth didn't seem encouraged. Ms. Johnson had everyone take their positions, the music would start, and she pointed to Kenneth and Ellen. Ellen was the best singer in class, and played the role of Sarah Brown.

Kenneth mumbled something which vaguely sounded like a tune, but Ellen sang out with her strong voice.

"No, no, no, Kenneth. You have to sing. Pretend like you are trying to be heard at the back wall." She restarted the music and he squeaked out something that sounded like a cat in the last throes of life. "Okay, you guys practice your dances while Kenneth and I work on his songs."

Michael knew the words to all of the songs. He loved the whole play because it took him back to the fondest memory he had, performing with Tommy while the two boys sang and danced. With his opera tenor voice, Tommy would play Nicely-Nicely Johnson. Michael imagined bowing on stage with Tommy, listening to the crowd applaud.

He wasn't sure if he could sing like Marty, but Michael felt certain he wouldn't clam up like Kenneth. Kenneth didn't want the role, so why wouldn't anyone ask him? But with a week before show time, the teacher would not call on him. Kenneth it was, whether he liked it or not.

Saturday night arrived, and the dancers gathered in the community center with Ms. Johnson and Ms. Thomas. Michael peeked out into the auditorium. "It looks like the whole town is here," he said with delight. Kenneth groaned at the thought. He sat in the chair and rocked as he hugged himself.

"This is our big night," announced Ms. Johnson. "You all have worked so hard, I know your parents will be proud of you. I'm proud of you." She looked down at the knot that once resembled Kenneth. "What's wrong, Kenneth?"

Kenneth looked up, eyes wide. He looked like someone facing the bully. His lip began trembling and waves of fear started rippling through his body. "I can't do this," he cried.

Ms. Johnson knelt in front of him, "Yes you can. You have worked hard, and you'll do fine."

"I can't sing in front of all those people," he wailed. His wail raised to a deafening level when he shrieked, "I can't do it!"

"Look, Kenneth. You can do this. Don't worry about being perfect, just sing and dance like we have been doing. Pretend like you're in the studio with just us."

That probably wasn't a great solution because Kenneth didn't fare much better in the studio. His cries grew louder, and he made sounds resembling words, but were impossible to decipher.

"Oh, goodness!" Ms. Johnson rose and paced across the room. She knelt back down and looked the face of terror in the eyes. "Kenneth, you can do it. You can't back out on me now."

But Kenneth had already backed out. He was gone. He cried, "No," followed by a few pitiful sounds.

Ms. Johnson stood back up and paced with her hand on her forehead. "We are out of time. What am I going to do?"

"I can do it." Michael tried to stop the words from erupting, but they popped out like a gunshot. Ms. Johnson looked at him with the most doubtful expression he had ever seen. He felt like curling up and joining Kenneth.

The expression of his teacher eased into an assuring smile and she said, "Thank you, Michael. But you don't know the part."

"I do. I know the songs and the dance. It's my favorite play." He shrugged and toed the floor, "I pretend like I'm playing the part at night."

Ms. Johnson stood motionless for what seemed like minutes. She looked deep in thought, trying to assess the problem. At last she broke the silence, "Sing 'Follow the Fold' for me."

Michael closed his eyes, played the tune in his head and began, "Follow the fold and stray no more. Stray no more, stray no more." His voice sounded loud and strong, though he needed work on his pitch.

Ms. Johnson looked surprised. "Are you sure you won't be afraid to sing in front of all those people?" she said, sounding hopeful, but skeptical.

"I'm sure." He shook with nervousness, but he knew once the performance began, his mind would forget the people. The world of music and dancing would be the only thing he would see. The rush always energized him.

Looking at the clock, Ms. Johnson clapped her hands, "Let's go. Ms. Thomas, get the younger dancers into their background positions. Ellen, help Michael out if he forgets his lines." She looked at Kenneth. He uncurled from his armadillo state to make a miraculous recovery. He wiped his eyes on his sleeves. The teacher knelt before him, "Can you dance your old role with Susie Anne?"

"I think so, if I don't have to sing."

"No, you won't have to sing," she said. Kenneth appeared pleased. "Oh, Lord. Please don't let this be a disaster," Michael heard her whisper under her breath while scurrying past. "Okay, take your places. It's time for the show."

The voice of Ms. Johnson called out for Michael's attention. She tried to encourage him, probably needing to calm her own nerves. Michael didn't respond. He felt himself entering that magical world, and outside words were not getting through.

The music started and the dance began. He might be a shy little boy in the social world, but a different person stepped on the stage. Michael fell into the role, singing and dancing gracefully to the music. The play was his first big success. Even as a child, after this performance he knew the stage would be his future.

Michael's eyes were drawn back to the Christmas play in the park. The stage should have been his destiny. So why did he now wear filthy rags, and fight to gain control of his addiction. Instead of standing on Broadway, he sat on a park bench in New York watching a kids play. A play that reminded him of what he once gained, but now had lost.

Why is it that everything I see reminds me of the life I should have?

If life had not turned against him, he would be starring as Erik, he would be married to Raquel, and their future would be bright. The play before him testified of his own failures. Unable to bear watching the play any longer, he got up and staggered away. Not knowing where he would go, or how he would make it another day. The pain felt greater than anything he had known before.

I've fought to keep everyone out of my heart to avoid pain. But there is no greater pain than this. I've lost the only woman who ever loved me, and all I have to show for my life is failure. Dirty, stinking failure.

Up to this point, He'd held on with all his strength, but what's the use of fighting failure? His mind was being pulled by a force greater than himself. Control slipped away. Tired of fighting, he allowed himself to be carried by the overwhelming urge to feed the addiction. Michael's mind enveloped in a fog of desire for the drug, and soon the world lost focus. Getting a fix is all he could think about. Nothing else mattered.

Michael knocked on his supplier's door. A middle aged, balding man opened the door. "Hey. How much do you need today?"

"Whatever you can spare," Michael answered.

"Well, how much money do you have?"

Michael dug through his pockets, and gathered all his money together. "A dollar twenty-three," he said as he held the money out, palm up.

The man tilted his head and gave Michael a pitiful look. "That isn't enough to pay for a bag to put the ice in."

"Please. It's all I've got. It's too late in the day to make any money, so I'll get you the money tomorrow."

The man's face drooped into a scowl. "Then you'll get your stuff tomorrow. I don't sell on credit."

"I can't wait until tomorrow," Michael said, his voice echoing with desperation.

"No dice. No money, no ice," the man said with indifference.

Michael stepped forward to plead with the man, but he produced a handgun and pointed it at Michael while he stepped back.

"Don't even think about getting crazy on me. When you have the money, come back. Until then, no merchandise." He pushed Michael backward with his free hand, "And don't come into my house. Do you see that line," he said, pointing at the weather stripping lining the floor. "Nobody steps behind that line. Understand?"

Michael nodded, looking at the gun trained on his chest. He considered threatening to turn in the man, since handguns were banned in this city, but he pushed the thought aside knowing that it would not do anything to get him his drugs.

"Good," the man said. A loud slam left Michael staring at the cellophane Santa draped over the door.

Desperation pulsated through Michael as he set out to find a way to get the money for the drugs. He wanted to keep his life together, but the beast within had become too strong for him. He had willed it into submission, and thought he had it under control, but when the beast awoke, he discovered it was too powerful to tame. Feelings of hopelessness returned, and he wondered if it was even possible to conquer this monster, or regain control of his life.

Chapter Twenty-Eight

Michael felt sickened by his actions as he watched the man count the money, then hand him a ziplock bag containing several hits of meth. All efforts to become civilized failed. People didn't matter. Nor did his own life matter. The only thing he cared about was his cravings. Holding the bag to his chest like a treasure to protect, he hurried away from his supplier to find a secluded place.

Huddling in an alley corner, he pulled out a glass pipe and a lighter. He shook so hard, he had trouble keeping the flame on the pipe, but relief began to wash over him as the drug took its effect. Relief was all he felt. No thrill. No euphoria. No feelings of peace. Numbness dulled his senses, but he understood he had returned to a day to day existence, serving no other purpose than to get enough money to feel normal—at least as close to normal as he could get.

With his mind racing, Michael stuffed the pipe back into his pocket. Burying his head in his hands, he began wondering how long he could continue. This wasn't a life. It barely qualified as an existence. Why should he fight through the daily battle of finding money to feed the monster of his addiction? The monster had to be killed. But he didn't have the power to destroy it. The beast was inside. The only way to get rid of it is to destroy the body that housed it. What would he lose if he ended his life, since it wasn't really a life anyway?

Climbing to his feet, Michael stumbled out of the alley. He tugged on his pants and held them up on his hips with one hand. At one time, these pants fit, but now he barely kept them up. The sagging pants served as proof to the number of meals Michael had sacrificed to buy a dose of what Alec had called the wonder drug. Is Alec going through a similar hell? Or is he even alive? Could Alec have already been devoured by the demon in the pipe?

His foot hit something, and it skittered down the alley. He bent down to have a look and saw a toy pistol. It looked realistic, except for the red cap on the end.

An unusual toy, for a city that has so little tolerance for guns.

A thought dawned on him. He grabbed a broken bottle and whittled the red end off the pistol. The supplier carried a gun and seemed more than willing to use it. If he attempted to rob the man, he would be forced to defend himself, and would shoot back. This would be the easiest way to end his life since he couldn't get his hands on a real firearm.

Michael knocked on the door of his supplier's apartment. When the door opened, he raised the gun, but it slipped from his shaking fingers, tumbling out of his hand, and onto the floor, bouncing at the balding man's feet. It made a plastic clack on the floor. Both men looked down at the gun.

The supplier cocked his head. "You trying to rob me with a toy gun?"

"I just want you to shoot me. I can't take it anymore," Michael said, his voice rising to a shriek.

"Are you crazy?"

Michael grabbed for the man's arm and cried, "Please shoot me! I just want to die!"

"You're nuts," the man said as he pushed Michael backward, sending him stumbling to the ground. "You are out of your mind. Hey, I have appreciated the business, but now you are too unstable to be trusted. Do *not* come here again."

The door slammed, leaving the broken man on his knees, begging for death. Michael buried his face in his hands, crying, and no longer able to control his emotions. Feeding the monster no longer kept his sanity. He was beyond help.

He didn't know how long he had been sitting outside the supplier's door. It may have been five minutes. It might have been an hour. Time lost significance. He wandered down the street and an idea hit him. Maybe he could just drift off to sleep in the cold night. It would be painless and effective.

Lights from the corner drug store welcomed him. Michael spent the last of his money on two boxes of sleeping pills and a soda. He wandered to a secluded place in Central Park and wrote a note.

Good-bye Raquel. Thank you for being a true friend. I hope your life reaches the heights. We are opposites and our lives went in opposite directions. Please don't be sad, I had to end the pain. It's better this way. Michael.

The smell of buttermilk biscuits swept through the house, teasing Raquel's appetite. She had missed eating her mom's biscuits. They were the best in Bristol. Gathering at the table with her family for breakfast, Raquel noticed the sad expressions of her brother and sister.

"Why the long faces? I'll be coming back the next time I get a break," she said.

"When will that be," Johanna said while poking at the egg she'd selected to bear the punishment for her sorrow.

"I'm not sure, but I'll let you know." Raquel tried to sound cheerful. She already missed them at the thought of leaving, but she put on a happy face. "Maybe when summer arrives, you all can come and watch me on Broadway."

Stewart sat up straight. "Can we?" He turned to his mother, "Can we go to Broadway, mom? Please?"

"We'll see," Raquel's mother said, avoiding commitment.

Somewhere between her mouth and Stewart's ears the words must have changed, because he shouted with excitement, "Hotdog! We're going to New York!"

"Yea!" Johanna cheered.

"I didn't say we were going. I said, we'll see," his mother corrected.

The two faces drooped back toward their plates until Raquel brightened them again by leaning over and whispering, "You'll get to go. I promise you."

Their mother stood at the far end of the kitchen, her back facing the table. She spoke to the pot she was stirring on the stove. "Don't think I can't here you whispering, Raquel."

Raquel gave a wink and a knowing smile at her brother and sister, causing them to snicker through their fingers.

Rising from the table, Raquel grabbed the luggage beside the front door and prepared to carry it to the car. The phone on the wall rang. Raquel knew who it was. Her mother put her hand over the receiver and opened her mouth, but Raquel spoke first.

"Tell Robert I am at the mall. Say I went to catch more after Christmas sales with Margaret, or something."

Her mother shrugged and returned to the phone while Raquel turned to carry out her remaining suitcases.

This will keep him looking elsewhere until I get out of town.

It's hard to believe another Christmas has passed. These three days flew by. Merging onto highway 81, Raquel turned north toward New York. Somehow she had managed to avoid Robert until she could get out of Bristol. With his gift of observation, Robert figured out she'd come home, but with the city now in her rear view mirror, and Robert watching the mall, she felt safe. By the time he realized she had given him the slip, she would again be too far away to track down.

Scanning the cars in her mirror, Raquel felt relieved.

No red trucks. She felt a little paranoid, but after years of his escalating behavior, she couldn't help worrying about him tailing her now. Traffic was light and none of the few cars behind her looked like something he would drive.

She changed lanes to get past a slow-moving cargo truck. A yellow car behind her changed into her lane. Feeling silly, she pushed her concern aside. Robert didn't have a yellow car, besides, the car remained a quarter of a mile behind her. After a few minutes, Raquel changed lanes again. The car in the distant background did the same. Concern began to trouble her mind. She changed lanes again, but the yellow car did not. Relieved it was all a coincidence, she put her attention on the road ahead.

Maybe listening to the radio will distract my mind.

Fumbling with the dials, she settled on a talk station. Hearing someone discuss issues will surely take her mind off the stalker from Bristol. Glancing in the mirror, she saw the yellow car in her lane again.

What am I thinking? Robert wouldn't drive all the way to New York. My mind is playing games.

Several hours into her drive, the yellow car remained behind her. When she sped up or slowed, it matched her speed. Raquel looked at her gas gauge when she crossed into West Virginia. It's time to fill up. She glanced from the mirror, to the tank, and back into the mirror. The thought of exiting the safety of a public highway sent fear through her, but running out of gas wasn't an option. Her mind raced through the scenarios of what would happen if Robert followed her off the highway. If it is Robert. One thing is certain, she needed enough gas after dark so she wouldn't have to stop.

The reflective green sign read, "West Virginia Airport, Exit 1 mile." Martinsburg is another ten miles beyond the airport. Maybe she could lose the yellow car. She pushed the gas and moved to the left lane, passing a large truck. She remained in the left lane until the yellow car followed her, matching her speed. When the car pulled beside the eighteen-wheeled truck, Raquel swerved across three lanes and braked hard, trying to make the airport exit.

A horn blared as she cut off another driver before darting onto the exit ramp. The yellow car could not clear the truck in time, and missed the exit. Raquel let out a long exhale, relieved to see the car disappearing from view. Maybe it wasn't Robert, but it's good to know whoever it is, they are far down the highway by now. If it is Robert, he would wait for her to pass and would resume tailing her when she got back onto Highway 81. To avoid crossing paths again, Raquel would take State Road 11 to Martinsburg, fill up, then continue on SR11 until she rejoined the interstate after Hagerstown. It would add time to her drive, but at least she could be certain to avoid the yellow car again.

When Raquel's Manhattan apartment came into view, she felt a sense of relief. It had been a long day. Driving is always tiring, but the stress of looking over her shoulder made Raquel's fatigue all the worse. Talking with Joseph on the phone along the way made her feel a little safer. But it didn't eliminate her feelings of paranoia.

Pulling into the parking space outside of her apartment, she saw Joseph. He waited on the curb, watching her apartment. When she spoke to him on the phone during the drive, she didn't expect him to meet her, but relief flooded her emotions at the sight of him. A sudden urge to cry arose, and she fought to blink back the tears. *Am I really that afraid. Come on Raquel. Don't be such a chicken.*

The clock on the dash showed 11:14 p.m. She parked,

and looked back down the road. No cars turned down the road behind her. Joseph rose from the curb and walked toward her car.

Fortunately, she'd lost Robert in West Virginia. He probably would have no idea where to start looking for her. She would not have to think about him unless she returned to Bristol.

Maybe I won't go back to Bristol again. My family can visit me here.

Even with the relief of being hundreds of miles from Robert, an odd feeling crept over her. It was the same feeling she experienced when Robert watched her during their dating years. She looked around and saw no one but Joseph. Though the stalker lurked several states away, she felt spooked, and glad to have someone to see her into the apartment.

The car door opened. "Need a little help with the luggage?" Joseph asked.

"What are you doing out here this late at night?"

"You sounded so worried. I decided to drop by and see you into your apartment."

When she stepped out of the car, she said, "You didn't have to do that." She gave him a hug. "But I am very glad to see you." Raquel pulled back and saw his warm smile. "Thank you, Joseph."

"It is the least I could do." He looked at her for a long moment, and then glanced at the back seat. "I see you packed everything in the apartment and took it with you. Can I help you carry it back in?"

A smile spread across her face and she nodded. They talked about business and holidays while carrying luggage from the car to the building. On the third trip, Raquel had to laugh.

"I guess I did carry a lot of stuff with me, didn't I?"

A pleasant laugh flowed from Joseph. "Yep. I'm glad I'm not a woman. I carry one bag and a laptop. If I can't cram it into the bag, I figure I don't need it." He repositioned both hands for a better grip on her suitcases and smiled. "Guys can get away with that." A soft thud echoed when he dropped the last two pieces of luggage on the kitchen floor. "Looks like that's it."

"I guess six suitcases is a lot, huh?" She felt sheepish, but Joseph disarmed her embarrassment with a smile. A long awkward silence filled the space between them, and Raquel wondered how to proceed. Drowsiness took over her mind, but she didn't want to rush him off and appear ungrateful. Her eyes darted to the clock. Eleven-thirty-two. "It's been a long day, so I guess I better think about getting some rest."

Joseph checked his watch. "Yes. I better be going."

The two strolled to the door and Joseph stepped outside, then turned around.

Raquel spoke first. "Thanks again for meeting me. I was a little afraid, and you were a godsend."

"It was my pleasure." Joseph reached out and took her hand. "Can I call you tomorrow?"

Raquel looked at Joseph, smiled, and nodded. He stepped forward and gently pulled her hand, drawing her close. Standing inches from him, her mind raced. Her heart followed. *He's going to try to kiss me.* Part of her welcomed the thought. Part of her struggled with her feelings for Dancer. She had already determined to let go of the hope of being reunited with him, but was it too soon to allow her heart to be swept away by another man?

Joseph's green eyes drew her in. He looked down at her lips. The moment of decision. Turn away? Do a preemptive hug? Or let the relationship take its course? Slow motion. He leaned forward. She didn't move. His warm lips met hers and she returned the kiss. Time seemed to stand still, or did it race forward? It was hard to tell if they held together for seconds or minutes.

Joseph pulled away and gave her another warm smile.

"I'll call you."

Another nod from Raquel, and Joseph turned to walk away. Several steps later, he turned to wave, and she waved back. She held the door and caught her breath. *Joseph seems so perfect.* Always a gentleman, eager to help, and he cared enough to come out to protect her during the late hours of the night. So why did she feel apprehensive? Part of her wanted to pull up the anchors and let the wind carry this relationship where it's meant to go. But the other part of her didn't want to cut the ties of the past.

Lord. I don't know what to do. I don't even know what I should think.

A fear chilled Raquel, and her eyes were drawn to a parking area to her left. Nothing. After studying the area for several moments, she assured herself that nothing looked unusual. But why the fear? Why should her instincts be on high alert. And why did her eyes keep getting drawn to the same group of parked cars? She stepped back into the apartment and bolted the door. Somewhere in the darkness, she felt someone's calculating eyes watching her. Raquel didn't know how she knew, but someone definitely watched.

Chapter Twenty-Nine

After walking for hours, Michael felt he'd cleared his mind enough to make a firm decision. Destroying the beast is the right thing to do. He walked down an alley, put his knapsack on the frozen ground, and sat on top of it. Pushing each sleeping pill out of the package, he emptied both boxes into a bag, then poured them into his hand. Twenty-four pills. He removed his coat, and laid it on the ground. Waves of shivers rushed through his body.

This should be enough. Even if the pills don't kill me, at least I'll freeze quietly in my sleep. No pain, no suffering.

Unfolding the note he left for Raquel, he examined his final message. "Oh, yeah," he said.

Digging in his pocket, he took out a pen and wrote *Orren* at an angle after Raquel's name. No one would be able to notify her without a last name. After folding the note back up, he tucked it under the front of his shirt where it would be found. Michael took the handful of pills, and with shivering hands, poured them into his mouth. Took a swig of soda to wash it down. His thoughts kept drawing his attention, calling him to the business card in his pocket. The urge to swallow became almost overwhelming, but he decided to hold it for a moment while he dug for the card. Feeling the sharp corners of the business card, Michael pulled it out. In the dim moonlight, he could see the name, Kenyon Pamella.

The words of Kenyon returned to him, "If you need help, call me anytime, day or night."

For weeks, this persistent preacher had been chasing him around, but Michael managed to avoid Kenyon for several days, and had nearly forgotten about the man, and the card in his pocket. But tonight he remembered.

A bitter taste assaulted his taste buds, drawing his

attention back to the suicidal task at hand. He thought for a moment. He had no more money, so wasting these pills would be a loss, but then again, he could steal the money to buy more. Or he could just steal the pills. He looked down at his boots and remembered the kindness of the man. Hadn't the preacher said God sent these to show His love? But if God loved him, why is life so miserable? He needed to swallow and all the misery would be gone. But what if God waited on the other side? Did he need to do something to make peace before he faced God?

The bitterness in his mouth grew stronger, and Michael fought to resist the urge to gag. Should he swallow, or should he waste the pills? A voice in his head said, "Just swallow." He prepared to choke down the cocktail, but something kept drawing him, calling his heart beyond the life of drugs. Drugs had destroyed his life, and now he was about to surrender his last breath to a mouthful of them. It would be a willing defeat. Swallowing would be to say, "You win," to the monster inside him. Drugs win, Michael loses.

He had already tried to live without drugs, and the addiction just reached out with its powerful grip, and pulled him back. He felt helpless against its grasp. Hadn't drugs already won? Or would this be the final victory for the monster? Reason said this addiction would always be his master, and the grave is the only place to escape it. But something else whispered its call among the thoughts shouting in his head. It was like a quiet voice, whispering among the orchestra of noise in his conscious mind. He had to talk to Kenyon.

Spitting out the pills, Michael gagged from the bitter taste. He drank the soda, swished, and spit. After expending the bottle, he still felt the bitterness in his mouth, but it was tolerable. Now shivering uncontrollably, he slipped on his coat, grabbed his satchel, and went to look for a nearby hotel where he could use a courtesy phone.

An elbow nudged Kenyon, and he began to stir out of sleep.

"Kenyon, is that your phone?" his wife called from beside him and poked at his ribs.

"What?" his delirious voice replied.

"Is that your phone? Your phone's ringing."

With a yawn, he slid out of the bed and staggered toward the device charging on the dresser. It stopped ringing before he arrived.

The cold floor chilled his feet. "I don't know who would call me at this hour. I'll check the messages in the morning," Kenyon said, and slid back under the warm covers. The phone started ringing again. After letting out a sigh, he climbed back out of bed. "Hello?"

"Is this Kenyon?" came a voice from over the phone.

"Yes." He rubbed his face, trying to arouse his conscious mind.

"This is Micha... I mean DB. Do you remember me?"

It took Kenyon's mind a moment to interpret the words. *DB?* "Oh, yeah. DB. Of course, I remember you."

"I need to talk to you."

"Do you know what time it is?"

"Um, no."

"It's not even three a.m."

"Oh," Michael said. "I'm sorry, but you said to call you anytime, day or night."

Kenyon smiled. "I did say that, didn't I."

After finishing the brief conversation, Kenyon left to meet Michael at the hotel.

When Kenyon saw DB's appearance, a wave of shock ran through him. He had always looked disheveled, but now dark circles ran deep under his eyes and his face looked gaunt. The last few weeks had not been good for the drug addict. Trying to keep his face from showing the concern he felt, Kenyon said, "How's life treating you?" He reached out a hand to shake, but dropped it when DB looked down.

"Not good, preacher. I couldn't keep my life together," DB said as he lowered his head. "I promised God I would do better." He looked up, "I tried. I really tried. But I just can't drive out my personal demons."

"You misunderstand," Kenyon began. "God is not looking for your efforts. He doesn't want you to do your best. The Lord wants your all, warts, moles, filth, everything. He is asking for you to give him your worthless life so He can give you a new life in Christ. Even if you could fix it up, it would still not be good enough." He looked directly into DB's sunken eyes, "DB, it's not your work or your efforts, it is his work. Jesus once said, 'This is the work of God, that you believe on Me'. Just put your trust in Him and believe in the work Jesus has finished for you. Believe on Christ."

DB dropped his eyes back to the floor. "This all sounds good, but you don't understand. I'm a horrible person. I've done things that should have put me in prison. Things that give me nightmares when I close my eyes. I can't forgive myself, and I know God can't forgive me either."

"Actually, DB, you are closer to salvation than those who have not done the things you have," Kenyon said. "It's hard for people to see their need when their lives are *normal*. Do you know what the worst sin is in the Bible?" DB shook his head and Kenyon continued, "Pride. Pride is the one sin everyone struggles with, and it blinds us, preventing us from seeing our need for redemption. You see your need, and that's a big first step."

Kenyon continued explaining to DB the grace, mercy, and forgiveness of God. The homeless man prayed with Kenyon, and even asked Jesus to save him. But said he didn't feel any different. Kenyon's heart went out to DB. The man was trying, but just couldn't trust the Lord. Maybe because he doesn't trust anyone. There seemed to be no right words to make DB get it. He finally seemed to grow frustrated.

"I appreciate you coming to meet me, preach. I'm sorry, but religion is not working for me. I've gone too far, and God will not forgive someone like me."

After a long talk with Kenyon, Michael stood to leave. This discussion on religion seemed to get nowhere. Things looked hopeless. The sinner's prayer had not been answered because God could not love someone so far gone. Though Michael said the words and felt sure he said the right words, the burden still weighed on his heart and the aching pain would not let go.

Kenyon kept explaining, but since God remained silent, Michael already knew the answer. God had rejected him. The weight of life will remain on his back, and the crushing feeling in his chest would not be lifted.

Before parting for the evening, Kenyon gave Michael a pat on the back, and handed him a Bible. Michael walked out of the motel with a heart that felt too heavy to carry. God had cast him away, into the darkness, yet he still felt a longing for something he couldn't understand. Why? What unseen voice kept taunting him with unattainable hope?

Chapter Thirty

The music of this morning's praise caused Kenyon's heart to forget the weight of a hard week. It had been a long week, but the rising of the morning daylight gave birth to a new day, filled with hope. Kenyon looked around the room. The church's congregation was a small group from many backgrounds, but they were united in their faith and love fore each other. People sang with joyful hearts, expressing each one's gratitude for the love of God they were experiencing.

By modern standards, the small church wouldn't be considered a success. They weren't drawing in large crowds or expanding into bigger buildings. When the church began, Kenyon knew this would not be a road to recognition. His calling is to reach the downtrodden and outcasts of society. Not an easy work. It would never be easy work. These people had little or no money, hope, or resources. Street people are elusive, suspicious, and often have problems that reach deep into their emotional makeup. Results were usually slow, and bringing in those who are weary drives most church people away.

It was challenging to stay focused on the mission of the church when each church leader gave opinions and different methods he should follow. They didn't understand why his goal was to reach the unreachable, not build a church empire. Enduring the criticism of his fellow pastors, Kenyon had determined to follow the heart of the Lord only.

Though he might be able to fill up the church by offering what the people wanted, the Lord had made it clear that the mission would be to reach those the Lord was calling out of their broken lives. It would not give him fame, but Kenyon decided not to allow the church to become a social club that could draw members, but not change lives.

His humble work would not lead to wealth, but there's little doubt people were being reached. Vashan came with his family, and Kenyon could see he hungered for the scriptures and the knowledge of God. It had been a month now, and Vashan testified about his changed life and deliverance from alcoholism. The ex-drunk's broken family had begun the process of healing. Hope could be seen on the faces of his wife and son. This testimony stood as affirmation that the church was having the right kind of impact.

Half of Kenyon's congregation were former addicts and street people. Who would reach these people if he did not remain faithful and be willing to stay close to the ground level? It would not give him glory on earth, but isn't it better to have twenty people with changed lives than to shoot for the masses and never see the miracle of these transformations?

One thing about those who had been pulled from the pit of their own failures, they truly appreciated the love of God. These recognized their need and the grace given to them. Almost everyone here had friends or loved ones stuck in the mire, and it was the mission of the Church at Central Park to reach out to them. At each service, the church would gather at the altar and pray for someone in need. Today they will be praying for Raquel's friend. She asked prayer for Michael each week, but this week they would gather after the music and all agree as a church in prayer, asking God to touch this man.

Kenyon thought about DB. Perhaps next week they would pray for him. This man's heart seemed hardened and so calloused he could not respond, even though he acted as if he wanted to. The world is filled with people like DB, but they could only reach out to individuals as opportunity arose. Kenyon kept crossing paths with this man, so there must be a reason for the chance encounters. But how would grace break through such a hardened heart?

Tossing an emptied purse into a dumpster, Michael stuffed the valuables in his knapsack and leaned into the wind, making his way toward his supplier. Seventy-three dollars would give him enough money to get the hits he needed, and still leave plenty for food. The howling wind cut through his clothes while he knocked, and stood outside the door, waiting for the supplier to answer.

The door opened and the balding man's face grew hard. "I thought I told you that you're no longer welcomed here?" He pointed an angry finger at the center of Michael's chest and commanded, "You need to leave. Now!"

"I'm sorry. I was a little depressed the other day, but I won't be doing that again. I just need to buy a little—"

"You need to leave," the man interrupted, pointing toward the road and preparing to close the door.

Michael pressed one hand against the door and held up a fist full of cash in the other. "I have seventy-three dollars. I'll give it all to you for one bag. Please." The man forced the door shut. Michael hammered his fist into the door, "Please. I just need a little."

A muffled voice called from the other side of the door, "I don't do business with robbers. You're not to be trusted. Don't come back here again."

Michael began slamming both fist into the door, "I never intended to rob you. Please." Silence followed and Michael continued hammering at the door, pleading for anything. "Please," he cried in desperation. "At least tell me where else I can get it."

The sound of a metal clink behind the door indicated the man had chambered a round in his pistol, ready to defend his home. Michael considered busting through the door so the man would have to shoot him, but instead, he dropped to his knees and wept at the front door.

Cold streams of tears stung his cheeks and Michael

wondered why he still hung on. What he had was not life. He wasn't sure if it even qualified as an existence. Grabbing his bag, Michael wandered back toward Central Park, unsure of what to do next. His body gasped for the numbing effect of the meth, and without it, he was crashing hard. Any moment his chest would implode.

With rage, Michael thrust a fist into the air and shouted toward heaven, "Why are you doing this to me?" Dropping to his knees, he looked up to the sky and wept, "Why don't you just kill me? Kill me and get it over with!"

Falling forward, he buried his face in his knapsack and cried in a weak voice, "Help me. If you are out there, please help me." He could feel the corner of the Bible the preacher had given him, and he pulled it out of the knapsack. "I don't know where to look. Show me something," he said. After wiping his eyes on his coat sleeve, he looked at the book.

Cautiously, he eased open the cover as if something dreadful would emerge from the Bible. He flipped it open and the pages blew in the wind. He slapped his hand on the book, stopping the pages from turning. He read the passage under his palm.

"Ho! Everyone who thirsts, Come to the waters; And you who have no money, Come, buy and eat. Yes, come, buy wine and milk, Without money and without price. Why do you spend money for what is not bread, And your wages for what does not satisfy?"

That's my life in a nutshell. I have been spending everything on something that does not satisfy. I've been going hungry because I spend money on this cursed drug and can't afford food. "Lord, what do I buy without money? I am thirsty. My soul is bone dry. What is the wine and milk this book is talking about?"

Continuing down the page Michael read, "Listen carefully to Me, and eat what is good, And let your soul delight itself in abundance. Incline your ear, and come to Me. Hear, and your soul shall live; And I will make an everlasting covenant with you—The sure mercies of David."

"I'm listening. I have nothing else I can do. Where is your abundance? What are the mercies of David?" Michael said, staring at the page.

The next words struck him like a blow to the heart. "Let the wicked forsake his way, And the unrighteous man his thoughts; Let him return to the LORD, And He will have mercy on him; And to our God, For He will abundantly pardon."

Michael buried his face onto the page as his vision blurred from the stinging tears which echoed his tormented heart. "If I forsake my way, can you have mercy on me? If I turn, will you abundantly pardon me? Lord, I have nothing. I am nothing. I turn away from my life. My ways. Please pardon me. Please have mercy on me. I don't have money. I don't even have a life to give. Please give me this mercy and the thing you said satisfies without price. All I can do is give myself to you—as I am. My broken life, I give to you. What little is left, it's yours."

A lifetime of buried emotions broke loose and a wave began in the pit of his stomach and spread until he shook uncontrollably, tears dotting the pages below him. "I can't keep my life together. I can't do anything to please you. All I can do is lay myself before you. And ask for mercy."

Michael wept, and could not stop a lifetime of tears from pouring out of his heart. Oblivious to those who stared as they walked past, he lifted his voice toward heaven. A weight began to lift off his back. The sinking feeling in his chest disappeared, and his mind felt like the chains which held him to his past fell away. He was free! He didn't know how he knew, but Michael understood he'd been set free from the chains binding him to his old life, and from the drugs that ruled him. He could not stop the tears from flowing, but the bitterness faded, and his tears became a flow of sweet relief.

Though he didn't understand what had happened, he

had to tell someone his life changed. With his vision still blurred from the tears, Michael climbed to his feet. He looked around to get his bearings, then rushed toward 111th Street.

Wiping the tears away from her eyes, Raquel rose from her knees while the congregation returned to their seats. It felt good to have each person agreeing in prayer for Michael, and for the first time, she had a real peace in her heart for him. She could feel something in her spirit confirming their prayers were not in vain.

Tedra embraced her and they walked from the altar. Raquel took a seat between Tedra and Joseph. Joseph looked at her and smiled, but she could tell by his eyes he didn't understand. Church was a new experience, and clearly he didn't know what to think about it all.

Kenyon spoke while walking toward the pulpit. "Speaking of prayer, don't forget our upcoming *pray in the new month* service next week. It's hard to believe another month has flashed by. This time it will be the day after New Years, so save some celebration for our prayer night."

He took his place behind the podium and began his sermon. "Don't lose heart. Sometimes God answers prayers in ways we don't expect—"

The door of the church flew open, and a cold wind rushed through the room. Every head spun to see a frizzy faced man in vile clothing standing in the doorway. Kenyon recognized the drug addict from the park. The man's eyes sparkled and the way he stood testified that something was different about him.

"You were right, preacher," he proclaimed. "I *am* a new

creation!"

"DB?" Kenyon said.

"Michael?" Raquel said.

Their eyes met. He knew she went to church, but did not expect to see her here. He tried to keep his composure, but tears began welling up in his eyes again. Through the blur he could see her rise and begin rushing toward him.

"I can't believe it! I should have known, but I just can't believe it," she said and wrapped her arms around him.

After a long tearful embrace, Michael said, "I'm sorry. I know I stink."

Raquel laughed through her tears and wiped the water from Michael's face. "Yep." She smiled brightly and wiped her own tears. "But it's a wonderful stink. What's outside can wash off. I'm just glad you're clean in here," she said, patting her hand on his heart.

"Some sermons don't need words from the preacher," Kenyon said with a wide grin. "I think we need to gather back to the altar to thank God, and to pray for DB," he laughed and then said, "I mean Michael. See? God indeed works in ways we do not expect."

For his entire life, Michael felt dead inside, but now he felt alive. Turning to Raquel, he said, "For the first time I actually feel like I have a heart."

Today is a day to rejoice, but Michael understood much needed to be done. He remembered the pain he had caused others. Most people were unknown strangers, but some fences could be mended. There might be a cost, but he had to reach out to those he'd harmed.

Chapter Thirty-One

Michael examined his face in the mirror and felt encouraged to see evidence of health returning to his complexion. Flush color returned to his face, and the gaunt look faded as he gained weight.

Amazing what rest and good nutrition can do.

The beard was gone. He wanted to keep it, but Raquel insisted on seeing his face. The first time he looked in the mirror, he was shocked by his own appearance. He had avoided his reflection for the last few years, and it surprised him to see how sunken his face had become. Also, he had more acne than an adolescent. Everything began to change, and the last few weeks had transformed him inside and out.

Today was payday, and he had saved enough money to take care of something that had been on his heart. The first two people he wanted to repay were the tenants of the apartments he had broken into. He especially wanted to see the old man he attacked. He pulled two envelopes out of his drawer and counted the cash. A thousand dollars each. This is the result of two meager jobs, a lot of overtime, and saving every penny he got his hands onto. The shelter gave him low cost housing and meals, allowing him to save most of his money.

While walking up to the apartment door, he thought about the possible consequences. The man could call the police and report him once Michael explained why he was giving him the money. It's a chance he had to take. Inhaling deeply, Michael knocked on the door. After a few moments, the door eased open and a woman peeked out.

"I'm looking for the old man who lives here." He tried to

give a reassuring smile.

"There is not an old man here," the woman answered.

Michael felt the air squeeze out of him. Is the old man alive? "Do you know where he moved to?"

"I have only lived here a few weeks. I don't know anything about who lived here before."

"Thank you. Sorry to bother you," he said and she closed the door.

Stepping to the next apartment, Michael knocked on the door of the other residence he had broken into. He remembered a woman and a child leaving before he broke in. He wondered if she's a single mother. The door cracked open.

"Hi, sorry to bother you, but do you know what happened to the old man who lived next door?"

"He left to live with his children. I think in Florida," she said.

Relief flooded through Michael when he realized the man had survived. "Do you know how I can get in touch with him?"

"I'm sorry, I don't know anything other than his family came to get him. He decided to move after being robbed a few months ago."

Regret washed over Michael. Had he caused this man to live in fear so he could no longer stay alone? The woman said something, but Michael was lost in thought. She began to close the door.

"Wait," Michael said, "I have something I need to give you." The woman cracked the door open and peeked over the safety chain. All Michael could see was her eyes. They gave a look of uncertainty. "Here," Michael said and pushed the envelope through the opening.

"What's this," she said as she stepped back, avoiding the object.

"It's money. I want to give back what I took from you— with a little interest."

Michael stood, holding the envelope and waiting for the woman to gain enough trust to take it. Feeling the need to justify his actions, he tried to explain his past drug addiction, and why his life had changed. He's now trying to restore some of the money he had taken. Rattling off about the Church at Central Park and the preacher who chased him, Michael realized he wasn't making sense.

It's hard to give a life story in a few seconds.

After concluding his explanation, he said, "I don't blame you for not trusting me, but please take the envelope. Nothing is in it but money." Michael held the envelope open for her to see and flipped the bills with his thumb. "See, there is nothing but money from my paycheck. I have a job now. Actually two. And I want to pay you back." Pushing the envelope back into the door with care, he felt relieved when the woman took it.

"Thank you," she said with an uncertain voice and closed the door.

After he walked away, mixed emotions swirled in his head. Michael felt glad to give the money to the woman, but confused about the rest of the cash. He felt certain he needed to set this money aside for a reason, but didn't know what to do. Maybe he could use this money at his discretion.

Michael wandered through the shops off 5th avenue. It felt good to walk through these stores without looking over his shoulder while searching for an opportunity to steal. It's also relaxing to browse without looking like a vagrant. Technically, he was still homeless since he resided in a shelter, but at least he was off the streets and cleaned up. Life now has hope and a future—though he had no idea what that future might be.

Strolling into an upscale shop, he browsed through several racks of coats. The smelly coat he'd worn for years had been replaced with a hand-me-down coat someone at church had given him. It would be nice to have one of these nice new coats. One jumped out at him.

Wow, look at that!

It's the last jacket of this style remaining after the Christmas shoppers finished picking through the place. He gasped when he looked at the price tag. Almost a thousand dollars! He pulled out the envelope and eyed the money. The after Christmas sale price is ten percent off, so the total would be about what he had in the envelope plus the little in his pocket. Maybe the money is intended as a gift from the Lord.

With his boxed up coat in hand, Michael walked out of Tip Top Coats. An odd feeling of fear struck him. Something in the back of his mind sounded an alert. After looking around, a man caught his attention. A figure observed the crowds as if looking for someone. The face looked familiar. Then he remembered him from high school. The years had sharpened his features, but there was no mistaken the face of Robert, the man who had tried to end his dancing career on the side of the road in Bristol.

At least he won't be able to recognize me. Michael ran his fingers over his smooth face and remembered that whiskers no longer hid him from public recognition.

Perceiving someone watching him, Robert turned, and their eyes met. For a moment his eyes widened, locked in recognition upon Michael, then Robert hustled down the sidewalk.

What is Robert doing in Manhattan and why did he act like a kid caught in mischief? Was he afraid of retaliation after all these years?

Something in Michael's gut told him Robert wasn't just sightseeing in New York. The uneasy feeling he felt went beyond the awkwardness of childhood enemies. After years on the streets, Michael had learned to perceive subtle suggestions in body language. Sometimes these hints were imperceptible to the mind, but instinct and street smarts had taught him to stay in tune with what his gut told him.

This man is up to no good.

The daily monotony of rehearsals seemed somehow more enjoyable, and Raquel felt full of life and hope. The last few months in New York were filled with heartbreaking lows, and wonderful highs. The January air may be bitter cold, but to Raquel, the days were declaring a new year with new beginnings. When rehearsals ended, Raquel saw Richard Barnhouse. She could feel her temperature rising, but then a thought struck her.

Approaching the reporter, she said, "Hi, Mr. Barnhouse."

"Well," he said with a startled look, "isn't this a surprise. I thought you didn't speak to us nasty reporters."

Raquel gave a sheepish smile and said, "I know. I've been cold to you. It's because of the story you ran on my friend, Michael Camp."

"The guy under the bridge," he said and nodded. "It is a sad story, but you have to remember, my job is to bring the news. Good and bad."

"That's what I want to talk to you about, Mr. Barnhouse—"

"Please. Call me Richard." His face scrunched up. "Mr. Barnhouse sounds so... formal shall we say for lack of a better term. The way you say it makes me feel like I should be sitting in a chair with a pipe." His face spread into a wide grin, seeming amused at such a thought.

Raquel took her eyes off his cleft chin and smiled. "Okay, Richard. You said you need to report the good and the bad. If you are really interested in the good, I have another chapter in Michael's life, and I think you will find a story that New Yorkers will love to see."

It was the first Saturday night of the month and Raquel hurried from their evening's performance to get ready to meet Michael at the little church off Central Park. She loved the church, but now church life became sweeter knowing Michael would be waiting. She rode with Tedra to her apartment where they were transformed from sweaty dancers back into ladies. When she glanced at the clock, Raquel realized service would begin in fifteen minutes, but Tedra was twenty minutes away from completing her metamorphosis.

"I want to meet Michael before service gets underway. Do you mind if I go ahead of you?" Raquel called through the bathroom door.

"No, but are you sure you want to walk alone in the middle of the night?" Tedra's muffled voice called back.

"I'll be okay. It's just a short walk."

"Alright, I'll meet you there. But be careful."

Raquel wrapped her scarf around her neck and stepped into the brisk wind, sloshing through the day-old snow on 110th Street, heading toward Central Park. The temperature remained near freezing and falling, but after a week of near record cold, this temperature was a welcomed change.

Another feeling of being watched sent a chill through Raquel. The alley she used to cut across to 111th came into view, but her attention kept being drawn toward Central Park. She quickened her pace. Looking over her shoulder and scanning the area, she felt more at ease. For a moment, it sounded like footsteps, but nothing seemed out of the ordinary under the buzzing streetlights. In the distance, she could see someone walking away from her, but no pedestrians were in the area where she walked.

Her heart began to thump in her chest. Each sound seemed to approach her from behind, but a glance over her shoulder revealed nothing. The wind rushing across her ears made it hard to identify the night sounds. She cut down a side street to 111th street, and let out a comforting sigh when the door of the church came into view. She lowered her head and plowed into the wind for the last fifty yards of her journey.

Her eyes caught site of a pole in front of her and she raised her head up to dodge the obstacle. "Hello, Raquel," a voice called out, causing her to jump to attention and gulp in a breath of cold air. The object she'd mistaken for a light pole had a voice. Robert.

"Good grief, Robert. You startled me," she said, trying to act as though his presence wasn't unusual.

"If I didn't know better, I would think you were trying to avoid me," he said.

Raquel stood, her mind searching for a reasonable answer, but words drained from her mind.

Stepping forward, Robert said, "You lied to me. Twice. Why did you tell me to meet you for breakfast, and then rush out of Bristol? Without even saying good-bye." Robert furrowed his eyes. The shadows lengthened his features, amplifying the anger engraved on his face. "Fool me once, shame on you," he said, and though his eyes remained angry, his lips curled into a wide grin before continuing, "but you didn't fool me the second time."

As Robert talked, Raquel fished for her phone in her coat pocket. She began pushing buttons, hoping her fingers were pressing 9-1-1.

"You know how to hunt down a doe?" Robert asked. "It's simple. You just have to know where she's going and then it is easy to track her down." Chuckling to himself, he said, "Raquel, you are so predictable. The last couple of weeks you have taken the same paths, usually at the same times. Since high school, I've been tracking you, and I always know where you're going. You are a creature of habit."

"I'm sorry," was all she could think to say. She could hear her voice squeak out the words.

Waving his arm in the air, he said, "Oh, you had me for a short time when you came to New York after lying to me about going to Virginia. I admit, I didn't think you would stand me up when you promised to meet me at the cafe back in the fall. But I made sure you didn't fool me again." His eyes filled with bottled rage. "Did you really think I was too stupid to know when your mother lied about you going shopping?" He laughed. "I watched you load your car while your mom said you weren't home." Robert wrapped a hand around Raquel's arm and pulled her near, "Raquel. I don't like being lied to. You showed a lot of disrespect, and it's time you learned a lesson."

Raquel tried to jerk her arm back, but Robert tightened his grip. "You don't own me," she said as she pulled harder and cried, "let me go!"

Leaning close, Robert's whisper echoed in her ear, "Oh, yes. I do own you. You're mine."

Raquel wrenched her arm free for a moment and turned to run, but Robert reached out and caught her coat, pulling her back. He heard a faint voice coming from her pocket. He looked down and shook his head.

"That will do you no good today."

He pulled the phone out of her pocket and disconnected the call. Robert snatched the phone back when she reached for it, but it slipped from his grip. The phone fell and busted on the sidewalk. She reached down for the phone, but Robert wrapped a muscular arm around her waist and lifted her from the sidewalk. He placed his hand over her mouth, and carried her toward his car. She tried to cry out, but the wind carried her muffled voice into the night.

Oh, God! What's Robert going to do?

Chapter Thirty-Two

Tedra slipped through the door of the church and took a seat beside Michael, holding Raquel's phone in her hand. "Where is Raquel?" she whispered to Michael.

"She hasn't gotten here yet, I thought she would be coming with you," he said. Michael had a dreadful feeling when he saw Tedra's expression. "What is it?"

"She left about fifteen minutes before me." Holding up the broken cell phone, Tedra said, "I found her phone on the sidewalk a few yards from the church!"

"It's Robert!" he said as he jumped to his feet. "I knew something was wrong when I saw him near the park." Michael rushed out the door, then scanned the park and the alleys. "Oh Lord, please let Raquel be all right," he cried as he scanned the area. Michael hunted while the church spread out and searched. He could hear people praying. *Where would Robert take her?* He started toward Central Park, but stopped, *No, he wouldn't go to the park. He would be afraid of being spotted near where Raquel was taken. Where would a Bristol redneck in Manhattan go?*

Turning in a slow circle, he tried to imagine what Robert would be thinking and where he would go. "Lord," he prayed out loud. "Where would the deer hunter from Bristol take his prize catch?"

Weaving through the wooded bank, Robert drove around the yellow gate, passing the 'Park Closed' sign, heading into Riverside Campgrounds. The freeze hardened ground provided traction for his tires to grip, and though the car slid and banged into a few trees, the vehicle made it through the snowy terrain with surprising ease.

After bringing the car to a stop, Robert exited the vehicle and snatched Raquel from the passenger side. Twisting her right arm behind her back, he forced her to fall hard across the car's hood. He then twisted her left arm behind her and began binding her hands with Duct tape. His motions were hard and cruel, not caring if she felt pain or fear. The duct tape made a tearing sound as Robert rolled it around Raquel's wrists.

"A thousand and one uses. I wonder if they had this in mind?" The idea caused him to chuckle.

"Look, Robert. I'm sorry for avoiding you," Raquel said.

Robert grabbed a handful of hair and snatched her head back. He seethed in her ear, "It's too late for sorry." His voice sounded quiet and raspy, but he made sure the sound shouted through her soul. He pushed her forward again and made another pass with the tape.

"Please let me go," she said, her voice cracking.

Cold tears ran down her cheeks, then dotted the car's hood. A violent shiver ran through her. It might have been the cutting cold of the winter night air, but Robert suspected it was her fear. Even in the pale moonlight, he could see the pulsing of her heart through the veins in her neck. The rapid pulse showed fear. Robert's heart grew colder than the frozen ground they stood on.

"Please. I'll do anything." The tremble in her voice confirmed the depth of her fear.

"We both know this relationship is over. I tried to love you, but you just kicked me to the curb," Robert said. "It looks like I am going to have to break up with you. For good. I've got my eye on someone else. She'll love me. And respect me. But first, I need to bring our relationship to a close."

"Why can't you just let me go and move on, then?" she said. "I promise to forget about this. No one will ever know."

He laughed. "Do you really not get it? I never lose. You lose, but not me. No one just walks away with my heart. We are one, and till death do us part?"

Robert's firm hand snatched the shoulder of her coat, and spun her to face him. With pleasure, he studied Raquel's expression. He watched her face melt when she looked into his eyes of steel. A smile etched itself onto his expression. Pride rose in his heart. It felt empowering. Trembling, her legs sank, but Robert lifted her by the coat. Weak knees proved she recognized his power. It was a painful lesson. Her last lesson.

It felt good, and he could feel his smile expanding until laughter erupted from deep inside. She deserved this. All of it. The choice had been hers, not his. "You thought you could disrespect me." Another laugh popped out. Few things were better than turning the tables on someone who thought they could outsmart him. "Do you know the best part? Not a soul knows I'm in New York. You will just be a random victim of a city crime." Raquel's lip began to quiver. The fear on her face energized him. Almost more excitement than he could contain. Now she respected him. No more did she think her little game was cute. The best moves had been played. The cafe had surprised him, and her maneuver on the highway was impressive, but her silly games were no match for his skill. She had put up a good fight—for a woman. But the end result remained the same - checkmate. "Just a random crime. What do you think of that?"

Seeing that Raquel could no longer speak testified to the power of his presence. He was in control, and she knew it.

Pulling her close to his face, he breathed out the words, "If I can't have you..." He paused to let the words sink in. It made him smile knowing she anticipated the next words. She knew the words he was about to speak. She dreaded them. Wanted to prevent them. But remained powerless to stop the voice speaking them. Robert knew her emotions. He could feel it. Felt her dread. Without words, she was begging him not to finish the sentence, though she knew it was inevitable. A hard smile chiseled across his face. Robert leaned closer, pressing his cheek against her face. Letting her feel the scraping of his masculine stubble. Sliding his bristled mouth close to her ear, he exhaled the rest of the sentence. "No one can."

Raquel shivered at the words. He felt it.

Pulling back, he smiled and released her coat, allowing her to sink to her knees. He retrieved a shotgun from the car and grabbed the shoulder of Raquel's coat to lift her back up. He reached behind her, gripped the sleeve of the coat, and hurried toward the river. She fought to keep her legs underneath her to ease the pressure on her arm. A cry of pain erupted from her when she stumbled, putting pressure on the arms still bound behind her back.

When he reached the river, Robert stopped and turned Raquel to face him. "After I kill you, I'll break the ice and push you under. No one will find you for months."

Raquel trembled again, and seemed to be struggling to keep strength in her legs. "Please, Robert." Her words squeaked out.

Go on, beg for your life. You thought you could shame me. Now who is the fool? Raising the barrel up to her chin, he looked through the sights at her face. *I'll bet that's cold steel.*

He chuckled to himself, thinking about how this woman who would not look at him or speak to him, now couldn't take her eyes off him. Without words, she was pleading, attempting to get his attention, hoping to return to the way things were. They both knew this wasn't possible. Nothing could ever go back to the way it was before. He released the safety and moved the barrel to her forehead. Raquel's eyes clamped shut. Tears squeezed from the corners of each eye.

"Bam!" he shouted, causing Raquel to jump.

He laughed out loud at his joke.

Raquel opened her eyes and tried to focus on the man before her. The wind burned her face, and tears blurred her vision. She wondered how this man could be taking such pleasure in this cruelty. He's a psychopath with no pity. His pride had been wounded, and his entire life balanced on that fragile ego. She now realized how unstable he had always been. How could she have been so blind. When Robert's pride had been wounded, everything in his life lost balance.

The worst thing you can do to someone like Robert is to make him feel shame. He would do anything to recapture his feelings of superiority. Certainly, he acted boastful, but it's nothing more than a mask to hide his insecurities. Leaving him at the cafe waiting for her, and feeling like a fool had been the worst of all possible situations for him. Insulting his ego had been a misstep on her part. The cost would probably be her life.

Since high school, Robert's behavior had been escalating. Raquel thought one day she might have to face Robert again, but nothing prepared her for the meltdown she now witnessed. Her thoughts shifted back to Dancer. At least she could die in peace knowing the love of her life will now become the man she always knew he could be.

Will Dancer ever find out what happened to me?

Shifting her mind to her family in Bristol, Raquel thought about her little sister. During Christmas, Johanna had demonstrated her dance moves, and declared her goal of following in Raquel's footsteps. A smile surfaced when her life flashed before her, causing her briefly to block out the peril of eminent death. She saw her brother leaping from the house with his parachute. That was almost as dumb as the time he played *Mission Impossible* and jumped from the roof to a tree branch, which broke, and he plummeted to the ground. The only thing his mission accomplished was sending him to the emergency room.

The goofball. What is it about jumping from roofs that he finds so tempting? If he survives childhood, he's going to be a stunt man.

"What are you smiling at?" The voice of Robert brought her mind back into the peril before her. A puzzled expression flashed across his face, but he wiped it away and pressed the barrel hard against her forehead, forcing her neck back. "What's so amusing? Don't you know you're about to die?"

It became obvious to her that Robert wanted to recapture the thrill of seeing her in fear for her life. When the reminder of death didn't draw a response, he pressed the barrel harder into her forehead, and Raquel struggled to keep from falling backward.

"I know you're afraid," he said.

A grin merged into his angry expression, but confusion showed in his eyes. The truth is that she had a strange peace about this situation. If the Lord did not intervene, she was ready to go.

Raquel wondered at the realization that fear had departed. She understood it wasn't dying that made her afraid, since she knew her eternal destination was secure. The shock of the situation had caused the terror. It was confusion and surprise of being abducted. And the fear of not knowing what to expect from Robert. Now the threat had been revealed, and his intentions were clear. Raquel resolved herself to the reality of death. The shock faded. Accepting death, and releasing her life into the Lord's hands now brought peace.

Taking a deep breath, she said, "I'm not afraid."

"Yeah, right," Robert said. "I could see you shaking like a cat in a pen full of dogs."

"I was. But now I'm at peace. It is you who should be afraid, for you will be the one answering before God." Her voice cracked a little, but fear continued to lose its grip.

Robert kept his hands on the rifle and a finger on the

trigger, while moving his head in a sweeping gesture. "Out here, *I am* god. Your life is in my hands, and I alone have the power over your life and death."

"Not a sparrow falls to the ground without God's approval," she whispered to herself.

"What?"

"I said, a sparrow cannot fall to the ground without the Lord's approval. If you kill me, he must allow it. Precious in His eyes are the death of his saints. I will be at peace. I pray you too will find mercy."

"Shut up!" he shouted. "It is time to die. Not even God can save you now."

Robert looked around. Realizing that killing her in the campground would leave evidence, he decided to complete his task on the ice in the river. The edges of the river were frozen, but the current flowed twenty feet off shore. He stepped on the ice and tapped it with the barrel of the gun. He shuffled away from the shore until he heard the ice beginning to crack.

If he shot her on the ice, the evidence would be covered by the next snow and would melt into the river. But he needed to make sure the body wasn't in plain sight. Hiding her under the ice looked like the best option.

To get her body below the ice, he would have to make a hole closer to shore where he could push her under the surface without the risk of falling in himself. He poked at the ice extending from the shore until he found a spot solid enough to hold his weight, but thin enough to break through. He aimed his shotgun toward the ice and fired. The ice shattered. He chipped away a large portion with his barrel until the hole expanded enough to receive her body.

Michael borrowed a church member's car, and drove along Riverside Park's roads. It's the closest campground from where Raquel had disappeared. And it seemed like the only logical place where Robert would feel comfortable in the area. With the door open, he leaned out and looked for evidence of fresh tire tracks or footprints. The moonlight provided a little light, but not enough to determine whether there were certain patterns in the sun beaten snow. Unsure of whether his hunch had been correct, he prayed for guidance. He had to find Raquel fast. Then he heard it. The unmistakable sound of a shotgun.

Numbing fear pulsed through his veins. "Oh, God! Please don't let Raquel be dead." Michael's heart ached at the thought. Surely he didn't come this far just to see her die. Hope had emerged in his life, but he didn't think he could live with the pain of her dying at the hands of Robert.

He drove toward the sound of the blast until he ran out of open road. A yellow gate blocked his way. Michael parked the car and ran past the gate, toward the campgrounds.

Robert chipped away at the ice until satisfied with the size of the hole before returning to Raquel. He poked the shotgun in her back. "Get up and move to the river." He reached down and gripped the collar of the coat, lifted her, and marched her forward. He positioned her in front of the hole in the ice and said, "I've had my fun, now its time to end our little affair." He raised the barrel, thought for a moment, then lowered to where he could look her in the eye. "You know, this is your own doing. Things could have turned out differently. We could have been happy together, but this is all your fault."

Raquel didn't answer.

"Do you hear me?" he demanded.

Raquel held her peace. Was this little wench resolving herself to die, pretending not to have fear. *She's afraid. I can see her shaking, and it ain't just the cold.* He knew her peaceful look had to be just an act. She's just trying to keep him from detecting her fear.

You won't win this game. I won't be denied. "Answer me!" he screamed, eyes bulging in rage. Raquel looked at peace as she closed her eyes. "Fine." Robert jerked up the barrel, placing his finger on the trigger.

"Don't do it, Robert!" a voice shouted from the darkness. Michael emerged from the shadows, and cautiously walked into the milky moonlight. "Don't shoot her."

Thoughts raced through Robert's mind, but the only words he seized upon were, "How did you know we were here?"

"Many years ago, someone gave me a piece of advice on the side of the road in Bristol. He said, 'You know how to hunt down a wild buck? It's simple. You just have to know where he's going, and then it is easy to track him down.' You were very predictable, Robert," Michael said. "I knew you wouldn't go to Central Park, and this is the closest park where a sportsman would feel at home. I got close, and the sound of your shotgun helped narrow the search."

Robert looked at the hole in the ice behind Raquel and shook his head. Looking back to Michael he said, "I was hoping you didn't recognize me the other day, but it looks like you did. Now I am going to have to kill both of you." Realizing he had to be strategic, He knew the first shot had to take out Michael, or he would flee into the woods. Moving the barrel to Raquel's chest, Robert said, "Ladies first!"

"No!" Michael raised his palms as he stepped forward. "Please don't." Keeping both hands up, he took a careful step forward and said, "Don't do it Robert. We can work this out."

"Sorry. I Can't hear you in this wind," Robert said, turning his face toward Raquel but watching Michael through the corner of his eye. He could see Michael stepping closer. He now stood only about fifty feet away. "One more step and you're a dead man," he whispered.

He pressed the barrel under Raquel's chin and lowered his cheek on the stock as if taking aim. In a quick motion, Robert jerked around to face Michael and fired. His foot slipped on the ice and Michael dove as the blast erupted. Robert knew he didn't get a clean shot, but also knew Michael couldn't have gotten completely out of the wide path of the lead pellets.

Michael rolled to his feet and scurried for cover, holding his side. Robert cursed while he reloaded the gun. He had to get to Michael before he could escape. He stopped and looked toward Raquel.

"He won't leave you, so I'll just wait for him to come back." Robert looked toward the shadows and called out. "She's going in." He stepped toward Raquel and pushed her, causing her to stumble backward and fall into the hole in the ice. "Hey, Mr. Dancer. Her arms are tied, so she doesn't have long."

Michael fought down his rising panic when he heard the agonizing sound of Raquel thrashing in the icy waters. Choking gulps echoed into the night air. "Oh, God! What do I do?" If he rushed to her rescue, Robert waited to blast him, and he would die with her. But if he didn't act immediately, she would drown.

He had to think fast. Bending down, he scooped up a handful of snow and rushed out of the woods toward Raquel. As he ran toward the river's edge, he packed the snow into a ball and launched it with all his strength at the shadow of Robert, kneeling on the ice and aiming toward him.

The snowball caught Robert by surprise, and he instinctively fired. Michael dove onto the ice, and small pellets stung his back as he skidded across the frozen river's edge. He grappled to get his legs under him as he slid past the hole where Raquel gasped for air and kicked to get her head above the water. In the freezing water, she couldn't last long.

Warm blood oozed from his back before chilling against his shirt. Scrambling on slippery legs, he lunged toward Robert, slamming his head against the hunter's chin with as much force as he could manage with such little traction. Momentarily stunned, the rifle loosened in Robert's hands and Michael shoved it away. The two men tumbled onto the ice and the shotgun came to rest a few feet away.

Robert's hand reached for it, but Michael extended a foot and caught it with the tip of his toe, causing it to slide just beyond Robert's outstretched hand. When Robert stood, Michael wrapped his arms around both legs and tried to wrestle him back down. A sharp blow hit Michael in the head. Then another.

Pain screamed through Michael's cheek as the stalker hammered his plowboy fists against Michael's face. He realized he was no match against Robert's strength. Michael held on tightly as Robert pummeled him until he could no longer feel anything in his massacred face. Slipping free, Robert rushed toward the shotgun and Michael crawled to his knees and lunged forward, wrapping both arms around his ankles, and tackling him with a hard crash on the ice.

Raquel's thrashing grew weaker. Michael desperately needed to get to her, but this wouldn't be possible if Robert controlled the shotgun. Below him, a pinging sound rippled outward. They were too far from shore, and the ice began cracking. As the fractures expanded, the ice twanged an odd tune, warning all to abandon the area or sink.

A blunt blow to the head caused Michael to let go of Robert's feet. The stalker now had the shotgun. The pings of the fracturing ice alerted Robert to the danger of being so far from shore, and he climbed to his feet, preparing to flee the ice. When he put his weight on his feet, Michael heard a crash. Water flooded onto the ice, sending a cold, numbing wave over Michael. Looking back, he saw Robert flailing among the shattered chunks of ice, grappling toward Michael.

Laying as flat on his back as possible, Michael began working his body toward the shore, but a hand clasped his ankle, pulling him and the block of ice he floated on below the water's surface.

Michael rolled over to give himself a chance to grate his fingernails into the unbroken surface near him. The hand of Robert lost its grip and slipped away, and the ice floated up, lifting Michael's legs out of the water. He dug his fingernails into the ice and spread out, distributing his body weight as wide as possible. For a moment, Robert's fist thumped under a nearby block of ice, then ceased.

Michael scraped toward the place where Raquel once struggled. Panic rose and he scraped as fast as his uncooperative limbs would move. The only sounds were the wind, and his body dragging on the ice.

The numbing cold paralyzed his legs, but he fought to keep his arms moving. Michael's aching fingers felt the edge of the ice where Raquel fell and he pulled himself to the hole. A trembling head turned and gave him a frozen stare. Duct tape hung from one arm and a shaking, silent Raquel clung to the edge of the ice. She had freed one of her hands from the binding and pulled her head above the water. He wanted to smile, but his blue quivering lips wouldn't curl.

Michael grabbed her coat, rolled to his back and pulled with all his might. She slid up, then dropped back into the water. With a loud cry, Michael pulled with all his aching strength. Raquel tossed a leg feebly on the ice, and emerged from the water.

Cracks sounded in the ice, but Michael continued to

pull. Live or die, this would be their only chance. He shuffled toward shore and pulled again. Another grunting pull, and the rest of Raquel's body slid onto the ice. No time to relax, they had to get to the shore and out of the cold.

After an agonizing trip up the riverbank, Michael and Raquel crawled into Roberts car, cranked it, and blasted the heater on their bodies. Shaking fingers fumbled to disconnect Robert's cell phone. Help is on the way. Aching fingers and toes testified that life remained in his legs. He thanked God for delivering Raquel from the hand of Robert, then began to think about his relationship with Raquel. Could there be a future a has-been dancer could give to the woman beside him?

The events over the last few months made Michael's head spin. What kind of life could be on Broadway for a washed-out dancer? His heart flowed with gratitude, knowing he no longer lived in the gutter, but what direction could he go from here?

Peeking a glance at Raquel, he saw her brown eyes brighten, and she passed him a shivering smile. He didn't want to deliver pizzas for the rest of his life, and felt Raquel deserved someone with a real future. Dancing is the only thing he really knew, and with that opportunity squandered, he wondered if he could ever have anything of value in his life worth offering to this woman?

Chapter Thirty-Three

Now that Richard Barnhouse had expressed interest in the story of a dancer lifted by grace, Raquel decided to take her idea to her producer. He'd agreed to meet her at three o'clock. She walked down the hall where her journey began nearly four months ago. Almost as nervous as she had felt on her first meeting. When turning the corner, she saw Joseph Rodney exiting the producer's office. When he saw her, his green eyes lit up.

"Hi, Raquel!"

"Hi," she said. They stood for a moment in an awkward silence. This wasn't an encounter she'd looked forward to. Allowing any further romance in their relationship wasn't possible, but she didn't know how to break it off. When she had wanted to break up with guys in her past, it was easier. Most of the time, they were jerks and it felt right to end a dating relationship. But it was different with Joseph. Raquel cared about him. Why had she led him on? Or allowed him to lead her into a deeper relationship before knowing if her heart was available?

Her care for Joseph wasn't in the same way he cared for her. At no time did she discourage his advances, and when he asked about Michael, she had said the homeless man was just a friend. Now things had changed. No, things had returned to the way they were supposed to be. So how would she tell Joseph? How would she unsay the things she had said? Knots began to tighten in her stomach.

"You love him don't you?" Joseph asked.

"What?"

A warm smile spread across Joseph's face. "You love him. I could see it in your eyes the first time I saw you look at the man. At Michael."

Raquel nodded and looked to the floor.

Joseph placed a warm hand on her face and lifted her eyes to meet him. "It's okay." He gave a quick nod. "Oh, I'm a little disappointed. I can't deny that. But to see you happy makes me feel good. I'm glad to see his life taking a turn for the better. I'm glad for him, but I'm more glad for you."

Emotions tried to emerge, but Raquel blinked them back. "Thank you, Joseph," she whispered.

"I hope one day I have someone look at me the way you look at him. He's a lucky man to have someone with such a strong love."

His words sent a dart of guilt through Raquel. She felt as if she had betrayed Michael. After all, she had said he was nothing more than a friend, and she did everything within her power to push him out of her heart. Those memories ached inside her. Emotions began to emerge again.

"At least I have the satisfaction of knowing I kissed the prettiest girl on Broadway." Joseph tapped his mouth with a finger and said, "I'll never wash these lips again."

They both laughed.

Putting a gentle hand on Raquel's face again, he wiped a tear off her cheek with his thumb. Joseph leaned forward, and she thought he might try to kiss her, but he turned his head and gave a firm embrace. He spoke quietly in her ear. "Pull yourself together and take Marcus by the horns. Michael deserves it."

Raquel leaned back and gave a puzzled look, and Joseph smiled.

"I heard you talking to Richard and I think you're doing the right thing. Michael deserves another chance. Marcus will pretend like it's too big of a risk. I've known Marcus for a long time, and he pretends to be a tough guy, but he's putty in your hands. Show him your beautiful smile and plead your case. He won't be able to resist, and you'll wrap him around your little finger. He has a daughter around your age, and you know how daddy's are."

Joseph put a hand on Raquel's shoulder and led her to the office door. "I've already chummed the waters. He knows all about Michael, his talent, and that he has been a leading man on Broadway before. The only thing you need to do is convince him Michael is willing to commit to it."

Raquel gave him a long embrace. "Thank you Joseph. You're a good man."

"Be sure and spread the word. We wouldn't want to keep that a secret."

She raised up on her toes and kissed Joseph on the cheek, then he opened Marcus' door. "Good luck," he said. He walked down the hall, leaving her to the task at hand.

Entering Marcus Davenport's office, Raquel took a seat on the chair across from him.

Marcus smiled when Raquel took her seat. "How are you, Raquel? What did you want to see me about?"

"I have something to propose." Raquel sat on her hands to stop them from fidgeting, but then remembered Joseph's words. She sat up, gave Marcus a bright smile and said, "A really big news story is about to break, and I believe it will draw a crowd. People love stories of inspiration and if you will work with Richard Barnhouse, I think we have the biggest show of the decade ahead of us."

"What kind of inspirational story did you have in mind?" His words posed a question, but his eyes smiled. He already knew what was coming next.

Excitement surged through Raquel, and she shared the details of Michael's story, his rise from the drug infested streets of New York, and the opportunity for what Richard Barnhouse had said would be *the story of the decade.*

Raquel concluded by saying, "Richard said he would work on the story and air it in time for opening night. This is a story which benefits everyone. Richard will follow Michael as the story unfolds, providing a behind the scenes look at his journey back, and he will air it to give us unprecedented free publicity." She looked up with her *daddy's little girl eyes* and smiled again. "What do you think, Marcus?"

Kenyon spread three books, his Bible, and a stack of papers across his lap and on the sofa beside him. He flipped open his notebook, and began writing when someone knocked at the door. Lost in study, he decided to ignore it since he didn't want to lose the order of his carefully placed notes.

"Can you get the door," a voice called from the kitchen. "I'm cooking."

Kenyon let out a sigh, put down his notebook, and began stacking the items on the floor. When he opened the door, a courier handed him a package and a clipboard.

"Please sign here."

"That's odd, I don't think we were expecting any packages," he said before signing for it and returning to the apartment.

"Who is it?" his wife called.

"A delivery man. Are you expecting something?" he asked while searching through a drawer for a pair of scissors. Cutting the box open, he pulled the packing tissue aside to reveal a yellow article of clothing. Kenyon pulled it out and lifted it up.

His wife emerged from the kitchen, wiping her hands on an apron. "What is it?"

With a stunned look, he said, "It's a Bogner Madoc ski jacket." He turned to his wife. "Do you know how much these cost?"

"Who sent it?"

A note lay in the box. Kenyon read it aloud. "Dear Kenyon, I don't know why, but I just felt led to buy this coat for you. You have given to others, so maybe the Lord is giving this to you."

His wife flipped over the lid of the box, "Who's it from?"

"It doesn't say," Kenyon said while examining the tag of the coat. "Whoever sent it knows my size." He put the coat on and straightened it. "Do I look stylish?"

"You look like a million bucks," she said with a smile.

"I've got to take a walk. Now is a good time for a prayer in the park—plus it will let me test it out in the cold."

"Don't be gone long, supper is cooking," she said. Before the door closed, she called out, "Now don't you go and give that one away!"

Chapter Thirty-Four

Michael looked across the stage of the Belasco Theater, feeling more nervous than he'd ever remembered. Weak knees hardly supported him, and for a moment, he had the urge to sneak out of the building. A glance over to Raquel provided encouragement. Her face beamed with joy when their eyes met. She turned her bright smile toward the stage, and Michael turned to face ahead.

Music began as the stage illuminated with soft purple and blue lights. The introduction of Starlight played before a hushed crowd. Michael thought about Ms. Johnson. In the audience, she watched the expanded version of her choreography coming alive, fulfilling the dream of a lifetime. How proud she must feel. *I'll bet she never thought Starlight would open on Broadway.*

Years of memories flooded through the dancer's mind until his thoughts were interrupted by the cue call in the music. Michael took three bouncing steps into the light, then a leap sent him through the air. He landed and spun into a pirouette, then lowered himself to his knees. He gathered the stars from the floor, and placed them into the heavens. Dots of white light appeared on the dark ceiling with each movement of his arm.

A boom of a drum called Raquel onto the stage, and she bounded into a leap with each beat. Her beauty struck him. The woman he once said would never see him fall, now rushed toward him on stage. Just as she had done on the stage of life. If not for her deep love, he would still be living in the mire. If he was even alive. He had fallen, but she had become the hand of encouragement that he needed.

Two more bounds and Raquel leaped high in the air. Michael rose to meet her, and her waist lighted in his hands. The music carried Michael around the stage, with his angel from heaven high overhead. Other dancers scurried onto the stage, but the world faded from view. The crowds disappeared, the stage lights blurred, and the music began to play from deep within. Occasional applause from the audience drifted in, but they were watching from another world. It was just Michael, Raquel, and the dance.

The script and choreography no longer mattered. Nor did time. Every rhythm, step, and song flowed from the heart, through the world of the dance. Dancing lasted for an eternity. Or was it only a moment?

Relevance of time only returned when the dance drew to a close. Beats in the music began beckoning them back to the world from which they had escaped. Michael and Raquel pirouetted on center-stage, reached into the heavens to retrieve the stars, and with a soft chiming of symbols, they placed the stars before them with a bow.

The crowd erupted to life, and the remaining cast joined them on stage as they bowed. Emotions overwhelmed Michael as he took in the reality that he was actually on the Broadway stage again. Raquel took his hand and bowed, reminding Michael of stage etiquette, and he bowed with her. For a moment, he wondered if it could be real. He glanced to Raquel's hand in his. He raised his eyes to meet her. Tears streamed down her cheeks, but a smile beamed in her face. Yes, it is real. Very real.

He had been delivered from his inner demons, the dead end streets of New York, love had found him, and now he stood on Broadway as a restored man.

Is it possible to be more blessed than this?

Chapter Thirty-Five

Raquel watched as her son twirled and leaped. "That's so cute!" The door opened and Michael walked in. "We've got to show Daddy what you can do! Michael, look at what your son is doing!"

Michael walked into the room and sat on the couch. Michael Jr. waved his arm, indicating he was ready for the music, and Raquel pressed play. The young boy began to leap and twirl around as he performed in sync with the rhythm of the music. "Isn't that so cute!" Raquel said. "He's going to be just like his daddy."

Michael took his son up in his arms and walked to the mantle where two trophies were displayed with prominence, between pictures of Ms. Johnson and the family of his Aunt Beth. "Do you know what these are?" Michael asked his son. The boy shook his head and Michael took one down. "Son, these are the Tony Awards mommy and I won in our first production, when I returned to Broadway." He held one close and continued, "This is the greatest award I have ever received, and do you see what I have etched at the bottom?" He began to read, "I live my life by the Master's plan - I know no other way." Placing the award back on the mantle, he looked at his son. "Whether you become a dancer or take another path, one thing you must always remember is that life only has value within the Master's plan."

Raquel placed a hand on his back as he replaced the award. "He's just four. I don't think he is going to be mapping out his life yet."

He reached out an arm and Raquel slid into his embrace. Michael said, "That may be true, but it's never too early to begin pointing him in the right direction." Looking back at his son, he said, "I want my son to avoid my pain and grow up knowing the mercy of the Lord."

Michael reached out a hand to touch the Tony Award. He ran his finger over the letters engraved in marble. "This isn't a testimony of talent, but of the triumph of God's love, grace, and mercy. It was a hard road back, but I never lost sight of this one thing - For Him alone." Turning back to his son, Michael concluded, "Nothing else matters."

Acknowledgments

I would like to give special acknowledgment to the following people:

You, the reader. Without your faithfulness to read, books like this wouldn't be possible. If you have enjoyed this book, please add a review on amazon.com so others can discover books like this.

My wife, Jennie. She is my first proofreader of every book and worked hard in the editing of this manuscript.

Audrey Stout. Thank you for taking the time to read the manuscript and for providing valuable feedback to help the story flow more clearly.

Tom Webster. Thank you for spending your time reading the manuscript and making helpful suggestions. I am grateful for the words of these songs, the demo CD and your gift for writing. Your work to create the lyrics of *Dancer* and *I Know No Other Way* paved the way for this story. Without your talent, the song, and willingness to help, this story would remain hidden in my imagination.

Tralena Walker. Thanks for giving your ideas on the book, singing, and writing *Dancer* and *I Know No Other Way*. Without these songs, this book would not exist.

I am grateful to the Lord for giving me the desire to write, and a desire for His word that inspires this story of redemption.

Thanks also goes out to the Christian Authors Guild (http://www.christianauthorsguild.org). The people, encouragement, and helpful advice of others inspired me to push higher and pursue my writing goals. The CAG critic team provided helpful suggestions on the manuscript. Many eyes looked at this work, and pointed out issues mine could not see.

My parents, Linda and George, and in-laws, Arch and

Mary, provided encouragement and feedback on my writing.

Finally, I would like to thank Carlos Acosta for his book *No Way Home*. His autobiography provided a valuable insight by showing the world of performing through a dancer's eyes.

Look for other books by this author by going to

http://www.eddiesnipes.com or http://www.gespublishing.com

Appendix

Below are the complete words of I KNOW NO OTHER
WAY:

You May Doubt
What I believe
You say I have more faith
Than I'll ever need
I hope you're there
On Judgment Day
And you're close enough
To hear me say

(Chorus)
I live my life
By the Master's plan
So I won't be judged
By mortal man
I praise my Lord
Each time I kneel and pray
I know he knows
I know no other way

Deep in my soul
Burns an eternal flame
That's why I say to you
In Jesus name
I'm a child of God
He is the Truth
My Father lives
I'm living proof

Repeat chorus

Tag line

I praise My Lord
Each time I kneel and pray
I know He knows
I know no other way

I know He knows
I know no other way

I know He knows
I know no other way
Written by Tralena Walker and Tom Webster